WHERE the WILD WIND BLOWS

Where the Wild Wind Blows

NANCY MORSE

ISBN 1-484-06502-6

CHAPTER 1

Somewhere along the Laramie, 1855

"Mind me now, Katie m'darlin'. I've never let ye down, have I?"

Tom McCabe's lusty voice, thick with an Irish brogue, filled the tiny cabin along the Laramie.

"Aye," came a girl's laughing reply, "and the moon's as green as the hills of Ireland."

"And how would ye know what the hills o' Ireland look like when ye was born and raised right here in the heart o' Indian country?"

"Because I've been hearing about them for as long as I can remember. I can't count the times you said you'd go back."

A tremor of guilt swept McCabe's hard-chiseled features. "To be sure, tis a promise I've been makin' myself."

A spiral of pewter smoke rose from the iron kettle dangling over the fire and traveled up the stone chimney as Katie ladled rabbit stew into two burl bowls. "Tisn't too late, Papa."

"We can't just pick up and leave Richard behind," her father said. "We're a family. The McCabe's stick together."

"Richard's got no mind to go to a place he's never seen," Katie said as she set a bowl down before him.

"Besides, he's got a family of his own now. It seems to me my brother likes playing Indian. Tis the wild life that suits him."

McCabe gave a shake of his head, rustling the hair that long ago had turned silver. "Tis true. But I'm thinkin', Katie m'darlin', that there's a mite too much o' the wild blood flowin' through yer veins, too."

She sat down across the table from him, and said, "You've only yourself to blame for it. What did you expect, raising two young ones out here in the wilds without a woman? When the cholera took Mama back in forty-nine, you could have taken an Indian wife. There's things a man needs."

"Don't go preachin' to me on that subject again, Kathleen McCabe," he complained. "And don't go tellin' me what I need."

"If Richard's children can be reared by one, why wasn't it good enough for yours?"

With one swift motion McCabe was on his feet, snapping his chair back so swiftly that it nearly toppled over backwards. "If the truth be known, one naggin' female is enough for the likes o' Tom McCabe." His boot heels struck the hard-packed earth of the cabin floor as he stomped to the door, jerked it open and left. Katie watched her father go, the glow from the coal-oil lamp illuminating her smile.

Her father was like the mountains that rose beyond the Laramie, sun-browned and strong, with craggy features and a snow-capped peak. She might not always agree with him, but she would follow him to the far corners of the earth, even to a place called Ireland if that was what he wanted.

Often she would sit amidst the dense solitude beneath the cottonwoods, her back pressed against the furrowed bark, daydreaming about a place she had never seen. Ireland. Even the name had the ring of fantasy to it. She imagined the ladies there wore pretty dresses of silk and lace made just for them by seamstresses whose careful measuring guaranteed a perfect fit.

She glanced down at the calico dress she sewed with tiny backhand stitches from the cloth her father had traded for at the fort. It was loose-fitting and did injustice to her blossoming body. She much preferred the hide dress with the beaded yoke and dangling cowrie shells she had gotten from a Sioux woman in Richard's band. The hide, tanned almost to whiteness, was soft and supple and fit her curves just right. Her father didn't want her wearing it to the fort. Why raise the eyebrows of those newly arrived emigrants who would mistake her for an Indian despite her red hair and green eyes and bring all kinds of trouble down on them?

She enjoyed accompanying her father to the fort and listening to the stories the traders told of the old days when they could ride for weeks without ever seeing another white man. Yet she often daydreamed of far-off places, of dancing at gay parties, of wearing her red hair swept up off her shoulders in an intricate twist instead of bound in braids or hanging loose and blowing in the wind.

Sometimes, in the evening, her father would sit in his old pine rocker, smoking his pipe and reminiscing about Ireland while the cabin filled with the sweet fragrance of sumac leaves and the bark of the dogwood, a mixture the Sioux called kinnikinnik. Yet as often as he vowed to one day return to the land of his birth, she suspected that his failure to do so had not so much to do with the fact that Richard was here, but with his own love of this place he called home.

It was a love that ran deeply in Katie's own heart, as well. Out here in the unforgiving wilderness along the Laramie there was not a single roar of thunder or driving blizzard that frightened her. Not even the Indians, with their strange customs and flamboyant behavior and the drama of their ceremonies, scared her. Fear only seemed to get in her way. At the age of seventeen she had absorbed a feel for the land and its inhabitants that many mountain men never came to know.

A short time later Katie glanced up from the buckskin shirt she was mending when her father came striding back inside. Laying aside the awl and sinew, and hiding her smile, she went to get the bowl she had wrapped in a cloth and put before the fire to keep warm, and set it down on the table.

"Lord, girl," McCabe managed between swallows, "ye sure can cook a good rabbit stew."

"Bone Bracelet taught me."

"I only wish Richard's wife could teach ye other things, like temperance and how to curb that saucy tongue o' yers.

Ah, Katie m'darling, the man who tries to tame that wild heart o' yers is in for one helluva fight."

Katie watched her father wolf down the stew. When she was certain his belly was full, she ventured, "Papa, can I go riding in the morning?"

"Ye knew ye can't go ridin' alone, not when there's Indians out there who don't know yer Tom McCabe's girl and might do ye harm. These're uncertain times, what with those whites pushin' harder every day and the Sioux not willin' to give up an inch of land. Things ain't been right since last summer when those soldiers marched into that Sioux village and shot their chief. And all because one of the braves stole a Mormon's cow and ate it. Damn 'em! What do they expect when they tell the Indians they can't go huntin' any more? How's a man supposed to feed his family without food? If they don't watch out, they'll wind up like those soldiers, massacred every last one of 'em."

He shook his head with dismay. "For more than twenty-five years I've traded with the Indians and never had a lick o' trouble with 'em. Treat 'em fair and they'll do like to ye. Course, not all of 'em are friendly. Some would like to use my back for target practice. But I hold no grudges, and I don't judge 'em. To me, they're just people, some good, some bad. Still, these're uncertain times. Those Indians are under pressure from the westward-movin' whites, and men under pressure sometimes forget who their friends are."

"What is it, Papa?" Katie asked. "Something's wrong. I've been sensing it since we left the fort."

"I heard at Laramie that all friendly Indians have been ordered to the agency. The soldiers have started up the Platte with their big wagon guns in search of hold-outs."

"But it will take time to gather them all together, and winter is coming. Can't they wait until spring?"

"By then it may be too late," McCabe said gravely. "I'm thinkin' it'd be a good time to visit Richard at the Brulè village. We'll leave in the mornin'."

***

Out upon the broken plain, perched high up on a jagged, pine-studded ridge, Black Moon sat astride his sorrel pony, surveying the village. Spirals of gray smoke curled into the air from cooking fires. The smell of onions and turnips boiling in the kettles drifted into his nostrils. The laughter of children carried up from the river. With a subtle tensing of his knees, he guided his pony down out of the hills towards the village.

He rode past war shields, lances, spears and other things of war hanging from tripods, the eagle feathers laced to them flicking about in the wind. Outside one of the lodges a group of men milled about, most stripped to breechcloth and moccasins in the sweltering summer heat. They clustered around one whose voice Black Moon recognized as he dismounted and approached.

"Peace," Fire Cloud urged. "We must make peace with the whites." His soft-spoken words brought a round of agreement from the crowd.

"Peace is not possible." One angry voice lashed out in open defiance, spinning heads in its direction with its mocking, knife-sharp tone.

Black Moon strode in amongst them, the ancient belligerence of the Lakota gleaming in his dark eyes. "The *wasichus* have seen to it."

Although he was younger than his brother Fire Cloud by two winters, it was invariably Black Moon who dominated by virtue of his looks that were distinctive in contrast to his tribesmen. His complexion was lighter, his nose straighter, his features more refined, his demeanor contrary and formidable. The others like to adorn themselves in beaded shirts and quilled leggings. Black Moon preferred plain buckskin. The others wore feathers in their hair to signify brave deeds. His unfeathered braids were wrapped in buffalo hide and hung over browned shoulders, his war record speaking for itself. In battle his face bore no paint, just a serious expression.

In a voice that sounded like an animal growl from deep in his throat, he said, "More and more the wagons of the *wasichus* come up the Platte road, filing up the lands along the Big Muddy, moving like ants right through our hunting grounds. The hunters come with their guns and shoot the buffalo, taking only the skins, leaving the meat, the hump, the tongue, for the wolves. At the soldier towns the dried skins are piled as high as lodges where they wait for the wagons that will take them east."

"East!" snorted Lone Horn, a Minniconjou warrior. "That is where all our good things go. First the beaver, now the buffalo."

"And the land," said Black Moon, ebony eyes flashing. "Those Indians along the Big Muddy were fools for selling their land to the *wasichus*. Now when they refuse to sell more, they are chased off their land. Some are so hot over it they are carrying the pipe around for war."

At the flurry of excited conversation that ensued, Black Moon turned and left.

Fire Cloud caught up with his brother and fell into place beside him. "Before you rush off to war, think of how many the whites are. For each one you kill, ten more will take his place."

"Then ten more will I kill," Black Moon responded without breaking stride.

"And you think killing is the answer?"

"If we do not fight, we will be nothing more than dust in the wind. I hear the soldier chief at Laramie is arming his men with the gun the traders call a breechloader. With such a gun I can reload from my running pony."

Fire Cloud's amazement shone on his broad brown face. He stopped in his tracks, his hand going out to catch his brother's arm. "You hate the whites, yet you would be like them by killing like them?"

Black Moon met his brother's gaze. "To fight the whites I must fight like them. To do that I need their weapons. Do you think they will come to me and offer their guns?" He laughed with sharp contempt. "No brother, I will have to take them. The whites give nothing away unless they have no use for it." He pulled his arm free and stormed off.

Fire Cloud hurried after him. "There is no arguing that the whites are a strange people, but even that is the work of the Great Spirit. Think, brother. The Great Spirit is within all things—the trees, the rivers, the mountains, the four-legged ones, the winged ones, even these strange white men."

"In the big treaty they made with our people they told us we can no longer make war on our Pawnee enemies, not even on those Crow dogs who steal our ponies and our women. Do they not know that by taking away the spirit of war the fighting men of the Lakota will be no more? And what would they take next? The hunters? And after that the men of peace?" Black Moon saw the tremor that passed over Fire Cloud's swarthy face. "Yes, brother, even you." Bitterly, he reiterated, "Peace is not possible."

These past seasons Black Moon's eyes had been on the Holy Road, the one the whites called the Oregon Trail. With each passing moon the wagon tracks grew deeper, until what started as a slow trickle was now like the spring river that washes over its banks when the high snows melt. Hard times were ahead. The clouds of war were already gathering.

CHAPTER 2

*T*he drumming of pony feet on the hard earth stirred Katie out of her slumber. Shouts from outside bolted her upright. She ran to the entrance of the lodge, flung the flap aside and stared at the scene outside in wide-eyed terror.

From over the rise came the walking soldiers, the one in front holding the red, white and blue flag. Behind them came the long-range rifles of the pony soldiers.

McCabe and Richard rushed from the lodge, still pulling on their moccasins.

Long Spear, the Brulè chief, emerged from his lodge carrying the large American flag that had been given to him as a gift by the Indian agent. He hurriedly tied it to the end of a long pole, then stood with feet braced, holding the pole, the flag flapping in the morning breeze.

The infantry came straight on. A force of mounted dragoons came up the creek to their rear. The warriors, armed with bows and arrows, held off the soldiers so that the people could flee. The women were crying. The children were screaming. Dropping everything, they ran to the safety of Long Spear's flag. But the soldiers did not stop their charge.

Unarmed, Long Spear ran forward, hands raised in protest against the oncoming soldiers. In the ensuing instant he lay dead, riddled with gunshot.

Something inside of Katie snapped when she saw all those people huddled beneath the flag. Dashing back into the lodge, she emerged with her father's loaded rifle. Moving outside of herself, she fired into the ranks of charging soldiers. When the rifle jammed, she threw it to the ground and grabbed one from the hands of a dead soldier. When that one was used up, she grasped it by its wooden stock and swung wildly at anything in a blue uniform. Then, dropping the rifle, she turned and fled, following the people as they made their escape up the creek.

Half a mile up the creek they stopped, gasping for breath, only to be surrounded again. Pulling themselves to their feet, they stumbled across the water and through the tangled brush. Some fell from exhaustion, others from the soldiers' guns.

Katie choked on the air that was thick and black and putrid from the smell of the soldiers' guns. Everywhere she looked Lakota blood clung to rocks and seeped into the earth from the white men's wrath.

***

The same stench of death caught Black Moon's attention. Jerking hard on the jaw rope, he brought his pony to a stiff halt. Faint white columns of smoke rose against the dark base of the hills in the distance, coming from the direction of Blue Water Creek where the Brulès were camped. His nostrils stung with the smell of gunpowder and burning hides. Applying quirt and heels he sped his pony to the place.

By the time he reached the creek darkness was falling, hastened by gathering storm clouds. Hiding his sorrel in a ravine, he crept to the summit of a hill overlooking the encampment. His fury exploded within him as his eyes seared upon the scene.

Parfleches, robes, shields, cradles and other things were strewn about in wild disarray. Some were still smoking. The lodges had holes blown clear through them. Even the earth all around was torn up, rocks splintered into fragments by the big guns, some pulverized into powder from the impact. The odor of death hung in the air.

He forced himself to move through the decimated village. He found the trader, McCabe, sprawled in a grotesque manner, gunshot holes in front of him and behind. Dead in a little clump nearby was the trader's son, the one called Red Beard, his pregnant wife and young daughter.

Black Moon returned to his pony and mounted. Along the creek he found tracks made by small moccasins indicating women and children. They were spaced far apart, and he knew they had been running. He kept to the low ground, careful to remain hidden.

At the top of a rise he dismounted and crept silently forward to spy on the moving shapes below. The bluecoats rode in a straggly line back to the fort. With them went the shuffling figures of the captured ones, the women in tightlipped silence, the children whimpering.

At the rear of the column, a good distance behind the others, rode two bluecoats.

"I got three scalps. Ya hear that, Virg?"

"Yeah? Well, lookit what I got." He jerked his thumb behind them to where his captive trudged along, hands bound, led by a length of coarse rope around her neck. "Ain't never seen no Injun with red hair before. Could be a breed. Whaddaya think?"

"I think we should find out."

Avid, greedy chuckles came from them as they reined their horses away from the column and slipped away unseen in the direction of a stand of dense pines. When they were concealed among the trees, they brought their horses to a halt and dismounted. It took some doing just getting hold of their captive. She kicked and scratched and fought as hard as she could, but eventually her strength gave out and they had no trouble overpowering her.

Unable to scream because of the dirty cloth they stuffed into her mouth, Katie closed her eyes and wished silently to die. Her mind cried in outrage at the rough hands that tore at her deerskin dress, ripping the sinew that held the beading at the yoke and sending the cowrie shells arcing into the darkness. Their rough, gluttonous hands inflicted pain on her arms and legs as they threw her to the ground. One of them landed on top of her with a thud that took her breath away. All she could do was shut her eyes tight and will herself far, far away from what was about to happen.

Somewhere beyond the tumult that raged in her mind she heard a brisk whirring sound, like the wind passing overhead. The man on top of her grunted and went suddenly limp, falling off to the side. And then, everything went silent.

Breathing hard, she gathered up the courage to open her eyes and nearly choked on her own gasp to see two inert shapes on the ground beside her. From each man's back protruded three feather-tipped arrows.

A new wave of terror gripped her. She scrambled to her knees, pulled her torn dress back down and jumped up to flee. A strong hand darted out of the shadows to staunch her flight. It was dark and she could not see the face of this newest menace. She struggled to get away, but he held tight.

With his free hand he reached for her face. She flinched in anticipation of the blow that did not come. Instead, he pulled the cloth away from her mouth and threw it to the ground.

Katie gulped in the air as if it were water. When she felt his grip ease on her arm, her panic turned to confusion. Eyes big and full of fear, she spoke in a raspy whisper.

"Who are you?"

The only reply she received was a tightening of his fingers and a rough yank forward.

He half-dragged her to where his horse waited. His hands encircled her waist to lift her into the air and plunk her down on his horse's back. In one swift and silent motion he was in place behind her. His arm was tight across her breasts. The strength in those taut muscles sent a cold chill through her despite the warm summer night. His other hand went around her to grasp the jaw rope. With a subtle tensing of his thighs he set the horse in motion.

When they emerged from the cover of the trees, the first faint drops of rain began to fall. Katie turned to look at him over her shoulder. Overhead, a flash of lightning illuminated his face, and she sucked in her breath to find herself looking into the coal-dark eyes of an Indian.

"Where are you taking me?"

He did not answer. And strangely, she did not care. Her eyelids were already beginning to droop. She was unaware of her head falling back against his smooth-skinned chest, or his strong arm winding tight around her to keep her from falling off the horse, or that the gentle patter of rain had turned into a downpour. She was aware only of the dark sleep that came on wings of mercy to shelter her from the grim reality of this day.

CHAPTER 3

𝒦atie awoke to a crackling fire.

Overhead, a ceiling of rock stared down at her. Dark, sinister walls loomed into the blackness farther than she could see. Eerie shadows danced over them whenever an imperceptible breeze set the yellow flames in motion. There was a dull ache at her temples. Her muscles torn, her flesh bruised, she was too tired to feel fear, too wrapped up in remembering to care about where she was.

With a shudder she recalled the tense and worried look on her father's face the night before the attack. It had made him look far older than his fifty years. For the first time she'd gotten a glimpse into his mortality, and it had frightened her. She tried to make sense out of what had happened but scarcely knew where to begin. It all seemed like a bad dream from which she was only just now awakening. But if it had been only a dream, how could she explain this pounding in her head and the ache in every bone? Most of all, how could she account for the burning hole deep down inside of her?

As her gaze moved cautiously about the cave, it came to rest upon a figure seated across the flames.

There was nothing friendly about him. He sat without moving, deceptively relaxed in a cross-legged position, puffing silently on a long-stemmed pipe. The fire sent shadows flickering across his face and bare chest and cast him in an ominous light. There was a menace about him, an undisguised hostility and a proud arrogance. The colors and design of the beaded bag that hung from his rawhide belt confirmed that he was Lakota.

Her voice sounded small and childlike when it slipped into the space between them. "How long was I sleeping?"

If he was surprised that she spoke his language, he gave no indication of it. Tossing a stick on the fire, he said stoically, "The sun has risen and fallen once."

A day. She had slept an entire day. It seemed incredible until she recalled just how much there was to forget. She began to tremble, and into the darkness she raged at the utter senselessness of it all. "Why did they have to die like that?"

A muscle twitched in his high-boned cheek. His voice came low and reeking of bitterness from across the flames. "Word of this killing will spread like wildfire and many others will be asking that question."

Remembering what her father always told her about the Indian way, Katie swallowed down the lump in her throat and said in a voice that quavered, "My father will have many fine gifts for you for helping me to escape."

"Your father is dead."

She did not hear him. "He will be very grateful to you."

He repeated, "Your father is dead."

This time she could not block it out. His cold, flat words were the awful confirmation of what she had already sensed in the depths of her being. They had a final, absolute ring to them.

"Richard." She uttered the name as part statement, part question, aimed at no one in particular.

He tapped the spent ashes out of the pipe bowl, saying as he did, "The one with hair the color of the red dog is dead."

It wasn't that he referred to Richard as a fox that caused her to flinch, but the casual way in which he said it. Tears began to form, hot, stinging tears of disbelief, outrage and sorrow. Her shoulders started to shake as great sobs seized her. Like water from a broken beaver dam the tears rushed from her eyes and she wept into her hands. First, her mother was taken from her, leaving a void that would never be filled. Now, her father and brother, and with them, dreams of Ireland and a life that was never to be fulfilled. The world was suddenly a dark and lonely place, with death and destruction as the only rewards for living.

Black Moon watched her from across the embers. "Death is a part of the circle of life," he said. "Man moves in a sun-wise direction. He comes from the south, the source of all life, and moves toward the west, the setting sun of his life. As he grows older, he approaches the cold north where the white hairs wait. If he lives long enough, he comes to the source of light and understanding that is the east. From there he returns to the place where his life began, to his mother, the Earth. We all return to the place of our beginning. Only the weak ones cry." There was no pity in his voice, no compassion, only a hint of mocking.

Katie lifted her chin and glared back at him. With tear-stained cheeks and eyes wild and bright, she declared with a sudden burst of pride, "I am not weak. I am strong."

His face remained implacable. He gave an indolent shrug, and said, "Is that why you shake like a frightened long-ears? Tell me, little red-haired long-ears just how strong you are."

"I am no rabbit," she said. "Do not call me that."

His jaw tightened at her insolence. "I will call you whatever I please."

"I have a name. It is Katie."

"Names can be changed. A boy is known by his cradle name until he earns a new one."

"But I am a woman, and even among the Lakota a woman does not change the name she receives at birth. My name is Katie and I will answer to no other."

From the storm clouds she saw gathering in his smoky eyes she expected him to draw his knife from its hide sheath and silence her with it for speaking so boldly. But he made no move toward his weapon.

They lapsed into silence. Katie had no idea how long she sat there with her knees pulled up to her chest, her arms hugging them tight. During the indeterminate hours that passed in which neither of them spoke, she scrutinized him from across the flickering flames.

His hair, unbound and hanging long and straight over his shoulders, was blacker than the recesses of the cave. The fire illuminated a face that bore the stamp of power and sheer force of will. With its high cheekbones, straight nose and well defined mouth, its handsomeness was compelling. It drew her toward it, much like the glazed windows of her father's cabin on the Laramie had often drawn magpies that flew against them with a thud and an explosion of feathers.

She could not help but notice that his legs were slim and hard, made for wrapping around a horse's bare back. A lean, tough belly showed not a hint of extra flesh. His bare narrow shoulders seemed perfectly made for slipping easily through thick groves and brush. His arms were well-muscled from a lifetime of drawing taut bowstrings. A band of red-dyed porcupine quills spanned one forearm. The hands that held the pipe, with their long, tapered fingers, were almost too beautiful to belong to a man.

Yet despite the physical appeal of him that she found so compelling, there was a hardness about him, of angular features and taut muscles and the suggestion of an inflexible spirit. But it was his eyes, in which the flames of the fire shone so brightly, that burned with such undisguised hatred it sent chills through her and forced her to turn her face away.

The silence stretched on and on.

After a while Black Moon drew from his rawhide bag a few hump ribs that had been flavored with melted back fat and tossed them into the fire. The fat sputtered and smoked and sent a savory aroma into the air. He speared one of the ribs with the tip of his knife and held it out to her, drawing her attention with a low grunt.

She made no move to take it.

With a shrug of indifference, he bit into the meat. When he had eaten his fill, he picked up his long-stemmed pipe and placed into the red stone bowl a pinch of fragrant willow bark and a little leafy tobacco.

"I have not thanked you for saving my life," Katie said grudgingly.

"I need no thanks from you," he replied as he coaxed spirals of smoke into the overhead darkness.

"Still, you did save my life. I suppose that makes us friends."

"I am no friend of the whites!"

The abruptness of his reply startled her. She responded with a flash of anger. "You speak as though all whites are as bad as the ones who killed those people on Blue Water Creek. That is as foolish as saying that all Lakota are as bad as the ones who killed the soldiers over the Mormon's cow."

"Whose voice first sounded in this land?" he exclaimed. "The voice of the Indian who had only bows and arrows. What has been done to our country we did not ask for and we do not want. When the white man comes into our country, he leaves a trail of blood and death behind him. Blue Water is proof of that."

Katie pushed the sleeve of her deerskin dress up past the elbow and thrust out her arm. "Look! Do you see the color of this skin? It is white. If you hate all whites so much, why did you save this one?"

He looked at her for several long, tense moments before answering. "Perhaps it was for the pleasure it gave me to kill those bluecoats."

An unearthly silence pervaded the cave after that.

Gradually, Katie's anger abated and the cold sting of despair set in. A chill sent her body into shivers despite the warmth generated by the fire. From across the fluttering flames she watched with cautious eyes as his gaze wandered about the cave, climbing high upon the walls into the darkness and wandering all about the ground as if he were alone and idling the time away. Several times she caught his eyes stray to her, and then look away in haste.

After a while he rose from his spot and went to the place where his blanket of blue trade cloth was spread over the ground. Dropping to his knees upon it, he removed a buckskin bag from his belt. The bag was beaded front and back in a colorful geometric pattern on a white background, with quilled drops ending in tin cones and tufts of dyed horse hair. The tenderness with which he handled the bag ran contrary to the overall fierceness of his demeanor. She could only guess at what the bag contained. The talon of an eagle perhaps, or a stone from the base of grizzly butte. Things of importance only to him. As he knelt there running his fingers over the powerful medicine, she knew he would rather die than reveal it to her.

But that was all right. She had no interest in him or the contents of his bag.

Her teeth were chattering with cold and her eyelids drooped with exhaustion. The next thing Katie knew, a hand was at her shoulder shaking her awake. He stood over her, wearing only a breechcloth, the fire flickering across his long, lean legs and near nakedness, the blanket of blue trade cloth dangling from his hand.

He tossed the blanket to the ground beside her. "Even a white woman must have warmth."

Katie snatched the blanket and hurled it at him. "If you can stand the cold, so can I."

With a shrug, he returned to his spot across the fire, laid down and pulled the blanket up over him.

Some time later, when the fire had burned down to a few smoldering embers, he came to her again, trailing the blanket behind him. Without a word, he dropped to the ground beside her and drew the blanket up over them both, using the heat of his lean, muscular body to chase the chill from hers. This time she made no protest. The raw masculine scent of him, mingled with the smell of sweet grass that emanated from his hair, filled her senses. Drawing in a deep sigh, she snuggled against him, closed her eyes and sank into a dark dream.

Two days later they rode into the Oglala village on the Running Water. Black Moon halted his pony before an unadorned lodge. Sliding off its rump, he walked to its side, placed his hands about Katie's waist and pulled her to the ground. He left her standing there while he disappeared inside.

From all around dark, curious, distrustful eyes peered at her. She'd never been afraid of the Sioux before. Her father had traded with them without any trouble, and her brother had married into Bone Bracelet's clan. Her visits to the Brulè village had always been happy, joyous times. But now, she felt suddenly like an intruder among hostile people who understood her even less than she understood them. Despite her circumstance, she straightened her back and stood as tall as she could, making eye contact with no one, feeling isolated and alone, so unbearably alone.

After what felt like an eternity Black Moon emerged from the lodge. "Some argue to send you back to the whites," he told her. "But Turning Hawk says your place is here." He shrugged, as if it made no difference to him. "The choice is yours."

Katie cast a wary glance around at the scores of eyes upon her. Unconsciously, she inched closer to him, feeling somehow safer in his shadow. He made no move to step away.

"What will become of me if I stay here?" she asked.

He looked down into those eyes that were the color of a new leaf, and said, "Turning Hawk has offered to take you into his lodge as his daughter. His woman is old. She has three sons but no daughters to help scrape the hides. He knows of the one you called father and says he was a good man." His expression darkened, telling her he was not convinced that any white man could be considered a good man. "Do you have a white family you can go to?"

Katie shook her head. "There is no one."

"You could go to the soldier town. Perhaps there someone would help you."

She had accompanied her father many times to Fort Laramie, but the thought of what the soldiers had done to Long Spear's village filled her with revulsion. No, there was no place for her at Laramie.

Privately, Katie assessed her options. McCabe was dead. Richard was dead. Bone Bracelet, Long Spear, and all the others she had known and loved were dead. For a reason that was unknown to her Providence had spared her life.

The question now was to which world did she belong, the white world to which she owed her heritage, or the Indian world to which she owed her life?

She looked up into his dark, intense eyes, and said, "I do not know your name."

He answered grudgingly, "My name is Black Moon."

"Is this your village?"

"My mother's lodge is at the end of the circle."

Despite what she sensed from his tone was his eagerness to be rid of her, the look in his eyes softened a little bit and seemed to beckon her to stay. He was fierce and imposing and made no secret of his hatred of the whites, and yet she felt no fear of him. He had saved her life when he could have let the soldiers have their way and then dispose of her. Was it really for the pleasure it had given him to kill them? Yes, she suspected it was. But there was more to it than that, and she need only to look past the savagery in his ebony eyes to the passionate man beneath to know that they shared a common bond, a wild, tempestuous nature and a love for this untamed land.

Where else could she gallop her pony across the plains and thrill to the feel of the wild wind blowing though her hair? Where but here would she ever find a welcome such as she knew these people would extend to her?

"Treat 'em fair and they'll do like to ye", her father used to say. They were, after all, just people, no better, no worse than anyone else.

And then there was Black Moon, whose handsomeness stole her breath away. Black Moon, her savior, fierce, violent, yet who she sensed was fair and just in his beliefs.

Black Moon, whose dusky eyes were searching hers for an answer.

For one incomprehensible moment Katie stood straddling both worlds, belonging to neither and feeling adrift with no one to guide her. For many long, silent minutes she grappled with doubt. Then, drawing in a deep, uncertain breath, and deriving strength from the Oglala warrior standing beside her, Katie made her choice.

CHAPTER 4

*B*lack Moon lay on his back on a hillside in the warm sunshine, watching the light in the sky flicker behind a passing cloud and breathing in the fragrance of sweet spring grass mingled with the smell onions and turnips in the cooking kettles. The dry wind that blew all morning settled into a gentle little breeze that teased the tips of his braids.

Having heard enough of his brother's talk of peace for one day, he complained, "You spend too much time with Turning Hawk, listening that old one's words of peace. When will you learn that battles are won with strong clubs and fast arrows, not with words?"

From where he lay beside him on the rocky ground tossing pebbles into the air, Fire Cloud turned his head lazily toward his brother. "That is just one way to deal with this problem with the whites. We can always learn to live in peace with them."

"You mean their big guns will force us to live in peace," his brother jibed. "Do you remember the time we climbed to the top of a rise and spied down on the bluecoats as they aimed one of their wagon guns out over the prairie? When the smoke cleared, the land was strewn with the bleeding carcasses of what had been a herd of pronghorns. That is what the big guns will do to us one day."

"Why are you always so serious?" asked Hail Storm, the brothers' reckless young cousin. "We would rather talk of girls. Have you noticed that just last season they were no more than plump little prairie chickens, but now they walk with straight backs and look at you with flirting eyes? They are like berries, ripe for the picking."

Black Moon's strong voice grew uncharacteristically quiet when the subject shifted to girls.

"Look at our bold friend here who hides his eyes at the talk of women," Yellow Hand said provokingly. "Can it be this brave Lakota warrior who speaks so strongly against the whites is ashamed to say that he desires the trader's daughter?"

Back Moon bristled. He had never liked Yellow Hand's fondness for taking more women than any man had a right to take. Of the dozens of women he had stolen, he hadn't paid for any of them. He just scoffed in the faces of the injured husbands, relying on his fierce war record to keep them from seeking retribution.

"The woman is *wasichu*," Black Moon snapped. "What use would I have for a white woman?"

"The same use Fire Cloud would have for my sister, Good Deeds," Yellow Hand replied.

"No woman would want a man whose skin is as pale as the white buffalo," Hail Storm teased.

Sensing his brother's discomfort, Fire Cloud sat up and turned to Hail Storm. "Did you never ask yourself why the Great Spirit made some of us different? Perhaps those are the ones He singles out for special things. It is not for us to wonder how greatness will show itself. It is enough for us to know only that it exists."

Black Moon looked up to find Fire Cloud's eyes upon him. Not only were the people divided over what should be done about the encroaching whites, but he and his brother were divided as well by virtue of their vastly different hearts. Fire Cloud's heart was too pure, his own too proud for them to ever stand together. In that brief moment an unspoken look passed between them, melting away the hostility and speaking of things that were becoming harder for them to say to each other with each passing moon. In less than a heartbeat it was shattered by Yellow Hand's obnoxious voice.

"They say the white girl holds much power. Why else would Turning Hawk have taken her into his lodge? Black Moon may have no use for her, or so he says, but I could find many uses for such power. I paid two ponies to the buffalo dreamer to make a flute out of cedar and decorate it with the carved body of a horse, the most ardent of all animal lovers. Once she hears the music from my flute, the woman, and the power, will be mine."

"The real power will be in the shirt," Fire Cloud said. "Turning Hawk has told me of a plan underfoot. Some Oglala headmen want to build a new chiefs' society to govern the people. It calls for seven older leaders, men who have seen more than forty winters, and four young men, to be chosen. They will be the owners of the people and will be given the bighorn shirts to wear."

"You will be one of the four," Hail Storm said confidently. "And after you are named shirt-wearer, Good Deeds' family will surely approve of you as a husband."

"The shirt is not yet on his back," Yellow Hand objected with a sneer. "For now, he is just the son of a holy man, without ponies or much else to give." He leveled a hard look at Fire Cloud. "My sister will go only to a man who wears the shirt or has a lot of ponies."

Knowing how desperately Fire Cloud desired both the bighorn shirt and Good Deeds, and disgusted by Yellow Hand's constant efforts to thwart the courtship, Black Moon got up and left.

He made his way to the stream where he went down on one knee and reached a cupped hand into the water for a drink. He was about to head back to the village when he spotted Katie coming down the path that led to the water.

He waited until she bent over the stream to fill the buffalo paunch with water before his laconic reflection came up behind her in the mirrored surface. It startled her, and she straightened up quickly, spilling water on her elk skin dress.

Black Moon's mouth widened into a grin, and he laughed, exposing flashing white teeth.

"Only a coward would laugh at something like that," she said, looking down at the wet stain on the front of her dress.

He could have sent her flying with one swipe of his hand for daring to speak to a warrior in such a disrespectful manner, but she looked so small and comical, like one of the little prairie chickens Hail Storm spoke of, that he let her vent her anger. And besides, the sound of her voice was pleasing to him.

She bent to pick up the paunch and aimed a sidelong look at him. "Perhaps what the people say about you is not true after all."

Amused, he asked, "And what do they say?"

"That the son of Claw is brave and one day will be a leader of the people."

He dismissed it with a shrug of a bare, sun-glistened shoulder. "My father has two sons."

"Yes, but the times are changing. One day the people will need a leader who does not cry for peace at every turn, but one to lead them in battle when peace is no longer possible. You and I both know that day is coming."

The smile faded from Black Moon's face. His eyes burned strongly into hers. He had never known a woman as bold as this one. Or as beautiful. Her hair was long, reaching nearly to her waist. Daylight danced along each strand, turning it as red as a setting sun. Beneath the skin of her dress he sensed the presence of willowy limbs and skin as soft as down. But it was her eyes that intrigued him the most. They were vibrant and alive and as green as the *Paha Sapa* in the spring moon. But there was more to her than what his eyes could see. How was it possible for her to know these things that troubled him and to echo them as clearly as though his own voice had spoken them?

"But it is too bad you will not be that man," she said

"And how do you know this? Did you see it in a vision?"

"The only vision I see is that of the arrogant man standing before me." She walked off with the half-filled paunch hanging heavy from her hands.

She was truly a strange woman, one moment amusing him, the next moment infuriating him. Her boldness, so much like a man's, impressed him. Her soft voice, so much like a woman's even in anger, thrilled him. He knew it was wrong to feel lust for a woman. Women were the bearers of life and were to be placed above the desires of men. But this one, with hair the color of the setting sun and her splendid green eyes, was driving a lance of indecision right through him. On one side stood respect and temperance, on the other selfishness and lust. It appalled him to think that he lusted after a white woman. He reminded himself again that she was his enemy. Yet looking into her green eyes was like looking into a pool of still water in which his image was reflected. The same wild spirit that ruled his heart dwelled also in hers. It was almost as if they were made of the same stuff despite the difference in the color of their skin. She was, without doubt, the most splendid woman he had ever seen, and while his sensibilities railed at the possibility, he knew it was useless to deny the strange attraction he had for the trader's daughter.

The sun glinted off Black Moon's smooth skin as he made his way to his pony staked before his mother's lodge. Jumping astride its bare back, he turned its head toward the prairie where he could be alone to think and to plan.

So many things were happening. The whites were taking his land and leaving a trail of Lakota blood in their wake. The buffalo herds were dwindling. The wagon tracks grew heavier each season on the Holy Road. Yesterday the scouts returned with news of bluecoats swarming like ants all along the flat-water. Little by little his country was shrinking. Soon it would be just a tiny island surrounded by a giant sea of white. With all these things troubling him, now there was this thing with the white woman who was slowly, inexorably working her way under his skin.

CHAPTER 5

*W*hen the days lengthened into heat and the sweet berries were ripe on the vines, all the bands came together in a ceremonial camp for the annual Sun Dance. Fire Cloud painted the sacred pole made from a cottonwood tree and decorated it with bundles of cherry sticks and tobacco offerings and a banner of reddened buffalo skin at its top. As a holy man, Claw worked with those warriors who had vows to fulfill and ordeals to endure in supplication to *Wakan Tanka.*

Everyone was busy preparing. Only Black Moon remained uninvolved. He felt no compunction to have his breast pierced with the sharp skewers attached by long thongs to buffalo skulls. The scars that formed after a man danced for hours under the weight of the skulls were an ever-constant reminder of what some men were willing to give of themselves.

Black Moon needed no such scars. He was willing to give more than mere pieces of flesh. He was willing to give up his life. His chance came when the ceremony and the days of feasting were over and he and the other warriors rode out of the village to go against their Crow enemies to avenge a killing from last summer.

His war pony was a powerful black creature whose coat

glinted from the slick bear's grease he rubbed into it. He bound up its tail in red flannel and painted a zigzag streak of yellow lightening across its muscular shoulder. His own hair and skin he left unadorned. Stripping down to breech cloth and moccasins, he mounted in one swift motion, muscles twitching at scent of danger in the air.

From their vantage point atop a hill overlooking the Crow village, Black Moon observed them turn their ponies out to graze. One sleek yellow pony caught his attention with its speed and beauty, and when the Lakota warriors rode down out of the hills to steal the horses, Black Moon claimed the yellow racer for his own.

The Crow warriors took out in hot pursuit. Black Moon raised his lance high over his head and gave out with a war whoop. "It is a good day to die!" he shouted. "Strong hearts, brave hearts to the front! Weak hearts and cowards to the rear!"

From out of the swirling dust the big black horse exploded, Black Moon clinging to its back, his heart racing with the excitement of war. Using the black's neck as a shield, he shot a succession of arrows as he raced into the enemy's ranks. Arrows whizzed through the air and bullets from Crow guns sang overhead, but Black Moon galloped on, zigzagging this way and that, nothing touching him but the wind, his thoughts racing ahead to the pride he would see in a certain pair of green eyes.

When the moon was fat again, the war party rode into the Oglala village. Pretty Shield's round face beamed with pride and she made a soft trilling of admiration for the Crow scalp Black Moon honored her with.

"Is Fire Cloud here?" Black Moon asked his mother. "I want to tell him of our victory."

Pretty Shield's eyes gave the answer even before she replied, her voice tenderly apologetic. "He is not here. He is in the hills with Turning Hawk." She saw his expression of eagerness change to disgust, and urged, "Try to understand him. To him killing of any kind is a bad thing. He can see no honor in it."

But Black Moon was beyond hearing. Turning away, he jerked the entrance flap aside and bent to enter the lodge.

Pretty Shield placed two crossed sticks before the entrance to signal to others that the one inside wished to be alone, and left her son to his private brooding.

When the night sun blossomed in the sky, the victorious warriors danced around a huge campfire in the center of the tribal crescent. Katie watched through a gap in the lodges, her wide-eyed gaze traveling up the long poles the women carried to where the remnants of human hair flicked about in the breeze.

Little had changed for her during the ten months she had been living with the Oglalas. As before, her days were filled with hard work and daydreams. It was only at night, when the nightmares came, that she was confronted with overwhelming loneliness and unbearable grief over the brutal loss of her white family. She would be forever grateful to Turning Hawk and his wife Kettle for taking her in, but *fitting* in was an entirely different matter.

Turning Hawk's sons brought meat to cook and hides to scrape, but it was Kettle to whom they brought them. Though she helped erect the lodge when the village moved to a new camping ground, the lodge belonged to Kettle. Other women had husbands, she had none. In the whole world there was nothing to call her own. Even her language was slowly slipping away. As time went by she found herself speaking and even thinking in their language until English had become something that flashed through her mind once in a while, like the memory of the life she used to know.

More and more her attention was drawn to Black Moon, the light-skinned Oglala with the fierce black eyes, who looked at her with disdain and yet who often looked her way. There was something about him that beckoned to her willful nature. She was undeniably attracted to him. His unbound hair, flowing like long thick ribbons over his shoulders, his handsome features and proud stance invariably made her throat go dry.

Even his feverish excitement for war was strangely thrilling to her. But she sensed a gentleness about him, as well. At times she thought she could see past his smoldering anger right down to the vital core of his heart that was soft and vulnerable, just as her own heart was.

Eagerly, she searched the faces dancing around the fire, looking for him. "Forget about him," she ordered herself. "Aye, he's a handsome devil, but he's no good for you. He's trouble." Muttering to herself, she turned her back on the brightly lit village and slipped into the darkness beyond the lodges.

She made her way to a grove of pines that stood like a massive black shadow against the night. The thick overhanging branches of the shaggy-leaf trees obscured the face of the moon. The drums throbbed in the distance. The cool night air whispered across her flesh. Her ears filled with the sound of her own heart beating. She stood perfectly still, thrilling to the reverberations that reached clear to her fingertips.

A twig snapped faintly underfoot somewhere in the blackness that enveloped her. Her hand flew to her mouth in an instinctive gesture as her eyes scanned the darkness. A rustle of leaves sent her whirling to flee. With a thud she ran smack into the hard wall of a chest that barred her flight. She opened her mouth to scream, but a familiar voice froze the sound in her throat.

It was Yellow Hand. The fever of the dance burned in his wild eyes. The horse-hair roach atop his head bristled arrogantly in the midnight breeze. With his face painted black he looked like the devil just stepped out of the pit of hell. Without warning his lips came down over hers in a forceful kiss.

Memories of her experience at the hands of the soldiers surfaced with a vengeance. She beat at his chest with her fists, but he only laughed and crushed her against him. She was no match for him. Trapped in his arms, she was powerless to avoid his groping hands.

The sudden pressure of a grip on Yellow Hand's shoulder spun him around and propelled him backwards. When he regained his footing, he found himself looking into the furious eyes of Black Moon.

"You disgrace yourself and the woman with this kind of behavior," Black Moon charged.

A look reeking of hatred twisted Yellow Hand's face.

"What difference does it make? She is only a white woman."

In the blink of an eye Black Moon's knife was at Yellow Hand's throat.

Katie lunged for Black Moon's arm. "No! Do not kill him. Not over me. Please. It is not worth the trouble it will bring."

For several tense seconds the world and everything in it seemed to stand deathly still. Then, with a shove, Black Moon released him.

Yellow Hand aimed a murderous glare at them. Mumbling an angry vow of revenge under his breath, he stalked off.

Black Moon replaced the blade in its hide sheath. His fingers closed painfully over Katie's arm to jerk her around to face him.

"You should know not to leave camp," he said. His face was stamped with fury. "Those Crow dogs love nothing better than to attack Lakota villages when the people are busy with the dance. You have been spared the experience of a Crow attack, but there are many who can tell you how they come charging in, killing and scalping and carrying off the women and children. Do you want to be one of those they take?"

Katie squirmed to free herself from his cruel grip. "You are only trying to frighten me. Why should I fear them? I am white, and everyone knows they are friendly to whites."

He held on tight. "A white woman living among the Lakota?" he scoffed. "Do you think it would make any difference to them?" He was pulling her closer as he spoke, so close his breath came in hot, rapid bursts against her cheek. "Forget what you have learned from the whites. You would do well to learn that you live among the Oglala now."

His arrogant, mocking tone infuriated her beyond reason. Without stopping to consider the consequence, she responded with a flurry of heated words. "You are a brute of a man! How dare you speak to me that way? You forget that I am here because I choose to be, and if I feel like leaving, I will do that, too. Do not tell me what to forget and what to learn. It seems to me you could learn something from the whites you hate so much. And you would do well to learn a thing or two from a woman!"

Her eyes blazed up at him and her chest heaved and strained against the tanned skin of her dress. A shaft of pain seared up to her shoulder in the ensuing moment when he pulled her hard up against his naked chest. Winding his arm around her waist, he crushed her body to his, taking her breath away with the strength of his hold. She opened her mouth to protest, but the sound was eclipsed by his lips that closed over hers in a hard, anger-filled kiss.

There was no tenderness in him, no gentleness. Holding her pinned against him, he kissed her harshly and thoroughly. She felt the bite of his arousal beneath his breech cloth and the hard muscles of his thighs wrapped in leggings of blue trade cloth. Her legs grew weak. Her thoughts began to spin out of control. Trapped in Black Moon's powerful embrace, Katie was unaware at first of the way her own body was responding.

It grew upon her slowly. The throbbing began somewhere deep down inside, spreading outward, racing like a wildfire through her bloodstream to every limb until the feverish pounding threatened to consume her. Her mind gave up its hold on reason, ceding control to her emotions. Without thinking, she lifted her arms and wound them around his neck.

His hand moved slowly up her back to caress the bare flesh at the nape of her neck beneath the heavy curtain of her hair. His fingers entwined themselves in the thick, red mass, crushing the silky softness in his palm.

Katie's head fell back, giving his lips access to the pulsing hollow of her throat. She made a little sound that vaguely resembled a moan. She struggled, but only halfheartedly. Something took hold of her that she didn't fully understand. In the arms of this half-naked man she was powerless to do anything but submit. She was all too conscious of the pressure of his lean, hard body, the heat of his flesh, the softness of his hair between her fingers.

His voice issued from a place deep in his chest, low and threatening at her ear. "If you know what is good for you, you will leave this place now. If you stay, you know what will happen."

Yes, she knew where this was leading, but she had not

the will to try to stop it. His kiss was hot and strong and sucked the breath right out of her lungs. She could scarcely breathe when he guided her to the ground.

She lay back, breathing in the fragrant scent of pine bark mingling with the heady aroma of leather clinging to his skin. Overhead the shaggy leaves murmured in the breeze. Moonlight sifted through the thick branches to dapple the ground. His lips moved lingeringly from her mouth to her neck where he buried his face in her thick hair while his hands moved over her buckskin dress, exploring the swells and hollows of her body. His strong fingers set into motion a million tiny nerve endings all over her body.

She forced herself to lie still as he undressed her, trying to be brave by telling herself that this was what she had wanted all along. Hadn't she come out here tonight half-expecting…hoping…to find him? She shivered against the cool night air that pranced across her naked flesh while a surge of warm embarrassment colored her cheeks, for her body had never before been looked upon by a man's eyes.

She made a feeble attempt to cover herself with her hands, but he pushed them aside and murmured, "I want to look at all of you."

Her stomach tightened, but she allowed his hungry eyes to gaze their fill, making no further protest, not even when his lips kissed every inch of her skin and his fingers sought the secret places of her body. She grew relaxed under his touch, until he rose and kicked off his leggings, and then she grew afraid. She had never been this close to a naked man before.

"Touch me," he coaxed.

Her hands moved haltingly across his broad shoulder, to his smooth-skinned chest, past his taut belly and over slim flanks, thrilling at the realization that a man's skin could be as soft as her own. With a curiosity borne of a naturally reckless heart she moved her hands along his lean, tight body, exploring its contours. She felt his muscles constrict involuntarily at her touch, and heard his soft gasp when her fingers closed around the hardness of him.

Winding his arms tightly around her, he rolled her onto her back and slid on top of her. He brought his face close to hers and whispered against her lips, "Now I will make you my woman."

He was gentle at first, with movements that were slow and pleasurable, lulling Katie into a false sense of security that was ultimately shattered with one hard thrust. Her body heaved upwards from the quick, sharp pain and her cry was lost in his kiss. Hearing her gasps of wonder and pain, he paused, moving his hand downward, his fingers caressing her until her panic subsided. And then he began to move inside of her, slowly at first, and then with thrusts that grew stronger and more urgent, the steady rhythm driving away all pain, fear and uncertainty.

By instinct she matched his movements until she could no longer tell in whose passion she was drowning, his or her own. A warmth covered her that was so beautiful and so powerful that she moved her body with the sheer joy of it.

A ragged whisper tore from his lips as his body shuddered. "*Mitawin. Mitawin.*"

Katie recognized the words. My woman. My woman.

This was good, and it was right, and it was what she had been waiting for from the moment she met him. Except for the initial pain of his penetration, which had turned into an explosion of pleasure, she knew he would never hurt her again. In the arms of this fierce Oglala warrior she felt safe and protected and bound by a common fire raging in both their hearts.

Afterwards, she lay in his arms on the soft, pine-scented ground, eyes closed, her breathing slowly returning to normal. Stars twinkled in the midnight sky, and somewhere in the distance the dance drums pulsated. Through the shadows she could see his scowling expression and felt the old shield of hostility once again up between them. Hurt and confused by his behavior, she got up and dressed in silence.

When they turned to leave that spot beneath the pines, her voice broke the stillness with a single word. "Why?"

In the hazy starlight that played across his face his jaw muscles tightened. "I have sworn to fight the whites," he said. "To defeat them and drive them from my land. Nothing will get in the way of that. Nothing."

Back at the village Black Moon waited until she slipped

unseen between the lodges. Then, with the night sun sending streamers of hazy blue light to guide his path, he made his way to the pony herd. Minutes later he headed for the hills at a gallop.

He stayed in the hills for seven suns seeking answers to the questions haunting him. Why was he such a slave to his body that he could not find the strength to resist this woman? When had she changed from an enemy whom he despised and mistrusted into a flame that ignited his blood? Despite everything, her spell had broken through, piercing his heart as surely as an enemy's arrow. She was still his enemy, but only to his heart, and one he could no longer do without.

Hail Storm and the others could laugh at him all they wanted. When had he ever cared what others thought of him? All he cared about was what he thought of himself. The girl was white and he had sworn to fight the whites. His desire for her was his only weakness. And yet, she was like him, strong-willed and resilient, tenacious and unafraid, so different from the Lakota girls who did as they were told and followed orders blindly. With such a woman at his side he could do anything. Where was the weakness in that? Yellow Hand wanted her for the power it was said she carried, but he wanted her for the way she made him feel—invincible. And for the way she looked at him with those splendid eyes, daring him to put his hatred of the whites aside and see her, only her.

He heaped severe reproaches on himself for what he had allowed to occur between them beneath the shaggy-leafs. It had been too easy for him to lose control of himself with her. Control was everything. He could afford no weakness in the battles he knew were coming. And yet, now that he had tasted the sweetness of her, there was no turning back.

By the time Black Moon came down from the hills he had made an important decision. He spoke to his father about it immediately upon his return. It was not until the new moon, however, that anything came of it.

It was one afternoon after returning home from going out again against his Crow enemies. The news awaiting him at his lodge made the Crow scalp dangling from the pommel of his hide saddle meaningless to him. His eyes grew large with disbelief and his anger burst from him like a hard-thrown lance.

"They will not let me have her?" he stormed. "You mean they will not let her go!" He stripped off his buckskin shirt and tossed it to the ground with a savage gesture. "They call her a Lakota, yet they will say what she can and cannot do?" He gave out with a snort of disgust. "Just like the *wasichus* who tell others how to live."

Claw sat silent, staring into the fire while his son vented his fury. Then he spoke. "I knew when you came to me and told me you wanted the girl that nothing good would come of this. Yet I did as you asked and went to Turning Hawk to speak in your behalf. And now you will not accept the answer. My son, you were born to the excitement and glory of the warpath. You have a sharp, quick mind for the planning. The young ones look to you with awe and admiration. The warriors hold you in high esteem. The women are attracted to your unusual handsomeness. All that, and still you want something you cannot have."

Claw sighed deeply. "When you were gone, the sons of Turning Hawk came here to say that you cannot have her without a fight."

Black Moon's fire-lit face came up in sharp surprise. "They are fools to bring bad feelings among the people over a woman."

"It is not the woman," Claw said.

"I know," his son hotly replied. "It is her power they wish to sell for the most ponies. So, tell me, father, who has offered the most ponies for her?"

Claw answered with hesitation. "Yellow Hand."

"I am not surprised. That one has always sought to have enough for ten men. Now he wants the woman's power to strengthen his own lodge."

Claw shrugged and tossed a stick onto the fire. "That may be, but they are prepared to fight to keep the power where they want it. Many helpless ones would get hurt." The fire crackled as the knotted stick sputtered into flame. "How many will suffer because you desire something that can never be yours?"

Black Moon's eyes met his father's across the yellow

flames in a flash of brilliance that made Claw tremble. "Never?" he seethed. "We will see about that."

CHAPTER 6

*W*hen the spring moon was fat, the ceremonial camp was set up, round as all sacred things are round. The council lodge was erected and painted with holy things. Inside, the headmen sat in a circle, smoking, passing the pipe from east to west. After deliberating they came outside and instructed a group of horsemen to circle the camp four times, each time stopping to pick out one of the four young men to become the shirt-wearers and protectors of the people.

The first two times around they stopped before the sons of two of the headmen. The third time around they reined up before Lone Horn, the Minniconjou.

The horsemen circled the camp for the fourth and final time. When they stopped before the lodge of Pretty Shield, Fire Cloud's heart began to pound. A name was called. It was not his. With a look of stunned disappointment on his face he watched his brother stride forward to accept the shirt.

With the bighorn shirt came Black Moon's triumph, for surely the sons of Turning Hawk would not dare turn him down when he went to them personally to ask for their adopted sister.

With the establishment of the chiefs' society and the choosing of the men to wear the bighorn shirts, Turning Hawk had a hard decision to make. That night the hot coals glowed over his seamed face. When Kettle came forward to prod the dimming embers, he took one of her gnarled hands in his and guided her to the ground to sit beside him on the skin.

"Do you have a preference for which man we should give our daughter to?"

"Several have asked," she said. "There is Gray Wolf."

"He already has two wives and treats them badly."

"There is Yellow Hand."

"That one is thirsty for power."

"There is Black Moon."

"That one is at war with himself over his hatred of the whites."

"Your councils have always been wise," she said. "I know you will make the right choice for her. She is a good girl, if not a little too headstrong. But are not all wild things so?"

Long after Kettle had slipped beneath her robe and was snoring peacefully, Turning Hawk sat before the fire, throwing an occasional piece of fat into the embers, encouraging smoke to waft out into the night through the smoke hole at the top of the lodge where the poles were gathered, while he pondered over what to do.

By dawn's light he had made up his mind, but he shrewdly waited until some of the warriors had ridden south to visit their Cheyenne allies and were gone several suns before telling anyone. And then the camp crier went through the village, announcing the news to one and all that Turning Hawk's daughter would go to Fire Cloud.

Stunned, Fire Cloud went at once to Turning Hawk to protest.

"It is your responsibility to preserve harmony within the tribe," the old man said.

"But how can my taking this woman do that when it will destroy the happiness of so many—my brother, your daughter, Good Deeds, and myself?

"The people are to be placed above everything else," Turning Hawk insisted, "including the selfish desires of a few."

When Katie heard of Turning Hawk's decision, she was plunged into a well of confusion and doubt over what to do. She owed a deep debt of gratitude to him for taking her in when she had no place else to go. But to marry a man she did not know or love? All she needed was a sign from Black

Moon, a single glance from his dark eyes asking her...telling her...willing her not to do it, and it would have stopped right then and there. But with Black Moon gone, she was left to the persuasiveness of Turning Hawk and to her own sense of obligation.

In the summer Moon of Ripe Berries Fire Cloud and Katie were married.

She found her husband to be a gentle, soft-spoken man, not at all like his fierce, hotheaded brother. In the weeks that followed she grew to like him for his kindness and respect him for his beliefs. But there was no sense in either of them denying that her heart belonged to another man and his heart belonged to another woman. And so, they came to an understanding to live as husband and wife in all ways except one, and to tell no one that they did not sleep beneath the same robe, not even Black Moon, so as not to bring disgrace upon Fire Cloud.

The thought of the night beneath the pines with Black Moon was seared forever on Katie's heart, haunting her with its memory of his fiery kisses and heated possession that had sealed the tempestuous bond between them. She had no idea what his reaction would be when he learned of her marriage to his brother, but she knew it would not be good.

One day when the chokecherries were ripening and Black Moon had been gone for many weeks, there came a scratching at the door to her lodge. Laying aside the hide shirt she was mending, she swept the flap aside and went outside to find Pretty Shield standing there holding the jaw rope of the magnificent yellow racer Black Moon had captured last summer.

"It is a wedding gift from my son," Pretty Shield explained in answer to Katie's questioning look.

Katie's eyes darted about anxiously for a sign of him. "When did he return?"

"Yesterday."

She bit her lip. "What did he say?"

"He said to give you the yellow pony. Then he packed his things and rode out."

Katie looked at the horse. "Why did he not bring it to me himself?"

Pretty Shield shrugged, and with a half-written apology in her dark eyes, said, "Who can understand that one's ways?"

Katie's heart sank, but what did she expect, that he would stay in the village and get used to the idea that his woman was now his brother's wife?

"You do not approve of this marriage," she said to her mother-in-law.

"Too many hearts are broken over this, and no good can come of that. But I am glad to have a daughter-in-law to help with the cooking on days of feasting and the scraping of the hides Black Moon brings home after a hunt." She handed the jaw rope over to Katie and walked away.

Katie stroked the racer's soft, fleshy muzzle, rubbing her face against his. As she had seen Black Moon do, she brought its nose to her mouth and breathed the horse's power into her being, then blew her own spirit into the horse's nose, making them as one.

The racer's deep golden color reminded her of the flame at the center of a fire. "Your name will be *Peta*," she whispered. "Fire."

When Fire Cloud returned to the lodge later that day, he just shrugged and accepted the fact that another man had given his wife a valuable gift. Katie said nothing, but inwardly she was disappointed that there was not the slightest show of jealousy on his part. Black Moon would have flown into a rage and insisted she return the horse.

The next afternoon, Katie ignored the onions and turnips she had dug up that morning for the cooking pot, and left the lodge. Jumping on *Peta's* bare back, she turned his head in the direction of the prairie.

He was a runner, born and bred for speed. With her slender legs wrapped around him, grasping a fistful of coarse, honey-colored mane, she galloped him up and down the flat, dry land. The wind rushed past her face and through her hair. Exhilaration surged through her blood. As she sped across the prairie, she was struck by a similarity. The excitement of racing *Peta* was akin to the emotion that Black Moon inspired in her. Now she understood why he had given her this fine animal, so that she would never be able to forget their one night of fierce passion, and remember always the tempestuous bond that existed between them.

She returned to the camp from her ride, cheeks flushed, breathless with excitement. Sliding from *Peta's* golden back, she picketed him in front of the lodge and worked with a piece of tanned hide to rub down his frothy coat, unaware of the eyes watching from the hillside.

As the Crow warrior's gaze traveled over the village, they stopped abruptly upon a sight that made them grow large. Picketed before one of the Lakota lodges was the yellow racer stolen from him last summer.

Slipping past the scouts he entered the unsuspecting village and made his way straight for the horse. He quickly untied the rope securing it to a stake in the ground and was about to lead it away when a sound from behind made him freeze in his tracks.

Katie emerged from the lodge just then. Her eyes flared wide when she saw the Crow warrior. She grabbed for the knife at her belt and opened her mouth to scream, but he lunged for her. Clamping a hand over her mouth, he pulled her back into the lodge, the heels of her moccasins dragging in the dirt.

Inside the lodge he threw her to ground and pounced on top of her. The weight of him forced the air out of her all at once. The knife fell from her hand as she gasped for breath and struggled to escape his hold. Her attempt to kick him in the soft vulnerable place between his legs only increased his fury.

Her teeth bit into the hand over her mouth. He grunted with pain and brandished his knife before her terrified eyes. Katie squeezed her eyes shut, preparing for the worst. In the darkness came flashes of memories, of her father, the cabin along the Laramie, of Richard and Bone Bracelet, of *Peta* and Fire Cloud, but most of all of Black Moon, whose image overpowered all others in her few remaining moments.

But the excruciating death she anticipated did not come. Instead, he shoved a small scrap of hide into her mouth and swiftly bound her wrists with the strips of rawhide she'd been using to mend a shirt.

With the squirming woman slung over his shoulder and

the yellow racer in hand, he slipped out of the village. It took some work getting her onto his pony, she thrashed about so, but when she was astride, he climbed up behind her, and with a savage kick to his pony's flanks, they were galloping away from the Oglala village.

CHAPTER 7

McCabe had always spoken well of the Crow. They were friendly to whites, he said, and made good trades. But it was not with them that Katie wished to be. Her life had taken yet another drastic turn, only this time, Providence had given her no choice in the matter.

Her captor, Big Belly was not actually a Crow at all, but a Gros Ventre who had been taken captive as a child and adopted into the tribe. He was a burly brute with calloused hands and a bellicose manner. His ponderous belly had earned him the name used teasingly by others. He had two wives who were sisters, Two Scalps, a gentle girl heavy with child, and her older sister, Corn Woman, who liked to lay with other men in the tall reeds. He had married them, reasoning that there would be less friction between his wives if they were sisters. Sometimes the method worked. In Big Belly's case, it did not.

For Katie, life in the Crow village was filled with thoughts of escape. As the weeks went by she secretly gathered bits of food which she wrapped in scraps of hide and hid beneath her robes. One day she found a knife, another time a flint with which to strike a fire, and buried them. When the time was right, she would take *Peta* and flee. She waited only for the right moment.

But Katie's hopes of escape were shattered when Big Belly returned to the lodge one evening and announced that he had sold her to another man for four ponies. Their meal was a tense affair. Big Belly slopped down his bowl of soup, grabbed the whiskey jug he had given the traders five beaver pelts for and went out to join the other braves in a game of hands.

Corn Woman was off in the corner making herself pretty for the man she was sneaking off to meet behind the lodges. Katie was locked behind a wall of numbed silence.

Only Two Scalps was happy, singing to herself and patting her swollen belly as she cleaned up around the lodge. "Why do you object to the man my husband has chosen for you?" she asked.

With the smattering of Crow that Katie knew and with the aid of hand signals, she replied, "Because I do not love him."

"I did not love Big Belly when he took me, but I have come to love him. A young woman does not fall in love and get married just to please herself. She must listen to her father and marry the man he chooses for her."

"But I do not even know the man he has chosen."

"You will like Watchful Fox," Two Scalps assured her. "He is young and handsome and he has many ponies."

Katie was unimpressed. "Then why does not someone else marry him?"

"Among our people a man may not take a woman from his own clan. Watchful Fox comes from a large clan. It is so large that it is nearly the whole village. There are not many women he can choose from. When you came along, it was right that he should ask for you."

"Do not forget the ponies he offered for her," came Corn Woman's sharp voice from the corner. "Our husband is fond of a large herd. Each year it grows fatter, just like his belly." Tugging on one of the lodge stakes until the wood loosened, she crawled under the lodge cover out into the waiting night.

"She speaks of him like that because she knows I am his favorite," Two Scalps said. "It is I who carry his child. I who have the right to paint my face when there is a feast or a dance. I am his favorite because I show him respect. Corn Woman does not. We share one husband but we are married to two different men. If Big Belly knew of her wanderings, he would cut off the tip of her nose in a sign for all to see that she is an unfaithful wife."

Katie sank into a well of desperation. Two Scalps' claim that the warrior called Watchful Fox was young and handsome failed to stir her interest. There was only one man she wanted, one man whose face she carried deep into her dreams at night, one man's name on her lips as she sat alone through another long and lonely night.

The sun was glinting off the treetops and a yellow warmth spread over the sky the next morning as Katie knelt by the stream to fill the paunch. A breeze flowed gently from the ridge, rifling the edges of the four-poled Crow lodges. In the distance rose a grizzled butte, the aged boulders at its summit looking lonely and detached, much the way Katie was feeling. High above the plain an eagle soared with spread wings on currents of air, screeching as it climbed the sky, passing before a white cloud and then disappearing beyond the horizon. Katie watched it go, wishing she could sprout wings and rise into the cloud like the warrior bird.

The wild, free times were gone. Among the Oglalas there had been much hard work to do, but she could jump astride her pony and gallop across the prairie and no one would try to stop her. Here among the Crow, her every move was watched. She was permitted only to go to the stream for water. Any attempt at escape would be noticed by the scouts. A feeling of desolation came over her, not unlike that which had followed in the wake of the massacre on Blue Water that had turned her life upside down. She had thought then that nothing more could be taken from her, but now she knew otherwise.

She'd found a home among the Oglalas, and in Black Moon a passion unlike anything she had ever known before. But that was gone now, and she was left with another empty, aching hole inside that nothing, not even the most handsome Crow warrior in the world, could fill.

Suddenly, a shadow loomed up beside her, scattering her thoughts like a flock of magpies. Glancing up, she saw Corn Woman standing over her, arms laden with small wood for the cooking fire.

Corn Woman dropped her load to the ground and knelt

beside Katie. "If you marry Watchful Fox, you will become just like me." Her voice carried a hint of warning. "I am not a good woman. I wander from man to man because the one I call husband is not the one I love. It is a hard life. For you it will be even harder. Watchful Fox is handsome, yes, but he is reckless and swiftly loses interest in a woman. There can be no happiness for you with him."

Katie regarded Corn Woman with suspicion. "Why are you telling me this?"

"Because I know what it is like to be in love. Yes, you are in love," she said in answer to Katie's look of surprise. "I can see it in your eyes. He is one you call husband?"

Katie shook her head. "He is not my husband, but I love him. His name is Black Moon. He is a Lakota warrior."

"Do you wish to return to him?"

"I would do anything to see him again."

Corn Woman bit her lip and cast a sly glance around. "Escape is not impossible," she whispered.

"You would help me?"

Corn Woman nodded. Rising, she gathered up her wood, and said, "In two suns the hunters will ride out for the greasy-grass where the scouts have spotted a big herd. That will be your chance. I will have a pony waiting for you in the trees." Her gaze strayed tellingly to a grove of shaggy leafs in the distance.

"What about Two Scalps?"

"You are wise not to trust my sister," Corn Woman said with a smirk. "I will see to it that she is busy."

"Some husbands take their wives with them on the hunt. Maybe Big Belly will take Two Scalps," Katie suggested.

"My husband would not bother to take a woman on the hunt. She would just get in his way. All we are good for is to clean his lodge, cook his meat and for him spill his seed into."

At the undisguised disgust in Corn Woman's voice, Katie remarked, "It is fortunate, then, that it is Two Scalps who carries his child."

Corn Woman laughed, rustling the cowrie shells on the yoke of her dress. "It is no mistake that the seed he spills into me has never grown into a child. The old woman who lives at the far end of the village will share her plants for a small price.

Her man died and she has no sons, so she lives alone. No one pays much attention to her. The food I bring keeps her alive and keeps Big Belly's seed from growing strong in me. My sister has made a little sand lizard that will contain her child's cord." She laughed again, this time harshly. "The little lizards are hard to kill, so she thinks its power will protect the infant after it is born, but nothing can protect it from Big Belly. That one cares for nothing but his food, his ponies and the fire water the traders bring. When he drinks enough of it, his anger knows no limits."

Katie felt a pang of sympathy for Corn Woman, trapped in a brutal, loveless marriage. Was it possible she had found a friend among these strangers? Dropping her voice to a conspiratorial whisper, she asked, "How will we plan this?"

"Be careful," Corn Woman cautioned. "The scout is watching."

Katie glanced over her shoulder to where the scout perched on the hillside had his eyes trained on the two women by the stream.

"We will meet again at this place to plan it," said Corn Woman.

For the first time since she'd been captured Katie felt hope stir in her heart. To see Black Moon again, to feel safe and protected by him, was all that mattered. Yes, he was hurt and angry that she had married his brother, and she knew how fierce his anger could be, but when she had a chance to explain to him the reason she had gone through with it, and how very much she loved him above all others, then surely he would let go of his rage and somehow, some way, they would find a way to be together. With Corn Woman's help she would get that chance.

CHAPTER 8

Black Moon's war pony pranced nervously beneath him as he held the far-seeing glasses to his eyes and surveyed the bridge across the North Platte. Beyond it was an army outpost.

"The bridge must be burned," he said. "Then we can cross at the shallow ford and attack the stockade. But first we must draw the bluecoats out."

The warriors rode down to lure the soldiers out of the fort, but it did not work. A Cheyenne called No Neck reined his pony close to Black Moon's, and signed, "The bluecoats are afraid to come out."

"They fear our wrath," Black Moon signed back.

"And well they should for attacking a defenseless Cheyenne village two moons back. Did they think we would let them get away with that?" But as No Neck spoke, the gates to the outpost swung open and a column of soldiers galloped out. "So, they have decided to come out and fight after all."

Black Moon stretched a lean arm in the direction of a wagon train slowly approaching from the east. "There is the reason they have come out."

Without further discussion, they urged their ponies into a gallop.

The wagons were already forming a circle when the warriors charged down out of the hills. Black Moon's familiar war cry pierced the air. "It is a good day to fight! A good day to die!"

For Black Moon, war was a path to honor and glory. With swift arrows and a fast horse he could almost forget the pain gnawing at his heart over Katie's marriage to his brother. It was to these faithful Cheyenne allies he had fled when he heard the news of it. For two moons he had lived with them in their village at a bend in river. He ate with them, hunted with them, and today he fought alongside them, and, if the Great Spirit wished it, he would die with them.

"Make them empty their guns!" he shouted as he lashed his pony straight toward the wagons.

Like the blizzard wind the warriors swept down upon the wagons, forcing the white men to fire rapidly and repeatedly, emptying their guns in a hurry. With Black Moon leading, the mixed force of Cheyenne and Lakota fighting men jumped their ponies over the barricades. The whites were outnumbered. In less than an hour the fighting was over, and the warriors rode back to the Cheyenne village at a slow pace, raising no dust.

In the days that followed Black Moon was inducted into the Crooked Lances, a Cheyenne warrior society, in recognition of his bravery in the recent fight and as a sign of the strong bond existing between him and his Cheyenne friends. A feast was made. Pitches of yellow flame from the big fire leapt high into the darkness and the Cheyenne drums echoed through the night.

While the others danced and sang of their bravery, Black Moon sat with the Cheyenne chiefs in council. On this night his usually laconic face brightened when Lone Horn entered, his face still dusty from the long ride south.

"Tell us what news you bring," said one of the Cheyenne headmen. As he did, he placed an ember in the bowl of a long-stemmed pipe and drew on it four times, four being a sacred number. "The pipe is the symbol of truth, a sacred thing through which all things come together." He held out the pipe to Lone Horn. "The pipe knows when you speak the truth."

Lone Horn accepted the pipe, puffed four times, then handed it to the man next to him, east to west in a sun-wise direction. His scarred chest glowed red from the hot coals. His eyelids were heavy, swollen, fixed in mid-descent, giving him a perpetual hooded look. Speaking and signing at the same time, he said, "The whites come into Lakota country and drive stakes in a row from the Platte clear up to the branched-horn river, the one they call the Yellowstone, right through the heart of our hunting grounds. The wagons and the horsemen follow the stakes north to the diggings in search of the yellow metal. They must be stopped."

"Our scouts have seen wagons heading up the Holy Road," said the Cheyenne. "Smoke signals have been sent up against the sky calling in our warriors. We will meet at Lodgepole Creek when the new moon is fat."

"Do nothing against those whites," Black Moon advised. "Make no hostile move against them. Let them see you fanned out over the rise. Whenever one man leaves the line, another must take his place. Have every man who owns a looking glass wear it at his breast so that it makes a great shining upon them. Have the lances and arrow tips rubbed to brightness. Blind them with your power by day. At night let them see your fires and hear the calls of the scouts. They call the Indians wolves. To us, the true-dog is another brother, one who uses up the dead things that would poison the earth. Let them wonder whether it is a four-legged enemy that prowls close to their campfires at night or a two-legged one. After many days of this their terror will be real. And in terror there is weakness. That will be the time to strike."

Heads nodded as the others slowly began to understand the cunning of Black Moon's plan.

"You must change your fighting ways," he told them. "You will never win against the whites with your usual hit or miss way of making war. Striking a first coup has always been an honor in any battle, but these whites are different. It is not enough for them to touch an enemy. When they strike, they strike to kill. They plan carefully the taking of every Indian life. They do not come tearing and hollering with each man fighting to win a personal honor. They come as one, moving like the wind over the grass."

He paused to look at each man in turn, the fire dancing in his dark eyes, daring any of them to refute him. "The time of our fathers is gone. A new way is before us. The way of the white man. On the one hand it threatens our existence, but on the other, it teaches us that if we want to win, we must fight like them. If we want to survive, we must think like them."

Black Moon rose fluidly to his feet and looked down at the circle of men whose faces glowed in the flickering flames. "The new way also teaches us that we must do these things if we want, above all, *not* to be like them. Think on these things, brothers. I have shown you the way. I have made you aware. The rest is up to you."

Lone Horn rose from his cross-legged position and followed Black Moon from the lodge out into the balmy night air. "It is good to see you again, *kola*," he said to his friend. "I see you are still counseling your strange ways of warfare."

"Is it strange to want to live?" Black Moon countered. "To want to see the old ones live out their days and the young ones grow to be old? Is it strange to want to protect our land from those who would steal it piece by piece until nothing is left?"

"I am not surprised to find our Cheyenne friends preparing for war, or that you are in the thick of it," Lone Horn said.

"You have taught me well."

"Iron Shell's winter count shows the year the sacred white buffalo was killed. I was just a boy at the time, but I remember the day the hunters returned to camp with the white buffalo robe. That night darkness covered the moon. It was the night you were born. It was right for you to take the name when you became a man. The child born on that strange day is now a man of twenty-five winters whose body is a perfect instrument for war and whose strong voice, cunning mind and fierce heart place him far apart from the others who look to him for guidance. I taught you well in the ways of hunting and warfare, but I am not responsible for that which was already there. Do you think they will listen to what you said?"

Black Moon shrugged, as if it made no difference to him, but the smile that spread across his lips hinted of triumph. "What brings you here, friend?"

"I have come in search of a reckless son whose mother is worried about him."

"My mother would worry about me even if my hair was as white as snow and I had ten grandchildren," Black Moon said with a laugh. "But tell me, how are my mother and father?"

"They are both well." Lone Horn let a long moment pass. "You have not asked about your brother."

Black Moon's features tightened. "You would do well not to mention that one's name to me."

Ignoring the warning he heard in his friend's voice, Lone Horn said, "Fire Cloud has gone into the hills."

"What is so unusual about that?" Black Moon scoffed. "He often goes into the hills to seek visions. No doubt, that is where he dreamed up the idea to steal my woman."

"*Your* woman?" the other man questioned. "You have already asked for her and been denied. By what right do you call yours something that will never be yours?"

Black Moon would not have tolerated such an arrogant assertion from anyone other than this teacher-friend. *The night I spent with her beneath the shaggy-leafs when I made her mine, that is by what right*, he wanted to say. But not even to this trusted ally would he reveal such a thing, not out of any concern for himself, but for concern over what others would think of Katie were it known that she had lain with him.

"It is I who rescued her from the bluecoats," he said instead. "I who desire her above all others." This last part, spoken in a voice scarcely above a whisper, almost as if he could not bear to say out loud what they both were thinking, that the woman was white and that as much as Black Moon hated the whites, he hated himself more for wanting one of them. "So, my brother goes into the hills and leaves such a woman alone at the lodge," he said, turning away with a look of disgust.

"She is the reason he went into the hills. He blames himself for what happened to her."

Black Moon's hot gaze swung back to him in an instant. "Something has happened to her? What?" It was more of a demand than a question.

The Minniconjou knew better than to evade it. "Fire Cloud returned to the village to find both the woman and the yellow racer gone. Crow moccasin tracks were in the dust."

Black Moon's blood began to bubble hotly like water in the cooking pot when steaming stones are dropped in to make it boil. "Some filthy Crow dog has stolen my woman?" he stormed. "Yes, *my* woman," he asserted, giving Lone Horn no chance to counter his claim. "No matter who she is married to, she will always be *my* woman. Do you dare to tell me it is not so?"

Lone Horn read the challenge smoking in Black Moon's eyes and stood his ground, but he wisely let the challenge go unanswered. "It would be foolish to let such a thing as a woman come between friends. It is as you say it is."

Black Moon gave out with a contemptuous laugh. "My brother is a fool for going off so often when such a prize waits back at his lodge."

They walked to a place on a hilltop and stood in silence looking down on the Cheyenne village. The hides glowed from the fires burning within the lodges. Overhead, in a cloud-streaked sky, the fat moon sent hazy streamers of light earthward, bathing the faces of the two men.

Lone Horn's deep voice cut through the tense stillness. "They will need you to lead them in this new way of fighting. When they assemble at Lodgepole Creek, will you be there to ride with them?"

"No. With the new sun I will return to my village."

Lone Horn's disapproval was evident in his angry tone. "You return to go after the woman? What good can there be in it?"

"If you are worried because she is my brother's wife—"

"I care not whose wife she is," his friend snapped. "I care only that she is *wasichu*, and that you are stuck somewhere in the middle of your hatred for the whites and your love for a white woman."

Love? Who had spoken anything about love? It was burning lust Black Moon felt for her in the pit of his loins that made his man part throb and his pulse race faster. Wasn't it? Or did his Minniconjou friend know his true heart better than he knew it himself? The night she had given herself to him and they had become one, hadn't he known then it was more than a man's lust that drew him to her? That it was her wild heart, so much like his own, her spirit, unquenchable in spite of all she had been through, the proud shining in her green eyes when he had been given the bighorn shirt. He realized now that he had been foolish to think it was merely lust and that all he wanted from her was the pleasure of her sweet-smelling body. Yes, it was that, but so much more. Lone Horn knew it. Why had it taken him this long to recognize it?

Black Moon leveled a hard look at his friend. "When I was made shirt-wearer, I made a vow to protect the people. My feelings for the woman will not get in the way of that. I will fight to protect the people. I will even give my life. But there is something I must do. When the new sun rises, I will ride my red horse back to my village. The black seed horse is yours. He will serve you well in battle."

Despite the gift of the stallion, Lone Horn did not try to keep his disapproval out of his tone. "Where will you look for her?"

"You said he took the yellow racer," Black Moon replied. "I will start with the village where I found the horse. Where has my village moved?"

With a sigh of resignation, Lone Horn said, "To War Bonnet Creek where the people prepare for the hunt."

Black Moon nodded. "When our Cheyenne friends gather at Lodgepole Creek, they will be led by you, my friend. Painted on the black's flank will be your symbol instead of mine."

By then, he would be far away, first putting heels and quirt to his pony to speed him to War Bonnet Creek, and then far to the north where the greasy-grass flowed and his red-haired woman waited. The thought of her living as a slave among his enemies turned his heart black. She would be forced to do the hard labor, maybe even beaten, or traded to another enemy, the Black Feet or the Assiniboine, each time used and discarded. If he did not find her in time, who knew what would become of her?

Without the liberty she had known among his people, how long would she last? Wild hearts such as hers needed the freedom to soar as high as the red-backed hawk. Without it, her spirit would wither and die. Or worse, she would become one of them, and lost to him forever.

Stay alive! His heart cried out to her. Stay alive! I am coming!

CHAPTER 9

*T*he one and only time Watchful Fox attempted to make love to Katie she bit him so hard on the lip that he did not bother to try again. Night after night, while he was off in the tall reeds with another woman, she slept in the lodge they shared with his mother, a mean-tempered old woman who made her do all the work. She felt empty and alone, and more than ever her thoughts converged on escape.

It was the time of year when the buffalo were growing new hair against the threat of cold, the women were busy pounding the pemmican after the hunt, and the men carved arrows and made snares of sedge reed and willow bark for catching rabbits. The days progressed at a torturously slow pace, all moving inexorably toward winter. The leaves were changing and the nights were growing colder. Katie had to get away soon or the winter snows would make escape impossible. She had not seen Corn Woman in many days, and her sense of urgency was growing.

One morning Corn Woman appeared at the stream. Katie glanced around furtively. Finding no watchful eyes upon them, she hastened over to where Corn Woman knelt filling the paunch. "Where have you been?"

Corn Woman looked up to reveal a large red bruise on her cheek.

"What happened?"

Sullenly, Corn Woman replied, "Big Belly caught me

sneaking out one night and used his quirt on me. Now he only lets me out to collect wood and water. At night he ties my leg to a stake in the ground like one of his ponies."

"What are we going to do?" Katie asked, trying to curb her panic. "You promised to help me escape."

"Escape is not possible. Not now. Maybe after the snows."

"But I cannot wait that long."

Corn Woman flashed a hateful look. "You selfish woman, thinking only of yourself. Do you not think how I suffer?"

"Why do you suffer?" Katie fired back. "Because you cannot lay in the reeds with other men? We both know that as soon as Big Belly is out cold from too much whiskey you will find a way to run off again to have your pleasure." Her green eyes spit fury as she watched her hope of escape slipping away, all because Corn Woman sought her pleasure with other men. "Do you take me for a fool? Do you think I do not know that it is Watchful Fox you meet at night and that you want him for yourself?" Her voice dropped to a dangerous whisper that did not disguise her wrath. "Be warned. If I am forced to remain here, I will be a true wife to him and bring him such pleasure that he will never want to be with you. If you do not help me escape back to the man I love, then I will have the one you love."

It was not true, of course. She had no intention of fulfilling her role as wife to that vain, pompous warrior, but she was frantic, and driven further into desperation when Corn Woman turned her back and stalked off. No longer able to count on her, Katie vowed to herself that she would escape, or die trying.

CHAPTER 10

Early in the Moon of Falling Leaves, as Katie was hunched over the hide she was scraping, a stranger's voice made her pause.

"*Sacre enfant de grace!*"

Looking up, she saw a white man ride by on a hardy gray Wyandot pony. He was dressed in a red flannel shirt, broad felt hat, moccasins, and trousers of deer skin trimmed along the side seams with long fringes. A skinning knife was stuck in his belt. Slung diagonally across his chest were a bullet pouch and powder horn. A double-barrel, smooth-bore rifle lay against the high pommel of his black Spanish saddle. Along a length of rope he led the tenacious mule that had prompted his exclamation of disgust.

Katie wrinkled her nose at the stench that followed him as he rode by. "That one has been too many days without a bath," she remarked to her neighbor. "Who is he?"

"His name is Chatillon," the other woman said. "We call him the bear because of all his hair. He rides often into our village. The women like him because they say his man part is big. The men like him because he brings the crazy-water."

Katie nodded toward a second man riding behind him. "Who is that one?"

"That one is Baptiste. Sometimes they come together, sometimes alone."

The man called Baptiste was tall and angular, with squinty blue eyes and a face that looked like it was carved out of rock.

Later that afternoon as Katie worked inside the lodge her attention was drawn to men's voices outside. A sly glance revealed the old woman asleep in the corner. She tiptoed to the entrance and peered outside to see what was going on.

A group of men was assembled outside. There was Big Belly, shifting his massive bulk from side to side as he squatted into a cross-legged position on the ground. Watchful Fox was also there, dressed in beaded shirt and leggings, with shell disks hanging from his ears. To keep his hair from blowing into his eyes he had put little balls of pitch into it so that it was matted together all around his head. It was obvious that he thought himself quite beautiful. Katie thought he looked like a fool.

Among them was Henri Chatillon, the French-Canadian half-breed who could neither read nor write but was a crack shot at fifty paces and could wield a knife as good as any Indian. "I bring jugs of whiskey," he announced.

There commenced a hearty babble of conversation as the jugs were uncorked and passed around.

Baptiste wiped whiskey from his mouth with the back of his hand and winked at Chatillon. "Geesis, I got a good idea. How about a game of hands?"

In no time, robes, beaded pipe bags, war bonnets and other things were brought forward and laid down as stakes. The pipe was lit and the game began.

Two rows of six men sat facing each other. Both sides had two bones, one marked, one unmarked. One man hid the bones in his hands after tossing them back and forth and mixing them up. His opponent had to guess which hand held the marked bone. A wrong guess resulted in the loss of one tally stick and a possession. When three tally sticks were lost, the man was out of the game.

Big Belly lost all three of his tally sticks in a matter of minutes.

Next it was Baptiste's turn. "I wager this good knife." He threw down the double-edged knife with an inlaid wooden handle that he had taken off a dead Cree Indian. His opponent chanted as he worked the bones. When they were thoroughly mixed up, the Crow thrust out his clenched fists.

Baptiste studied the brave's fists with squinty eyes and pointed to one. The palm opened to reveal an unmarked bone. The white man's wrong guess brought a whoop of victory from the Indians.

The game progressed into the afternoon. The faces of the men were flushed with too much whiskey and they were no longer laughing. One by one they dropped out of the game, some because they had lost too much, others because they were too drunk to go on. Big Belly swayed precariously over his shadow before slumping backwards, unconscious, his ponderous belly protruding like a mountain.

Soon only Chatillon and Watchful Fox were left playing. Watchful Fox threw down his lance case, a six foot long shaft of rawhide whose long fringes were hung with brass bells, and promptly lost it.

Chatillon moved the bones in his big hairy hands, in and out, over and under in a masterful display of handiwork. Finally, he held out his hands. Watchful Fox licked his lips nervously and nodded to the left hand. Slowly it opened to reveal an unmarked bone.

Watchful Fox handed over his otter skin quiver and bow case. With only one tally stick left, Watchful Fox began to chant.

Baptiste fidgeted with impatience.

"Let him sing, *mon ami*," Chatillon said.

From where she stood watching avidly off to the side, Corn Woman stepped forward to kneel beside Watchful Fox and whisper something in his ear.

Standing at the rear of the crowd, Katie froze when she heard her name called. With a puzzled expression, she came forward.

"Geesis," exclaimed Baptist. He poked an elbow into his companion's flabby ribs. "Would you look at that?"

Chatillion gasped. "*Mon Dieu*. What a *femme*."

Reluctantly, he peeled his eyes away from the woman and turned back to Watchful Fox. "You have one stick left. What will you wager?"

Watchful Fox hesitated. "I will wager my woman," he said in a slurred voice.

A treacherous feeling sifted over Katie like ice.

Chatillon smiled greedily and began to rub the bones between his palms, making them click together. Faster and faster he rubbed them, from hand to hand, in and out of sight, over and under his leg, coming at last to a halt.

Watchful Fox looked down at those two massive fists that looked like bear paws. Tiny blue veins popped out at his temples and the corded muscles of his neck were straining against the flesh. He swallowed hard and nodded toward Chatillon's right fist. With agonizing slowness those hairy fingers opened, just a slit at first, then wider.

Watchful Fox sat motionless as he stated down into the white man's open palm. The bone was unmarked.

"Geesis," gasped Baptiste. "The woman is yours."

Katie's mind careened out of control. This could not be happening!

When Watchful Fox rose stiffly to his feet and stalked off, she broke into a run after him.

"You cannot do this!" she screamed, tugging on his buckskin sleeve. "You cannot give me to that disgusting man!"

He shook her off like dust, and grumbled, "It is done."

"Then undo it!" she shrieked. "I will not be bargained off like a buffalo robe. You cannot do this to me." She began to pound furiously on his chest.

Watchful Fox grabbed her wrists and brought her flailing arms to a halt. "You are no longer my woman," he sneered, and released her with a shove that sent her stumbling backwards.

Hot tears stung her eyes and spilled onto her cheeks. Numbly, she watched as he went into the lodge, gathered up her things and dumped them on the ground outside in a sign for all to see that he was divorcing her.

"Go!" he spat. "You have brought me nothing but bad luck."

"Good riddance to you," she muttered hatefully as she bent to retrieve her things. "I will go, but not to that stinking man. I will die first."

It was then the thought came to her. This was it, the time for her to make her move. She had only to slip between the lodges, grab *Peta* and be off. Her heart beat wildly as she backed slowly away. Just a few more steps and she would be free.

"Going somewhere, *ma petite*?"

The next morning the two white men saddled up and were ready to go by the time the sun was rising over the treetops. It took some doing getting Katie aboard the Wyandot pony. She kicked and scratched like a wildcat. When she was up there, Chatillon climbed on behind her, pressing his great, furry body against hers.

"We will see if you are this spirited beneath the robes, eh green eyes?" He laughed, showering her with fetid breath as his arms went around her to grasp the reins.

At the lodge of Watchful Fox he halted to untie the beaver pelts that hung from his saddle. He tossed them to the ground at the feet of the Indian. "The beavers are yours. They will bring you fifty dollar apiece at the fort."

Hot, salty tears blinded Katie's vision as they rode out of the Crow Village. She did not see Watchful Fox bend down to snatch up the pelts, nor the figure of Corn Woman standing between the lodges, a triumphant little smile twisting her lips.

***

Night came on a cold, dark wind. A rabbit roasted on a spit over an open flame.

Katie's stomach churned for food, yet the thought of eating sickened her. When Chatillon held out a piece of meat to her on the tip of his knife, she turned her face away.

"Maybe she would rather eat boiled dog like a wild Indian," Baptiste said to his cohort with a laugh.

Chatillon uncorked the whiskey jug and took a swig. "We will see if she turns her nose up at food when she has had none for several days."

Baptiste aimed his squinty eyes at her, and asked, "Why do you live with those savages, anyway? Did they steal you from your white family?"

"They stole me from the Lakota," she said.

"So, you were stolen from your white family by the Sioux?"

"I chose to live with them after the massacre at Blue Water."

"Ach, Blue Water," Chatillon said with disgust. "That was a mess, eh?" He shook his head. "*Dommage. Dommage.*"

What Chatillon called *too bad* flowed like poison in Katie's veins even now, more than a year later. "My white father was killed there."

He scrutinized her from over the rim of the whiskey jug. "You look a little familiar to me. Who was your father? I know him, maybe?"

"My father was the trader, Tom McCabe."

Any hope she had of gaining comradeship with him through his and her father's common trade with the Indians was squashed when he wrinkled his nose and spat at the ground. "Ach, that one. He ruined many good trades for me. Sometimes I would ride into a village and the Indians would take my good whiskey and give me nothing in return but some worthless pipe bags and knives. What do I need with more knives? And when I ask where are the beaver pelts, they would say the red-hair was here and we gave them all to him, and all I'd be left with was a bunch of drunken Indians."

Baptiste cackled, a thin, reedy sound that sent goose bumps careening over Katie's flesh, and reminded his companion, "Your last trade with a drunken Indian was not so bad, eh?" His eyes focused on her, so narrow it was hard to see their blueness, but his meaning was obvious.

"My father didn't trade in whiskey," Katie said in McCabe's defense. "He used to say there's no honor in a drunken man." She said this even as Chatillon lifted the jug to his lips and took a deep swallow, but she didn't care. She had ceased caring long before this night. She got up from before the fire and went to a spot concealed in shadows where she did not have the warmth of the flames and they would not see the rage and despair that swept over her.

Once again her life had taken a drastic turn. All she could do now was clutch at the memories of happier times, before Blue Water, when she and her father lived their peaceful existence in their cabin along the Laramie, before the soldiers started ordering the bands to move close to the fort and the Indians began attacking the wagons on the Oregon Trail, and later, the seasons she spent among the Lakota, when a single glance from a handsome Oglala warrior made her heart sing, until that, too, came to and end when she was forced to marry a man she did not love.

Here she was, once again someone's captive. What would become of her when these white men were finished using her? Would they trade her at the first Indian village they came to? Would they leave her at one of the miners' camps where the only women the men saw were the ones to be had for a price? She shuddered to think too far in advance of this moment. For now, her thoughts converged on staying alive and keeping Chatillon and Baptiste at bay.

As the night dragged on, Katie prayed that Chatillon's awesome manliness that the Crow women alluded to would be rendered ineffective by the amount of whiskey he consumed. One small prayer was answered when he soon lay drunk and snoring.

Katie was exhausted. Her body ached for sleep. Her mind sought the sanctuary of the dream world. Yet she could not allow herself to close her eyes, not when Baptiste was still awake and leering at her from across the distance. Long into the night she stayed awake, fighting sleep. It was only after Baptiste had drunk himself into a stupor and passed out that she closed her weary eyes and slipped far, far away.

In the days that followed the only thing that gave Katie the courage to survive, even if it was only within herself, was the image she carried in her heart of Black Moon. She had managed to survive the rest of it—the tragedy on Blue Water, the consuming disappointment of her marriage to Fire Cloud, the terror of her capture by Big Belly, the stinging indifference of Watchful Fox, the scheming of Corn Woman, and now, the ever-constant threat from these two white men that robbed her of sleep at night and made her days an exercise in constantly looking over her shoulder. At times she thought she would go mad from it all. McCabe used to say that as long as a man knew what was the most he could lose, if he was prepared to lose that much, then nothing could hurt him. Katie had already lost everything else. There was just one thing left to lose that could destroy her. One thing capable of sending her heart to its knees. Never to see Black Moon again or feel his strong arms around her. To feel safe and protected by him. *That* would be the worst thing that could happen to her now.

"*Sacre femme*! Don't you understand *Anglais* when you hear it?"

It was several days later when they stopped to make camp for the night and Katie had already unpacked the mule, gathered wood, started a fire, fetched water from a stream, thrown coffee grinds into the pot, and skewered the rabbit Baptiste had caught and skinned earlier that afternoon. She was tired and wanted only to sit on a fallen log and rest, but her gaze snapped up from the ground and her thoughts scattered at Chatillon's harsh jibe.

"Maybe you understand me better if I speak to you in Crow or Sioux, eh? Have you forgotten that you are white underneath those hides?"

She expelled a desolate sigh, and answered, "I haven't forgotten. Sometimes I simply choose not to remember."

"Ach! *Stupide femme*," he growled. "Come over here and pull off my moccasins."

Katie obeyed, wrinkling her nose at Chatillon's smelly feet, then retreated back to the fallen log, where she sat for a long time watching him blow smoke from his pipe.

When the rabbit was roasted, Chatillon and Baptiste sliced off some pieces for themselves. Seeing Katie's hungry look, Chatillon taunted, "You are hungry, eh? And what would you give me for some of this tasty rabbit? A kiss for old Chatillon, maybe?"

Katie went cold inside. She had already noticed that he was not touching the jug tonight. Ignoring the growling sounds from her belly, she said, "I'm not hungry."

He shrugged his big shoulders beneath the red flannel shirt. "So starve, you stupid woman." He ripped a piece of meat from the skewer with his hands and stuffed it in his mouth.

Katie sat there without taking her eyes from him, hungry, but not so hungry that she would give him the kiss he wanted.

Baptiste was also watching Chatillon. When it became apparent to him, too, that Chatillon had no interest in whiskey, he took a loud swig from the jug. "Geesis, this sure is good whiskey." But it failed to entice his companion. Mumbling to himself, he took another swallow, and another, and before long he was flat on his back, unconscious.

After a while Katie crawled beneath her buffalo robe and pretended to sleep.

"I like you a whole lot, green eyes," said Chatillon as he plunked himself down beside her. He pulled the robe back from her face. "And you like me, maybe some?"

She shuddered and shut her eyes tight, withdrawing not only from him but from life itself.

"You cannot be so tired," he said. "And tonight I am not so full of whiskey." He reached for her, but she pulled away.

"Ah, maybe you are shy. Here, drink this."

He thrust the whiskey jug at her. It hit Katie's teeth hard and she had no choice but to open her mouth and swallow.

Suddenly, an idea came to her. Tossing her head back, she wiped the whiskey from her lips with the tip of her tongue and saw his eyes widen at the gesture. Forcing a seductive smile, she said, "You are right, Henri. I do need a drink. Maybe just a little one."

It took every bit of her willpower not to keep from retching as she drank. She lowered the jug and peered at him from over its rim. "Yes, it always seems to work. And you? Aren't you drinking?"

He ran his tongue over his thick lips. The smell of whiskey was on her breath. He eyed the jug covetously.

Sensing his hesitation, Katie goaded, "Of course, if you're worried that you cannot keep up with me..." She took another swallow.

He snatched the jug from her hands. "I can keep up with anyone." Tilting his head back, he drank in long, measured gulps.

From that point on it became a contest, Chatillon matching Katie swallow for swallow. She managed to stay conscious by sheer force of will. Chatillon, however, was not so lucky. Soon he was seeing too many images of her dancing before his eyes.

Katie knew better than to let her guard down until he finally slumped over. She nudged him with her foot to make sure he was unconscious. The air went out of her in one long, low whoosh of relief. And then her head began to spin. She felt sick to her stomach. She was disgustingly, miserably drunk. The last thing she saw before falling into unconsciousness was Black Moon's handsome face. The last thing she felt were the hot tears that fell from her eyes.

CHAPTER 11

Black Moon dreamed of the wolf, the protector of all warriors. When the morning broke tart and crisp, he took a wolf skin from his bag and carried it to a nearby hill. Facing the Four Winds, he called to the wolves, asking them the whereabouts of the enemy. Packing his gear, he made a tobacco offering to the wolves, then jumped astride his red pony and rode off.

With the wind coming from the north, he stayed to the south side of the trail, hunting small game along the way. Many suns came and went before he crossed into enemy territory. At night, with his pony hobbled close by, he made no fire and ate nothing, sniffing the air for the smell of fire or tobacco smoke and listening for the sound of a snorting horse that would signal the enemy.

He reached the Crow village two suns after entering their territory. Concealed on a hillside, he surveyed the camp. When nighttime came, he donned the Crow shirt he had taken from the enemy in an earlier battle. He waited in the thickets until he spied someone go out between the lodges, and then entered through the same passage so that those inside would think it was the same person returning.

The lodges were pitched close together, with many ponies left to wander within the circle. The best ponies had feathers in their manes and tails. But Black Moon had not come all this way to steal ponies. He moved through the Crow village, not finding what he was after, thinking he had better leave before his ruse was discovered when, suddenly, his eyes flared upon a familiar sight. There, before one of the lodges, was picketed the yellow racer.

The animal's ears pricked forward as Black Moon quietly approached. Its golden hide quivered when he placed his hand upon it. The light from the fire within the lodge showed no figures moving about. Inching closer, he went around back and tugged at one of the stakes until the wood loosened. Lifting the cover, he peered inside. In the far corner he spied a sleeping woman, a squirming infant on one side and her man on her other side, snoring loudly and stinking of fire water even from this distance. A quick scan of the lodge revealed no sign of Katie. Backing away, he left the Crow camp the same way he came in, stripping off the shirt and tossing it into the darkness.

On his way back to his pony he spied a woman emerging from the tall reeds. Acting on an instinct, he came up behind her.

Corn Woman had no time to react when a hand darted out of the shadows to clamp forcefully over her mouth. A strong arm dragged her into the sharp-biting thickets and far off the trail.

Black Moon spun her around with a painful twist of her arm and shoved her up against the rough bark of a tree with the flat of his palm. The blade of his knife gleamed in the half-light of the moon as he brandished it before her petrified eyes. To make certain she knew he would not hesitate to use it, he pricked the skin of her neck with the tip, causing a droplet of blood to slip down her throat.

Satisfied that she understood his intent, he placed the knife between his teeth where it would be ready in case he needed it, and signed in strong, angry motions, "You will tell me of the woman stolen from the Lakota or you will die."

Corn Woman cowered against the tree and signed back with trembling hands. "There are several Lakota women living among us. I do not know which one you mean."

He slapped her hands away with a burst of fury. "If I tell you her eyes are green and her hair is as red as flame, would you know then which one I mean?"

"You are Black Moon," she signed frantically with shaking hands. "The woman with the green eyes spoke of you only to me because she knew I could be trusted. I was helping her make a plan to escape."

From his belt Black Moon produced some strips of rawhide and hastily bound her to the tree, leaving her hands momentarily free to sign. Reaching down, he scooped up a handful of leaves and stuffed them between her lips and wound a piece of trade cloth securely over her mouth so that no sound would escape to alert the scouts.

"How far is your village from here?" he demanded, testing her for truthfulness.

She signed, "Two arrow flights from a strong bow and as far as a man can throw an arrow with his hand."

He already knew this to be true, so he ordered, "Tell me which lodge the woman is in."

Corn Woman hesitated.

"Which lodge?" he repeated threateningly.

"She is not in the village."

Black Moon's burning impatience increased his fury. Bringing his face close to hers, his gaze turned deadly. "Where is she?"

With awkward, fumbling motions Corn Woman told him about the game of hands.

His stomach tightened. Gone? He had come all this way only to find Katie gone? And with a white man! Once again, those miserable whites had stolen what was his. First the land, now his woman.

Black Moon had heard enough. Binding the hands of the Crow woman, he aimed a final scornful look at her and disappeared into the shadows as silently as he had appeared. But he did not head for his red pony hidden in a gully. Instead, he moved again in the direction of the Crow village.

When the fragrance of firewood was no longer in the air and he was confident that the village slept, he crept in again on noiseless feet. At the lodge of the man who had stolen his woman he could hear the sounds of those sleeping inside. His hand went instinctively to the knife at his belt. For several treacherous moments he stood there deciding what he would do. When his decision was made, he acted with swift vengeance.

The following morning Big Belly slipped his oreech cloth in place over his cumbersome belly and pulled on his moccasins with much huffing and puffing. A glance around the lodge revealed Corn Woman's absence. He growled at Two Scalps, "Where is your sister?"

The girl cringed. "Sh-she was up early this morning," she lied. "She is down by the water. I will go and get her." She ran out of the lodge before he could question her further.

Seconds later Two Scalps' screams brought Big Belly bounding out of the lodge.

She stood there screeching at the tops of her lungs, pointing.

His gaze flew in the direction of her outstretched, trembling finger. There, lying in a pool of dark, congealed blood was the yellow racer. Its eyes stared fixedly. Its throat was slit. From its golden, blood-splattered hide protruded a Lakota arrow.

CHAPTER 12

*T*he buffalo berries were frosted on the gray bushes, and snow whitened the Tongue River country overnight. As near as Katie could tell, it was November, or maybe December.

She was bent over a cooking fire brewing a pot of coffee when Chatillon approached rapidly on foot. Every muscle in her body went rigid with anxiety and her guard sprang up all around her.

He rushed towards a confused mass of blankets on the ground and gave it a sharp kick with the toe of his boot. Up sprang his squinty-eyed companion. He barked out some words in French.

"The pack mule is gone," Baptiste said in answer to Katie's questioning look.

"There, you see," snarled Chatillon. "Her tracks lead away from the campsite. The rope I used to stake her is frayed at the end. Something scared her and made her bolt."

He stomped to his horse, saddled up, grabbed his rifle and rode off.

When he returned, the mule was not with him.

Baptiste looked up from the blade he was sharpening. "Is she lost?"

Chatillon's thick features screwed up in a severe frown. "*Mort*. Her scavenged body lays in a gully two miles from here."

"Wolves?"

"Maybe."

With no pack mule to carry their supplies they were forced to leave some behind.

"Let the savages have them," Chatillon grumbled.

"We can trade the woman for more," Baptist suggested.

"*Jamais*," Chatillon snarled. "The woman is mine."

The rest of the day passed in tense silence, broken only by Chatillon's vengeful cursing over the loss of his mule.

The next morning Katie awoke to a fresh, damp smell in the air. Rising from beneath her robe, she stretched her arms up over her head and opened her mouth to yawn, but the breath froze in her lungs. Several yards away Chatillon's Wyandot pony lay on its side, legs pointing stiffly, eyes like glass.

She heard Chatillon stir and awaken, followed by his outraged bellow when he saw the horse. Its body was bloated, with not a mark on it, giving no clue as to what had brought it down in the night.

Baptiste came racing in yellow-stained long-johns. "Maybe the water is bad."

"We all drank from the same stream you idiot!" Chatillon roared. He turned his face from the gruesome sight. "Starting tonight we sleep in shifts. And keep your miserable eyes open. Something tells me we are not alone."

All day the tension grew thicker. With nerves on edge, they snapped at each other like jackals. That night they kept the campfire low and put it out as soon as the food was cooked to shiver the remainder of the night away without the warmth of the flames to protect them against the nip in the autumn air.

It was Baptiste's turn to keep watch. Long into the night he sat with his back pressed against a boulder, a rifle across his knees, the barrel ice cold to the touch. Several times his eyelids drooped, only to snap open at each shifting of the wind. After many hours in a cramped position he got up to stretch his legs.

Something struck him hard in the chest. A dark, sticky stain filled the front of his buckskin jacket. His eyes grew wide at the sight of the arrow protruding from the wall of his chest.

An expression of shock and fear contorted his features. His voice emerged as a strangled groan.

"Geesis!"

Then he fell forward, dead.

Morning broke overcast and cold. "Who plays this game of cat and mouse with us?" Chatillion grumbled as he piled stones over the body of Baptiste. "Maybe that stupid Crow warrior has tracked us to make me pay for my trickery in the hand game, eh? Or maybe it is the Assiniboine. We crossed into their territory some days back." He cast a hateful glance over at Katie. "My luck has been all bad since the day I won you in the game of hands. The first Indian village we come to, I will trade you off. I have already lost too much. I have no wish to lose my hair, too."

In the aftermath of Baptiste's death Chatillon's temper was even more violent. "Get that horse saddled," he ordered.

For several moments she remained fixed, staring at the pile of stones covering Baptiste's body.

"Damn you, bitch, I gave you an order." With that, he cuffed her and sent her sprawling.

Something inside of Katie snapped. "You vile dog," she spat. "Don't you ever strike me again!"

Chatillon lunged for her, catching her by the arm. Clapping a hand over her mouth he pinched her nostrils shut with his fingers until she came close to losing consciousness. When he felt her go limp, he released her with a shove. "Do not worry, I will not kill you. I will let these northern savages have you. Like the Crow, the Assiniboine are enemies of the Lakotas. Do you know what they will do to you? They will use you and beat you and you will wish you were still with Chatillon. And then they will kill you and eat you. Now mount up. We leave this place."

Hatred welled up inside of her for Henri Chatillon, more than she had ever hated anything in her life, and she swore to herself that if the chance came, she would kill him.

Riding together now on Baptiste's horse, Chatillon pointed to a bending in the grass, and grunted, "Deer." And to the footprints close by. "Assiniboine."

A chill careened down Katie's spine. Signs of a hunting party meant that their camp was not far away. Fearfully, she wondered if she was drawing to the close of one frightening chapter of her life only to begin another, final chapter. She had to think of something, and quick.

"I want to get down," she said. "My legs are stiff from riding."

In a humorless tone, he replied, "You can wrap them around me tonight. You have avoided me long enough. Tonight I will discover what you are hiding under that dress, eh?"

Katie swallowed her fear, and said, "Maybe we should find out right now."

A greedy chuckle issued from his throat. With a jerk on the reins, he guided the horse to a patch of trees. It was moist beneath the bare branches of the cottonwoods from a morning rain shower. Here and there a random ray of sunlight poked through the clouds to dapple the ground. He brought the horse to a halt and climbed down, pulling her along with him. He led her to a spot where the fallen leaves made a bed upon which to lay.

"Take off your dress," he ordered.

She tried to think logically, to plot her next move, but panic welled up inside of her. Her hands shook treacherously as she fumbled with the rawhide laces of her dress.

Chatillon grew impatient. "You begin to press my nerve," he warned. "Forget the damn dress. It can stay. Get on the ground."

She dared not disobey.

He stood over her, straddling her with his stance. Pulling down his deerskin trousers, he exposed his manly parts to her. She could not look upon him without feeling sick.

"Lift your dress."

She felt the air squeezed out of her lungs when his full weight came down on her.

He forced her legs apart with his knees. The hardness of his manhood grazed the flesh of her inner thigh. Revulsion gripped her. Her hands flew out to fend him off. She clawed at his hide jacket and scratched at his face in an effort to get away. In her frenzy her hand struck something solid. She knew in an instant what it was. Without hesitating, she grabbed the knife at his belt.

Chatillon let out a loud howl of pain when the sharp blade sliced into his shoulder, tearing through the hide jacket and red flannel shirt, to the flesh and muscle beneath. For a man so bulky he was on his feet amazingly fast. Blood spurt from the jagged tear in his flesh, filling up the fingers of the hand he clutched over it. His expression was a mixture of pain and surprise.

Katie scrambled to her feet and stood before him wild eyed, the knife grasped in her hand. Through clenched teeth she warned, "If you come near me, I'll kill you."

"*Sacre bleu!*" he cried. "I give you food and protection and this is how you repay me? Give me that knife, bitch."

She shook her head. Her hair was a wild mass of red about her face. "You'll have to kill me to get it."

"It can be arranged."

Fear only made Katie bolder. "Or maybe I will kill you," she taunted as she brandished the bloodied blade before him. She backed away from him, frantically endeavoring to stay calm. No mistakes, she cautioned herself. But in the ensuing instant the warning was lost when she tripped on a rock and lost her footing. In that moment he slammed into her.

They grappled on the ground, rolling over each other. Katie held on to the knife for dear life, screaming her hatred into his face.

"Stop that yowling! Shut it up!"

With a burst of strength she flung the knife away.

Chatillon sprang to his feet and darted after it.

Katie was already up and running towards the horse. Her foot was in the stirrup and she was in mid-ascent when he caught her and threw her to the ground with a jolt that sent her senses reeling. When her vision cleared, she looked up to see him looming over her. A sneer of hatred twisted his great, hairy features. The knife in his hand began its descent.

A strangled groan was all that emerged from Katie's throat. She shut her eyes tight and braced herself for the shaft of fierce pain that would end her life. But the blade of death did not come.

When she summoned the courage to open her eyes, she saw Chatillon standing frozen over her like a statue carved from stone. The knife was still locked in his grip. His eyes were fixed upon her in rock-hard hatred. All at once he began to sway. Like a tree whose trunk has been chiseled to a slender thread by beavers, he came crashing down beside her, raising much dust and scattering the leaves on the ground.

The color bled from Katie's face. She choked on her own gasp at the tomahawk imbedded deep in Chatillon's back. She stared dumbfounded as the blood seeped into his jacket, one ring of wetness after another, like circles upon water. She began to tremble.

"Why do you shake little long-ears?" A voice spoke softly beside her. "You are safe now."

The words, spoken in Lakota, seemed to come from out of a dream. Lifting her horror-stricken eyes off the dead man, she turned them slowly upwards in the direction of the voice that had spoken. Was she dreaming? Had she gone completely insane? Was Black Moon really standing there? It was only then that she began to cry.

He knelt beside her and wound a strong arm around her shoulders. A convulsive sob shook her hard. Warm, salty tears spilled from her eyes onto the front of his buckskin shirt.

"I dared not hope," she sobbed against his chest.

He held her like that until her sobs gradually eased. With firm but gentle fingers he grasped her chin and guided her tear-shiny eyes to his. "Come," he said, drawing her to her feet. "I will take you home."

CHAPTER 13

*T*he buffalo were moving southward in long, dark rows, and the scent of winter was in the air as they rode back toward Lakota country.

From all she'd been through, Katie had lost track of time. "What month is this?" she asked Black Moon.

"The frost is on the tipis," he answered.

December. Memories of Christmas returned with a pang. She recalled how McCabe used to drag a fresh-cut fir into the cabin, and she would decorate it with the bits of cloth and ribbon he brought back from Fort Laramie. Richard would come with Bone Bracelet who didn't understand the Christian holiday but nevertheless loved the small presents she would receive. One year Katie taught her sister-in-law the English words to Silent Night. McCabe had danced a lively Irish jig, and everyone, even Bone Bracelet, who was forbidden by custom to look at or address her father-in-law, had a good laugh over it.

Now the only indication Katie had that it was December was the snow on the ground and the sounds of popping trees when the frigid temperatures caused them to split.

High into the hills they rode, Black moon leading astride his sorrel pony, Katie following behind on Baptiste's horse, riding away from the calamity as they had ridden away from the tragedy on Blue Water Creek nearly two years ago. Once again he had killed for her, this time leaving a trail of destruction behind him.

On this day they followed a snaking stream clogged with beaver dams. A black-tailed deer came to drink. From out of a cluster of bushes a lean gray wolf sprang and pounced on the deer. Katie cried out, hoping to frighten the predator away, but it was too late. Tears stung her eyes. "Why did this have to happen? I hate that wolf for this."

"You cannot love the prey and hate the predator," Black Moon said harshly.

Since rescuing her from Chatillon he had scarcely spoken to her. When he did, it was only to scold her in that overbearing manner of his, as he did just now. She wondered bitterly why he had come such a long way to find her only to treat her as if he were sorry he had gone through the trouble.

Higher up in the hills they followed a broad, dusty path made by elk. Black Moon dismounted and knelt on one knee to examine the ground. The grass was trampled down by deer. He glanced around. Higher up were the rocky pinnacles where the eagle-catchers made their pits to snare the big winged ones. Below, the prairie ambled into the distance. A prairie swallow flew overhead with mud in its beak, a sign that water was not far off. Satisfied that this was a good place to camp for the night, he removed his bow and quiver from his hide saddle.

"See to the horses," he said to Katie. "I will hunt for our supper."

"Why is it always the woman who must do the unpleasant work?" she grumbled to herself as she lugged the heavy Spanish saddle from the back of Baptiste's horse. She was feeling sullen and irritable. Instead of words, all she received from Black Moon were grunts and orders. Rather than kindness, he showed only impatience and anger. It was as if he were trying hard not to like her. Had he forgotten the night they made love beneath the pines? Had it meant so little to him? Damn him and his heathen heart!

Night found them sitting around a crackling fire. Overhead, the moon was as thin as a taut bow. The tension in the air was thick enough to cut with a hunting knife.

The rabbit Black Moon caught was slowly roasting over the open flames. Katie was wrapped in her buffalo robe, not speaking, having learned by now how to retreat inwardly.

Black Moon's expression was unreadable as he stared into the flames.

The tantalizing aroma of cooking food was too much for Katie to ignore. The robe slipped from her shoulders when she rose from her spot and came forward. She gestured to the roasting meat, and said, "If you cook that rabbit any more, there will be nothing left but charred meat and ashes."

Dropping to her knees, she began to remove the meat from the skewer. As she did, a piece of fat dripped onto the flames, splattering her on the hand. She gave out with a little yelp and pulled her hand back, blowing on it for quick relief.

Black Moon removed one of the small buckskin bags hanging from the pommel of his hide saddle. Without speaking a word, he examined her hand by the light of the flames. Reaching into the bag, he took out a handful of leaves which he put in his mouth and chewed. He worked quickly to apply the paste of moist leaves to her burned flesh.

In seconds the pain began to subside. Without its distraction Katie was suddenly and acutely aware of his proximity. He was close, dangerously close. Her small hand was still trapped in his, although his movements had ground to a halt.

They were both kneeling, staring into each other's faces. Katie recognized the hunger in his black eyes. She knew the desperate battle he was waging with himself over that which he wanted and was not his to have. There was no denying the passion raging between them, but neither could they ignore the fact that she belonged to another man whose presence stood between them like a chasm too wide to bridge.

"Fire Cloud—" she began.

"No!" The force of his reaction startled her into silence. "I will tell you about Fire Cloud," he said, his handsome face twisted with scorn. "He has always been so good and pure. His tongue knows no harsh words. His heart knows no unkindness. He is everyone's friend. With one hand he clasps yours in friendship, while with the other he steals what is yours. My brother is not like the Crow thief who steals out of hatred and revenge. He is not like the whites who steal out of greed. Fire Cloud steals out of love, and that is much worse. Love and weakness. It was his own weakness that sent Good Deeds to Gray Wolf's lodge. Weakness took from him the woman he wanted, and weakness made him take mine." He got up and stalked off into the darkness beyond the fire's light.

Katie was stunned by the vehemence in his tone. It was wrong for a man to hate his brother for a reason that did not exist. One word from her would ease his suffering. But how could she tell him that Fire Cloud was not her husband in the true sense of the word without revealing a secret she had sworn not to tell? Fire Cloud's shame would be great if it was learned that he was not a real husband to his wife. Rising from the cooking fire, she went in search of him.

He had climbed to the top of a rise. His tall, lean body was silhouetted against a black sky lit by twinkling stars and a crescent moon. Even in his dark brooding he was proud-looking. He stood straight, arms at his sides, head held high, eyes scanning the heavens. The soft tanned hide of his leggings hugged his muscular thighs, the fringes along the side seams rustling in the midnight breeze. The ends of his blue-black braids flicked about on a gust of wind.

Katie approached cautiously, her gaze feasting on his handsomeness. Why was it that just the sight of him turned her to liquid? There was something darkly thrilling about him that simultaneously frightened her and intrigued her. Something warned her not to come any closer, yet dared her to stay away. Softly, she said to him, "Fire Cloud is not your enemy. The Crow, the Pawnee, the whites, but not your brother."

Without removing his stony gaze from the sky, he replied, "The Crow steal our women. The Snakes steal our ponies. The whites steal our land. My enemy is anyone who would steal from me what is mine."

"Fire Cloud has stolen nothing. It is not his way you should question, Black Moon, but that of the Great Spirit, and you know that His way is without question."

"The whites come to my people and say 'Here are beef, flour and blankets for the lands we are taking', and suddenly, the flat-water is gone. Again they come and say 'Here are the same beef, flour and blankets for more lands we are taking', and the running-water is gone. One day they will come to us and say 'Here are the same beef, flour and blankets for the rest of your land', and the Powder River, the Snow Hills, and the sacred *Paha Sapa* will be gone forever." He gave a contemptuous snort, and said, "My brother is no different. He comes to you and says, 'Here is my love and my friendship and all my good, peaceful thoughts', and suddenly, something you thought was yours is gone."

He turned to look at her then. "Why did you do it? Why did you go to him?"

"Please," she whispered imploringly, "you must understand why it had to be."

"Who said it had to be?"

"If it were up to me, it would have been different."

"It *was* up to you. A Lakota woman has the right to leave one husband for another."

She answered with a sigh. "It seems I gave up that right when Turning Hawk took me into his lodge. Those were hard times for me. He gave me a home and was good to me. I owed him much in return."

"So you went through with a marriage you did not want because you owed something to an old man?"

"I could not shame your brother in such a manner."

There was an imploring look in Black Moon's eyes, a pleading in his voice that she had never heard before. "Do you not want *me* for your husband?"

"Oh yes!" she cried. "Can you look into my eyes and doubt it?"

"And still you will not leave him?"

"I cannot." She turned away and started down the hill.

In several long, powerful strides he covered the distance between them. With a quick motion he yanked her back around, gathered her up and flung her over his shoulder.

He carried her to their campsite and placed her on the ground before the fire.

Beneath his rough, impatient hands the seams of Katie's hide dress gave way. In no time her smooth white flesh was bared to him. He grasped a handful of thick red hair and pulled her head back, forcing her to look into his eyes that were fiery bright. "I have not lived one day without wanting you," he said as he crushed her mouth beneath his.

His lips slid over her, kissing, licking, teasing, devouring. The sound of his breathless whisper sent chills down her spine. "*Mitawin*," he rasped.

He forced her to return every kiss and each caress with equal ardor and abandon until there was nothing she would not do for him, no part of herself she would not give. Their passion reached high into the night, like the flames of an uncontrollable fire, scorching them with ecstasy and the undeniable truth that they could not live without each other.

When they were spent and the sound of her breathing told him she was sleeping, he did not get up to sleep alone in his own robes as a warrior usually sleeps, but with his woman in his arms.

As he lay there he thought about the time in his youth when he had gone into the hills to seek a vision. He had stripped himself down to his breech cloth and stretched out on the ground without a blanket, placing stones beneath his back and between his toes to keep from falling asleep. For three days and nights he had remained like that, eyes searching the expanse above, heart and mind seeking the wisdom of the Great Spirit. He prayed and sang and waited, but no vision came. On the fourth day, weak from hunger, dizzy with exhaustion and sick with self-disgust, he had started back down the hill for home when, suddenly, the trees began to sway as if stirred by a rough wind. He had straightened up and sniffed the air but detected no scent of a storm. In all directions the sky was clear and blue. Only the small circle of sky directly above his head had grown black and forbidding.

From out of the gathering storm clouds rode a mounted warrior. Lances of lightning pierced the air all around him. Pellets of rain struck the ground at the feet of his pony, a big black creature with a zigzag streak of yellow lightning painted across its shoulder. The warrior himself wore no paint. Although his features were concealed by the storm, Black Moon felt that he somehow knew him. He could read his thoughts and feel the emotions in his heart. Just then, the sky lit up with a brilliant flash, and in that moment, Black Moon caught a glimpse of the warrior's face. It was his own. Since that day he had strived to make himself just like the warrior of his vision. In all these years the vision had not changed.

He turned his head to look at the woman sleeping beside him. This, too, had not changed. Since the first time he saw her a day did not go by that he did not want her. His thoughts turned to the day his father told him that his request for her had been denied. Claw had been right. What good came from wanting something that would never be his? For in the end, no matter what his feelings were, she was still his brother's wife. The terrible longing he carried inside was another thing that did not change.

She stirred beside him and reached for his hand, placing it over her breast. It was not for a man to caress a woman's breasts, for they were the symbol of motherhood, something for the child, not the man, to have. Yet he cupped their fullness and ran his thumbs across her nipples that were like hard little berries, and brought his mouth downward, suckling like the child suckles, but with a fever burning inside that only a man can know.

He covered his face with her long red hair and pressed his mouth against her neck, enjoying the smell of her skin as he moved his hands over the whole of her body, exhilarating in the feel of her.

The movements of her supple body only drove him deeper into his obsession to possess her. She was his and no other's. It was he who had taken her from girl to woman. He who needed her so desperately. He who would kill any man who tried to take her from him. He took her again, embedding himself deep within her, becoming a part of her.

She cried out softly, one breathless word against the night. "*Mihigna*."

The word reverberated through Black Moon's mind like a drum beat, chasing away his anger and filling him with joy such as he had never known.

Mihigna. Husband.

CHAPTER 14

A covering of frost lay upon Good Deeds' lodge. She bent to stoke with a stick the flames of the fire kept constantly burning but managed only to raise billows of smoke. An impatient hand snatched the stick away.

"You foolish woman," chided Little Day. "If Gray Wolf returns and finds the lodge so smoky, you will suffer for it."

Little Day's berating was echoed by her sister, Makes-the-Lodge, who turned on Good Deeds with a sneer. "You should know by now that our husband's hand strikes hard even when you have a child in your belly. Did he not strike you yesterday when you tracked snow into the lodge?"

Tears burst from Good Deeds' eyes and she ran from the lodge out into the frost-laden air. Her steps flew over the hard ground, speeding her as far away from those two as she could get. When she could run no further, she collapsed on the frozen ground, sobbing.

She had tried to hold her head high when she heard of Fire Cloud's marriage, but inside, her heart had broken into a thousand small pieces. Losing Fire Cloud was like losing the warmth of the sun, the light of the day. With the devastating news had come the kind of reckless impetuosity that often springs from a broken heart, and in desperate confusion she had acted rashly and unwisely by marrying Gray Wolf, an ill-humored man who already had two wives.

Good Deeds wept until there were no more tears to

shed. When she raised her head from the ground, her gaze fell upon her brother.

When Yellow Hand saw the ugly bruise on her cheek, a hard, tight line formed across his mouth.

"It was my fault," she said. "I gave my husband reason to strike me."

"I have never known you to say a false word against anyone," he said. 'Am I to believe that you are capable of arousing this kind of anger?"

"Yes, it was me. I tracked snow into the lodge. I deserved his anger."

"No!" he exclaimed. "You do not deserve this. Not you. But I know one who does."

"Please," she begged. "You must not act against Gray Wolf."

"Gray Wolf?" He laughed contemptuously. "Fear not, sister. Your husband will come to no harm from me. You knew the kind of man he was when you went to him. The beating you received from Gray Wolf is a matter left between a husband and his wife. No, I was thinking of another. The one responsible for your unhappiness, and mine. Yes," he added coldly in answer to her sharp intake of breath. "I speak of Fire Cloud. When he married the red-haired woman, I watched the power she carries go to one who did not even want it. Yes," he said scornfully, "Fire Cloud will pay for what he has done. A party of white miners has been sighted along Cherry Creek. Right now Fire Cloud sits in the council lodge urging the headmen to do nothing about it. In time, they, too, will see him for what he is, just a common thief, no better than those white men."

***

Inside the council lodge the fires burned brightly.

"Their little diggings hurt no one," Fire Cloud said. "Let the white men take as much of the yellow metal as they need and go."

"When did they ever take only what they need and go?" Black Moon's strong voice argued.

"Only more trouble will come if we attack them. If they know that we are not to be feared, perhaps then we can—"

"We can what?" his brother harshly interrupted. "Live side by side with them?" His laughter was riddled with contempt. "There can be no harmony between our nations. Only one can survive. The whites see that clearly. Why else would they try so hard to destroy us?"

In a firm but gentle tone Fire Cloud told his brother, "The council has decided. There will be no more war on the whites. The ones on Cherry Creek will be allowed to stay."

Black Moon's fury exploded. "How many more greedy whites will we allow into our country to shoot up the buffalo and dig up the hills in their crazy search for the yellow metal? How many more to rob the streams of all the beavers? How long will it be before the buffalo are gone? Has the council also decided how we will make our lodges and how we will eat when there are no more buffalo? And after the buffalo what will be left? What will you say to the hungry ones who come to you with shrunken bellies when they are starving?"

"We have seen hungry times before," Turning Hawk said.

"It is more than just the buffalo," Lone Horn spoke up. "It is the land. The whites see our struggle to keep the land as a fight to hold onto a possession. But the land is not something to be owned. Man belongs to the land, and the Earth possesses all men. She is our mother. I would kill anyone who tried to harm the old woman I call mother, so why should I not kill anyone who would destroy our mother Earth?"

"That is what we must make them understand," Fire Cloud urged. "But how can we do that if we wave clubs or shoot arrows at them? We must come to them in peace."

"A Lakota knows no such thing as peace," Black Moon said with a derisive snort. "War is what the people know. It is what they were born for. What they live for. We have been making war on our enemies since before the time of our grandfathers. The whites come to us with treaties that divide up the land, telling us they are doing this so that we will know who the land belongs to. The whites may not know!" he said with emotion, eyes fiery bright. "But we know!"

"You have always been quick to think the worst."

Black Moon turned on his brother with a snarl. "It was you who did not think the bluecoats would bring their big guns into the Brulè camp on Blue Water Creek three winters past, but those very guns killed their chief. It was you who did not think it was possible to rescue a woman from our Crow enemies, but it was I who brought your wife back to you. Now it is you who does not think it is a good thing for us to turn back the whites, and I say it *is* a good thing."

He turned his face away from his brother with disgust and rose in a fluid motion. Glaring down into their faces, he said arrogantly, "Brave hearts, strong hearts to the front. Cowards to the rear." He aimed a pointed look at his brother and stalked out of the lodge.

When the night sun was high and the fires of evening sent shadows dancing across the hide walls of the lodge, there came a soft scratching at the door to Pretty Shield's lodge.

Hail Storm entered.

Black Moon looked up from his pipe and gestured for his cousin to sit.

"You will ride against the whites tomorrow despite the wishes of the council?" Hail Storm asked.

"My mind is not changed because the others say it should be," he answered stoically.

"How many do you think will ride with you?"

With a shrug of unconcern, Black Moon replied, "I will have no trouble finding men to ride with me. Many have turned their ears away from the council."

"It is true. And they look to you to lead them."

"I lead no one. I do as I choose for myself. If any wish to follow, that is their choice." He cast a side-long look at his cousin and asked, "Is that why you came here tonight? To find out how many will ride with me? You have never questioned the odds before."

Hail Storm hesitated, then said in a whisper, "Last night the spirit of the dead came and threw stones at me in my sleep. Maybe it is the result of some charm," he brooded. "Or a bad spirit has climbed inside of me."

In a restrained voice, Black Moon said, "I, too, have seen the spirit of the dead in my dreams. People will die because I go to war. But it is the only way I know. I am a warrior, and all the words of peace spoken by men like Turning Hawk and Fire Cloud will not change what I am." He leveled a hard, but understanding, look at his cousin. "If you fear for your life, then do not come. Do what you feel you must." With that, he fell silent and emptied his pipe in a sign that the meeting was over.

A short time later there came another scratching at the door and another visitor entered. Black Moon's eyes took in all of her at once. She wore a dress of plain buckskin unadorned with beadwork or shells. Her neat braids, decorated with hair-ties, reached her elbows. She murmured a greeting to Pretty Shield in that soft woman's voice he heard calling to him each night in his dreams.

It was expected of him to maintain a friendly, even intimately joking, relationship with his sister-in-law, yet his heart felt no gaiety in her presence, only a shattering gravity he could not overcome. He was her true husband. Had she not said so? The joy it had brought him to hear it was like a crushing blow to his heart when they had returned to the village and he watched her enter the lodge she shared with his brother. She was a proud and stubborn woman, and the same qualities that made him proud of her also made him resent her, for she had refused to renounce Fire Cloud as her husband, perpetuating the torment for them both. Seeing her now unexpectedly like this only heightened the misery in his heart.

He returned his attention to the bowstring he was making with the sinew he'd cut from beneath the buffalo's shoulder. With three strands placed against a naked thigh, he rolled them with his palm, adding strands of sinew until they were interlocked. When this twisting was complete, he stretched the string and laid it aside to dry by the fire.

Only then did he look back up at her and ask sullenly, "Has my brother sent you here to change my mind?"

"He sent me, yes," Katie confessed.

She shot a quick look over at Pretty Shield who worked

quietly in the corner. Her gaze returned to Black Moon's. The fire cast a rosy glow over his hard-muscled body that was naked except for a breech cloth and a red quilled armband encircling a well-defined upper arm. The muscles of his bare thighs flexed involuntarily when she came closer and sat down beside him.

"He sees only the good in people," she said softly. "His heart will not allow him to see the evil that threatens us. For him, peace is the only answer."

"Fire Cloud thinks we take a great chance by riding to war with the new sun," he said. "And you? Do you think the chance is too great?"

She searched his eyes for many long, unspoken moments when there was no need for words between them. At last she answered in a husky whisper, "It is the heart afraid of losing that cannot win."

"Are those my brother's words?" he asked.

"No. They are mine."

Black Moon's heart leapt for joy. Her faith in him gave him the courage to stand firm in his belief that going against the whites was the right way. When all the others opposed him, this woman, with her fiery beauty and boldness, stood by his side. She made him feel strong, powerful, and capable of defying the world.

Pretty Shield did not fail to see the look that raced back and forth between her son and daughter-in-law. Later that night, she whispered to her husband, "Those two say too much to each other with their eyes. You must speak to him. No good can come of his wanting her."

"Our son is not a man to be denied when there is something he wants as fiercely as he wants the red-haired woman," Claw said. "But it is his defiance of the council and the possible consequences that trouble me far more."

CHAPTER 15

*D*awn painted the sky red, calling the warriors away from the cold, dead ashes of their lodge-fires. By mid-sun a steady, freezing rain had turned the ground slick as bear's grease.

From where they watched at the top of a rise overlooking the miners' camp, Black Moon said, "I do not think it is such a good idea to fight today. The horses are slipping all over the place. We will not even be able to make a good charge."

Hail Storm lashed out with a sharp objection. "Are you calling off the fight? We can't go back now. Everyone will laugh at us. I have my good name to think of. You go back if you want, but I will stay and fight."

"Do not get so upset, little cousin," Black Moon said with a laugh. "We will stay and fight, but do not blame me if we get a good whipping. Wet bowstrings are no match against the far-shooting guns of the whites."

They fought hard, but the miners soon had them whipping their ponies to get away.

Black Moon and Hail Storm hung back. First one charged, then another, firing arrows into the oncoming whites, their ponies slipping and sliding, making it hard to escape the bullets. In the melee Hail Storm's pony stumbled when a bullet ripped through its front leg.

Black Moon leaped from his pony's back and shot a succession of arrows at the charging whites from the ground, trying to hold them off long enough for Hail Storm's injured pony to limp to safety. But Hail Storm was surrounded, fighting off whites from all sides.

"No!" Black Moon's voice tore from his throat as he raced to help him, but it was too late. There was a bullet wound in the youth's chest and blood was coming from his mouth. Their eyes met briefly before Hail Storm slid from his crippled horse and was lost in the wave of white men that swarmed over him.

It was not good for a dead warrior to remain unburied in enemy territory, so when the others mounted up and headed for home, Black Moon spurred his pony back to the battle site. The sky was darkening and the scent of snow was on the wind. He searched the ground, pushing aside bushes and looking behind rocks to find his cousin. He found him in a clump of brush. The youth's face was frozen white. His lips were blue. His eyes stared vacant, unseeing. He pulled the frozen body into his arms and hugged it long and hard. But he did not cry. There was too much coldness in his heart for warm tears to form.

The scouts sent up smoke signals to announce the return of the war party. The women made a loud trilling when the men rode in. Black Moon rode stony-eyed and grim-faced at the rear of the column astride his sorrel pony, with a body slumped over its shoulders, lifeless, like a sack of flour. He halted before his cousin's lodge. The women rushed forward to pull the dead warrior to the ground and knelt over his body, wailing and keening for their lost one, struck down in his nineteenth winter. Black Moon cast a long last look down at his cousin and then urged his pony to walk on past.

From where she stood watching, Katie took a step forward to go after him, but a hand on her arm stopped her.

"Let him go," said Fire Cloud. "He needs to be alone. He has much to think about."

There was a hard edge to his voice that she had never heard before which made her look at him, and say, "You blame him for this."

"He went against the wishes of the council, and look what happened."

"Hail Storm was not made to go," she argued. "He went because he wanted to."

"We do not speak the names of the ones who die," he said sharply. But then his tone softened a little. "He adored my brother and would have done anything for him. That is why he died."

"That was his choice," she reminded him.

Fire Cloud sighed in a burst of white frosty air. "It is cold. Come inside."

She pulled away from him. "I must go to him, since you will not."

He turned startled eyes upon her.

"Even a dog deserves to be comforted when it is hurting," she said. "When your dog stepped on a burr, you pulled it from his paw and soothed him. Would you do any less for your brother?"

"The dog did not try to bite my hand," Fire Cloud said. "My brother is not like a docile camp dog. He is more like the wolf who would die before letting anyone get close enough to comfort it."

"Perhaps you are right, but I must try."

***

Black Moon raced his pony across the snow-white plain, his face twisted with rage, a feeling of self-despising filling his heart. He wished the whites had killed him instead of his cousin. Then perhaps this ache in his heart would be no more.

He could not remember a time as an adult when he did not feel the dull throbbing in his heart. There was a time when he could ride for days without seeing another human being. Now, signs of encroachment were everywhere, in the big wooden walls of the soldier fort, the wagon ruts on the Holy Road, the streams and creeks littered with the leavings of the miners in their search for the yellow metal.

Then there was this hurting that came from wanting a woman who would never be truly his. Yes, she was his enemy, not because she was white, as he had once thought, but because she was a danger to his heart. That a brave warrior such as himself should be reduced to such pitiful longing over a woman filled him with self-disgust. And now this, the loss of a beloved young cousin, all because he had gone against the wishes of the council and put his own selfish interests ahead of everything else. He had done what he thought was best for himself, neither asking nor expecting others to follow, led by his own inner voice and by the burning knowledge that what he did was right. He did not wish to be any different or better than he was. He merely wished to be. But in doing so, he had brought misery upon others. He was no better than his brother.

He thumped his heels hard against his pony's flanks, trying to run as fast as he could away from the things that hurt him. Faster, faster, until the frothing mount could run no more and on its own slowed to a walk. Yet still there reverberated a drumbeat of hooves that grew louder and louder. He turned to look over his shoulder. A horse and rider were coming fast after him.

When she caught up to him and fell in place beside him, he gave her an unwelcoming look. "You do not belong here."

"I belong wherever you are," Katie said.

"Does my brother know you are here?"

"He knows."

"But he did not send you."

"Not this time."

Black Moon lifted his face and scanned the sky, his proud, unflinching profile etched against the gray light. "The wind is changing. More snow is coming. We should head back to the village before the storm breaks." But his time with her was so limited that he could not bring himself to pull the jaw rope and turn his pony's head around. "Are you ashamed of me for what I have done?" he asked.

"I could never be ashamed of you," she answered.

"But I have done a selfish thing, and now my cousin is dead and his family cries for him."

"You did the right thing by protecting the land. Without the land, the people are nothing. Why do you speak as if you wear a woman's dress instead of the bighorn shirt?"

Only she had the courage to speak to him in such a taunting manner. A freezing rain began to fall, but he did not notice. "How long do you think they will let me keep the shirt after what I have done?"

"I would love you if you wore no shirt at all," she said, raising her voice against the rattle of the wind. "In fact, I love you most when you are wearing no shirt at all."

He knew her meaning and felt a predictable surge in his loins. At another time he would have stopped his pony, pulled her down from hers and made love to her right there on the open prairie for all the winged ones flying overhead to see. But the cold rain now slanted against their faces, changing rapidly to snow, and he knew they had to find shelter.

The snowflakes were soon whirling all around them, making visibility harder. Katie let out a little yelp when the wind slapped her hard across the face. Black Moon reached over and grasped the rope to lead her horse along. The sheltered places had already begun filling with snow, the whiteness piling up in drifts all around them.

They rode with their heads down into the blinding snowstorm, Black Moon trusting his sorrel pony to find the surest footing. With the wind lashing at them from all sides, he spotted a thin shelter of brush just beyond and headed for it.

He jumped down and tied his pony to a snow-laden thicket, then hurried over to Katie. As soon as she was down her horse bolted and disappeared into the whiteness that engulfed them. From his pony's back he took the buffalo robe that was rolled up there, pulled Katie to the ground beside him, and drew the robe, fur side in, up over them.

They huddled like that while the wind whipped and howled all around them. After an indeterminate time Black Moon lifted the robe and peeked out. The wind had died and the snow was no longer flying in circles. Overhead the sky was brightening. He lowered the robe to a glistening silence. Close by, with ice crystals crusting the lashes of its brown eyes, the sorrel pony whinnied a gentle welcome.

The first thing Black Moon did was get a small fire going using his strike-a-light and a few pieces of dry kindling he kept wrapped in rawhide on his saddle. The flames he brought forth provided a little bit of warmth to chase the ice-cold chill from their bones, but they weren't enough to stop Katie's teeth from chattering. He wound his arms around her and pulled her against him, using the heat of his body to warm her.

He held her like that until he felt her shivering ease, and then, though he might have released her, he did not. Nor did she make any attempt to move. There came up from her hair the smell of bark and sweet grass, from her skin the fragrance of woman. When he turned his face downward to look at her, he found her eyes upon him, green and shining with hunger.

His lips were upon hers, teasing the coldness away until he felt them burn hot beneath his. Her mouth opened and he tasted the warm, wetness inside. Her breath mingled with his to create a fire that needed neither flint nor kindling, only the passion of two people who could not live without each other.

He laid her back against the robe, his lean, hard body covering hers, the warm buffalo fur surrounding them. Every doubt he had, every bit of self-loathing was lost amidst the sounds of her gasps as she clung to him, needing him, loving him, telling him with the movements of her exquisite body and her hand that guided his hardness into her, that no matter how many other hearts might turn against him, hers never would.

Later, he lay with her in his arms, the robe wrapped around their bodies as the sun slowly made its way behind the buttes on the horizon. The air had grown sharply cold again as twilight approached, but he didn't feel it. He fell asleep like that, only to awaken in those moments before dawn with a renewed urgency for her.

He stretched, and against her flesh he murmured, "I wish for my seed to grow inside of you so that you will always be mine."

Katie disentangled herself from him and reached for her dress. The peaks of her breasts stood out like hard unripe berries against the cold, drawing his eyes like hungry wolves. "My father used to say be careful what you wish for because it might not make you happy."

"Should I not wish it?" he questioned.

"I would be lying if I said I do not wish it, but what we wish for would bring much heartache to others."

She did not have mention Fire Cloud's name for him to know of whom she was speaking. Like wood burning to ash, his desire faded. He was up and at her side in a flash, his nakedness gleaming in the growing sunshine. "What about my heartache?" he angrily questioned. "Do you think it is easy for me knowing that you lay in his robes, in his arms? That his seed will create the life that should be ours?" Resentment tore through his voice like yesterday's blizzard despite the torment in his eyes.

"It is not what you think," she said. "Your brother has never known me in that way." In answer to the confusion troubling his handsome features, she softly confessed, "We agreed from the start that we would not live as a true husband and wife when we both love others."

Instead of relief, a slow fury built upon his face as the realization came over him. "You have known this all along and you let me think that you and my brother—" His breath came in rapid bursts that crystallized upon impact with the air, happy and furious at the same time. "And still you will not leave him?"

Her voice was small and weak beside his. "No."

Black Moon turned away and strode to the buffalo robe, kicking it across the snow as he reached for his clothes. "You are the most stubborn and foolish woman I know. I should find another, one who would be proud to call herself my wife." Yet even as he threatened it, he knew he would not do it, for no other woman would ever mean as much to him as this stubborn and foolish one.

He felt her hand slip into his and turned grudgingly toward her. "I would be proud to call myself your wife," she said softly.

His anger melted like snow in the sun. He reached up to stroke her face, running one strong, browned finger along the line of her jaw, caressing her with his eyes. "And I would be happy to have this wish come true."

They rode back to the village astride Black Moon's sorrel pony. When Pretty Shield saw them approaching, she ran forward.

"You must not be seen this way. Come, come," she urged her daughter-in-law.

Katie slid to the ground and followed her mother-in-law into the lodge while Black Moon rode off.

In the days that followed the ground was so frozen that a scaffold could not be erected for the brave young warrior who had died, so his body was hoisted into a tree. Around the base of the tree his family placed thorny branches and brambles to keep the wild animals away. His shield, lance and medicine pouch hung from a branch. The women wept and wailed. Some slashed their arms with sharp knives.

Black Moon stood in the distance watching their blood soak into the snow, turning it red. His heart was filled with sadness and shame over what he had done and with certainty over the repercussions he knew would be coming.

CHAPTER 16

A strong gust of wind from the south blew Pretty Shield's braids into her face. She glanced to the top of the lodge at the two flaps that served as windbreakers and went to raise the southern one to accommodate the shift in wind. She turned back around to see her son standing there, a grim look on his face. "What troubles you?" she asked.

"You know what it is," Fire Cloud answered.

She placed a hand on his arm. "You must try to understand his ways."

"But his ways lead the people toward death."

"Have you noticed how many follow him? He does not order it. The choice is theirs. Our bodies are the only things we truly own. Brave men offer bits of flesh to *Wakan Tanka* in the Sun Dance. They do it willingly. No one questions it. Why, then, do you question the needs of those who follow your brother to offer up their lives to protect the things they believe in?"

"Because I have seen too many get hurt. Who decides for those too small or too old to make their own choices?"

"What will you do?"

"What I must."

"My son," she said tenderly, "your heart knows only goodness. It has been so since you were a child. I am proud that you look to the Great Spirit for guidance. Black Moon is also seeking, but in a different way. He sees not always with his heart as you do, and so sometimes he sees things more clearly than you do. Continue your seeking. I ask only that you do not be disappointed by what you find. The days ahead will grow darker, and the people will endure great sadness before the world comes back into the Roundness again. The Great Spirit made the hoop of our people, and He will make it again when this one falls apart."

Pretty Shield's prophecy was ringing in Fire Cloud's ears later that day as he led the others back to his mother's lodge.

Black Moon knew why they had come. The tension was thick as he motioned for Pretty Shield to get the case containing the shirt of the bighorn. She carried it outside and handed it to Fire Cloud, her tears falling upon the stiff rawhide. Black Moon stood behind her, no tears in his eyes, only a fierce look that fell upon his brother like ice before he turned and disappeared inside.

No sooner was the shirt handed over to Fire Cloud than there was talk of putting it on someone else. Yellow Hand's name was mentioned. But Fire Cloud could not bring himself to do it. He passed the case quickly to someone else, getting rid of it as if it were something despicable.

The next day a new snowfall lay atop the old. The women were taking turns at skimming a ball along a slippery path. The boys were sliding down a steep slope in buffalo rib-cages. Fire Cloud sat by the stream with his back pressed against the trunk of a tree. The air cut his face with its stark chill as he contemplated what he had done.

To strip a man of the ceremonial shirt was to strip him of his honor, his pride, to force him to walk alone as if in mourning. Such a man was no longer entitled to smoke a long-stemmed pipe, but a short-stemmed one of stone as a constant reminder of his broken vow. In stripping Black Moon of the shirt, Fire Cloud knew he had lost him forever.

The one he called wife was too angry and hurt over this for their friendship to mend. With his action, he had done the very thing he punished Black Moon for doing, namely, not stopping to consider the sorrow it would bring to others. In his pursuit to banish pain and anger from the people's hearts, he had provided the perfect spawning ground for both, and had brought dishonor upon himself.

A frozen twig snapped on the ground, drawing Fire Cloud away from his tortured thoughts.

Yellow Hand approached, resentment shining in his hawkish features. "Can it be that you are finally feeling guilt for your treachery?"

With a beleaguered sigh, Fire Cloud said, "I did what had to be done."

"You are so busy doing what has to be done that you do not see the unhappiness you cause others. Or is it that you just do not care?"

"Is it others you are thinking about or is it yourself?"

"First you took the woman I wanted because it had to be done," Yellow Hand said with a snarl. "Now you deny me the shirt. When did your voice become so strong in council that the others do as you say?"

"If you are denied the shirt, it is because you are not worthy of it."

"And Black Moon was worthy? That one cares only for himself."

Fire Cloud rose to his feet to leave. "Not even your best can equal his worst."

The remark enflamed Yellow Hand's already heated emotions. "Your brother hates you for taking the woman. Can you be so blind that you do not see the way he looks at her? How long do you think it will be before he simply takes her from you? We all know what kind of man he is. What he wants, he takes." As he spoke his face contorted with rage, blue veins spiking his temples. "He hates you!" he exclaimed, aiming straight for Fire Cloud's sensitive heart.

Fire Cloud had difficulty swallowing down the lump in his throat that felt as large as a chokecherry. The estrangement between him and his brother may have reached its climax with the taking of the shirt, but its fate was sealed the day Fire Cloud married Katie. If there was any doubt before as to the pain he had caused, he had only to look at Black Moon's resentment, Good Deeds' unhappiness, Katie's disappointment, even his own stinging despair. But most of all, he saw his wrongdoing in the twisted rage on Yellow Hand's face. Drawing in a deep breath, he said, "My brother may hate me for what I have done, but you hate him for what he is. It only makes you see what you are not and never will be."

The words exploded upon Yellow Hand's brain, driving him beyond rationality. In moments too fleet to count, his knife was loosed from its sheath.

Later that afternoon the scouts found Fire Cloud. He was lying on his back. His eyes were closed as though he were asleep, but there was no breath cloud over him.

Black Moon helped prepare his brother's body for the scaffold, dressing him in his finest attire and slipping onto his feet the moccasins with the beaded soles. In his hair he placed eagle feathers, a right belonging to warriors, but who would be crazy enough to tell him he could not?

On a high hill a scaffold was erected out of four forked posts, high enough so that the wild animals could not reach it, over which was placed a cross frame of sturdy branches. The loved one, wrapped in his burial bundle, now traveled the spirit trail to the Land of Many Lodges where all things which had ever existed lived forever.

Seated beneath the scaffold on the cold ground, Claw ran pegs through his arms and legs and Pretty Shield slashed her limbs and Katie wept. Black Moon watched with a frozen heart, then jumped astride his sorrel pony and rode out of the village. This time Katie did not go after him.

High up into the hills he rode. Hobbling his pony, he spread his blanket over the hard ground, took from his pouch a few pinches of kinnikinik and placed it in the bowl of his short-stemmed pipe. He offered the pipe to the Four Winds, to the Sky, to his mother Earth, and then sat silently puffing, alone with his haunted thoughts. The sun crept high in the sky and then began its slow descent beyond the horizon, and still Black Moon sat there without eating, without drinking, without making a fire for warmth. When the grief became almost too much for him to bear, his head fell forward, his hair cascading like a black waterfall over his face, the only movement he made.

He had made many mistakes and broken a sacred vow, and although he heaped a load of blame upon himself for what had happened, try as he might he could not bring himself to beg the Great Spirit for His forgiveness. Hadn't the Great Spirit made him as he was for a purpose? All his life he thought he knew what that purpose was, but now he was not so sure. And still, he did not question the wisdom of *Wakan Tanka*. It was enough for him to know that there was a purpose and that he fulfilled it with every breath he took.

After a long time he got up and walked to the summit of the hill. Below him was spread the giant expanse of his country, the plains slowly emerging from the cover of snow, patches of brown earth showing here and there, the river winding its way toward the sacred *Paha Sapa*, the slim buttes in the distance looking like buffalo humps. Lifting his arms, he spread them wide to the heavens and silently implored the Great Spirit for an answer.

He remained in the hills for seven suns seeking an answer to the confusion that tormented him. Finally, feeling abandoned by the world, he jumped astride his pony and headed for home.

***

Pretty Shield sat in a corner without speaking, staring listlessly at the awl and sinew in her lap. Her once-beautiful long hair was chopped off in places, the self-inflicted gashes on her arms healing beneath dried medicinal paste.

"The headmen came to me this morning," Claw said. "They ask why you do not do your duty and take your brother's wife as your own in the Lakota way. One moon has passed since…" His voice choked. "…that day. A woman needs a man to bring her hides to flesh and meat to cook. A man to protect her. To plant the seeds that will become her children."

Black Moon looked up from the bowstring he was waxing, and said scornfully, "What about the time I asked for her and was denied?"

"What will happen to her if you refuse?"

"That one is a survivor."

"Yes, but a woman alone?"

"She will have no trouble finding a man to take her."

"If she remains here alone, her life will be hard," Claw said from across the flames. "It could be that she will choose to return to her world."

"*This* is her world," Black Moon said hotly. "She does not belong in a house made of wood surrounded by a fence of wood. She belongs here. This is what she is. Not that."

Claw tapped his pipe bowl into his palm and threw the spent ashes into the fire. The killing of his son had aged him. He lifted his weary gaze and looked into the proud, stubborn eyes of his other son. "She has put up a lodge at the end of the crescent. Go to her."

Black Moon's pulse began to quicken. Loosening the taut sinew on his bow, he placed it and its otter skin quiver of arrows aside, rose fluidly from his cross-legged position and left the lodge.

A sliver of pale frosty light lit his path. He stood for several minutes before her lodge unable to move, feeling apprehensive in a way that he was unaccustomed to feeling. The skins glowed red from the fire burning within. Into his nostrils drifted the smell of wood smoke and good things cooking. There was a soft rustling inside of someone moving about. He scratched at the hide door. The movements from within stopped, and a soft voice bade him enter.

Without speaking a word, he dropped like rainfall to the ground before the fire, legs crossed, eyes downcast. No words were exchanged between them. She ladled some food into a bighorn spoon and passed it to him. He accepted it without thanks. He offered a bit of the meat first to the Four Winds, then to the sky, then to his mother, the Earth. Then he ate in silence. Later, he sat smoking his short-stemmed pipe, watching her with guarded eyes as she moved about the lodge. It was strange to be here with her like this. Strange, but natural.

He was trying hard to maintain an air of indifference, while inwardly his heart tripped at the closeness of her. And yet he could not bring himself to speak to her, to say the words that burned upon his tongue.

After wanting her for so long she was his. His to hold, to gaze upon, to possess, to love as wildly as he had ever loved anything.

He stripped off his buckskin garments and lay down on a pile of robes. Sleep was slow in coming. He lay perfectly still, trying to concentrate on anything except the closeness of her. Eventually, his black lashes fluttered softly and he slept.

The fire died to a pile of simmering embers. Black Moon's eyes snapped open at the touch of a hand, soft and cool, against his bare chest. Every muscle in his body went rigid. His nostrils filled with the sweet smell of the cherry bark she had thrown on the fire lingering in her hair. Her touch ran across his chest, then up along his broad shoulder to his face to caress the smooth skin of his cheek. His breath caught in his throat when she placed her body, naked and soft, next to his.

"I will say the words you cannot say," she whispered, nuzzling against his ear. "Since that first day you found me, I have thought of no other man but you. Your brother was good to me." His body tensed, but she pressed on softly. "But he knew it was you I love. He loved you, too. Enough to let me come to you any time I wished."

He turned his head to look at her through the flickering darkness, disbelief in his ebony eyes.

"It is true," she confessed. "I could have come to you before this. It was I who made the pain stronger." She kissed him then, her sweet lips melting against his, her warm, mellifluent breath mingling with his. "And it is I who can ease that pain for you now."

Black Moon closed his eyes and pulled her close to him. The heat of her body merged with that of his to create a torch of warmth between them. All the pain they had caused one another was forgotten when a newer, sharper pain prevailed. It was the pain of sweet fulfillment.

He didn't care if she offered salvation or ruin as long as he could have her like this forever, writhing softly beneath him, calling his name in breathless whispers.

His own voice was low, almost threatening, when he pulled her head back, forcing her to look into his eyes, and said in a low growl, "There will be no more barriers between us. I want you more than anything in the world. And you? Tell me you want me."

Katie shuddered against him. "Yes," she said breathlessly. "Yes. I want you. I have always wanted you."

His heart drummed hard in his chest. "I will not lose you to another. Not again. You must know that I will do whatever I can to stop that from happening."

She answered him with her body, drawing him down on top of her and into her, making them one.

With Katie's expression of love, and the revelation that had come that day of the snow storm that she had never lain with his brother, Black Moon felt a sense of triumph in knowing that no other man had had her. Yet with that revelation came the sickening realization of how wrong he had been about his brother. He had been too blinded by his own jealousy to realize that Fire Cloud never meant to hurt him. He had simply been acting on a belief that was just as strong as Black Moon's own. Knowing this and not being able to ask his brother's forgiveness left him with a feeling of something incomplete, something he knew would invade every day of his life for as long as he lived.

They fell into an easy life together. By day, Black Moon hunted, bringing game back for his mother and his wife to cook and hides to scrape. Katie worked around the lodge, mending his buckskin shirts and moccasins and cooking his favorite foods. At night the flames of their passion reached as high as the smoke hole, threatening to set the whole world on fire.

One night a soft voice called at the door to the lodge. Good Deeds entered. She looked haggard and worn for one so young. Her eyes were red and swollen from crying. "I have come to beg for my brother's life."

"And who should I have begged for my brother's life?" Black Moon harshly questioned. "It was no Crow dog who did that killing as everyone thinks, and we both know it."

"He is my blood. You had a brother once. You know how it is."

Black Moon's eyes lit up with fury. "Yes, I had a brother, and today there is nothing left of him but a pile of bones atop the burial scaffold."

In a voice scarcely audible, she said, "There is something left. The child I gave birth to is his."

His eyes narrowed into slits of suspicion. "How do I know the child is not Gray Wolf's?"

"The seed was planted before I married Gray Wolf. In our own hearts your brother and I were already married. We saw no wrong in what we did."

The finality of his brother's death had stunned Black Moon in a way that was new to one who looked upon death as something inevitable and as much a part of life as living. Despite their differences, he had felt suddenly desolate. But now, a glimmer of hope resided with this frail, disillusioned girl. A part of his brother lived. Perhaps in the child Black Moon would find the forgiveness he sought.

He glanced over at Katie who sat without saying a word but whose green eyes carried a woman's understanding and a silent plea.

Turning back to Good Deeds, Black Moon said, "I will spare your brother's life…for now."

CHAPTER 17

*T*he grassy banks along the North Platte River where the Oglalas pitched their lodges for the summer reminded Katie of the quiet valley along the Laramie where she had lived with her father in a cabin made of wood, small and rudely chinked, the logs neither square nor barked, and the saddle notchings notoriously short-lived. She could not think of it without a knot forming in her throat. Until three years ago it had been her home.

She missed the winter nights when she sat before the spitting fire eating rabbit stew and the summers when she would run through knee-high grass and pick wildflowers for the window sill. Mostly, she missed the sound of her father's thick Irish brogue. It seemed a lifetime ago that Richard brought his new wife to visit, and how happy they all were when Bone Bracelet announced she was with child. But the future that had seemed so full of promise came crashing down on a sun-bright day along the Blue Water.

The wide-open plains were Katie's home now. She had become a nomad, packing up with scarcely any notice and moving with the rest of the village, following the trail of the ever-diminishing buffalo. She felt a sense of sadness in all this moving about, an uneasy feeling of impermanence. Once, just once, she wished they would stay in one place longer than a season. And it wouldn't hurt to have some of the things she used to have, like books to read, and the sweet treats McCabe used to bring back from the fort when he went to trade, and a dress made of something other than elk or deer skin. Oh yes, a beautiful dress of silk with appliqués at the neck and swirls at the hem and yards of velvet ribbon for trim, like the one she saw one of the general's wives wearing once when she accompanied her father to the fort. What would the folks at Fort Laramie think if they could see her now clad in plain buckskin and moccasins on her feet?

McCabe used to scold her for having her head in the clouds so much that she didn't get her chores done. It was just as true today as it was back then. Yet each time she thought of leaving the Oglala camp to follow her dreams of pretty dresses she had only to look into Black Moon's dark eyes or inhale the familiar male scent of his skin and the aroma of sweet grass in his long, dark hair. When he was present, there was never a need to dream beyond the ecstasy she found in his arms, but when he was away, as he was on this day scouting for buffalo, she could not stop her imagination from taking flight. Like a lover on a snow-white steed it carried her far away from these dusty plains to a place that existed only in daydreams.

"Kathleen McCabe!"

At the sound of her name Katie stopped in mid-motion over the hide shirt she was mending. It was the first time anyone had called her by her full name in a very long time.

A taut uneasiness gripped her. She sensed danger and recoiled from it. For many moments she remained immobile, uncertain whether or not she should answer the call. Sheer curiosity prompted her to place awl and sinew aside and lift the flap to step outside the lodge into the bright April sunshine.

Before her startled eyes was a company of mounted soldiers. The sunlight glanced off their sabers in a blinding flash. Her eyes swept over their ranks, searching for a hint of treachery as she warily approached. The soldier at the head of the column dismounted and came forward. Instinctively, she backed away.

"Kathleen McCabe?" he inquired. His voice was lower now, the tone noticeably softer.

She answered tentatively, "Aye."

Relief swarmed over his face, and it was only then she realized that the expression that had been there before had been one of fear. Fear was something Katie understood only too well, and it was perhaps that which made him seem a little more human to her.

"I'm sure glad we found you, ma'am," he said.

She assessed him as thoroughly as he was assessing her. He could not have been more than twenty-five or six, she judged. She had been to the fort enough times and seen enough blue uniforms to recognize the markings of rank on his sleeve. Was it inexperience or utter stupidity that prompted him to march his men into a hostile Oglala village?

Tersely, she said to him, "You took an awful big risk coming here, Lieutenant. Surely, you must know you aren't welcome."

He shifted nervously from foot to foot. "Yes, ma'am."

"Then why are you here?" Her tone was purposefully curt. She saw no reason to be friendly to him. He may have been young and handsome, but he was also white and a soldier, and she knew what a deadly combination that could be.

He slid his hand into a breast pocket and withdrew an envelope. "I have a letter for you." He was about to hand it to her, when he drew it back. "If you can't read, I'd be happy to read it for you."

Katie reached forward and snatched the envelope from his hand. "I can read."

She tore open the flap and hastily removed a letter from inside. Her eyes flew over the words. This could not be true. It simply wasn't possible. Her hands began to tremble.

The letter in Katie's quaking fingers was written by a woman in St. Louis who claimed to be her aunt. Katie recalled that her mother had an older sister back in Ireland. She wondered why McCabe never mentioned that the woman lived in St. Louis, and then realized it was probably because he hadn't known. All this time she assumed she had no white family left, yet here was proof to the contrary.

She read the letter over again, this time slowly. The letter mentioned matters to be settled. What matters could she have with a woman she'd never met? The handwriting had a regal, almost haughty, bearing, with sweeping strokes and elegant curlicues. The paper upon which the letter was written was of good quality. Katie tried to envision a face, but couldn't. Nevertheless, there was little doubt that this woman—her eyes sought out the signature—Virginia Devlin Beauregard—had the power and influence to have an army troop deliver her message.

Katie's mind spun as a world of possibilities suddenly opened before her, a world of books and sweet treats and pretty silk dresses.

"Miss McCabe? Ma'am?"

She looked up to find the lieutenant's anxious gaze upon her. "We'll wait until you gather a few things to leave."

The daydream vanished into thin air. "Leave?" she echoed sharply. "What are you talking about? I'm not going anywhere."

"My orders are to bring you back to Fort Laramie with me. I'm sure the General will explain everything to you."

Katie grew alarmed. "Perhaps you should come back in a month or two," she suggested, knowing that the village would have moved to another spot by then. "Or better still, I'll ride over to the fort when I'm ready."

His voice remained calm, but there was no mistaking the threat it held when he said, "My orders are to use force if necessary."

Katie's green eyes flashed and the color rushed to her cheeks. "How dare you march uninvited into this village and issue threats. I'll thank you not to use that bullying tone on me, Lieutenant. One word from me and you won't be riding out of this village alive."

It was an idle threat, and Katie knew it. Black Moon and most of the men had ridden off more than a week ago to hunt buffalo. The handful of braves and old men left were no match for these bluecoats. Was it luck or coincidence that they knew exactly where to find her at precisely the time when most of the men were away on the hunt?

Something told Katie not to underestimate the young army officer. Behind his polite exterior she sensed the presence of a strong will. If his order was to use force, she had no doubt he would not hesitate to do so. She glanced around at the unprotected village. Scores of innocent people would get hurt if she did not comply. She groaned inwardly at the thought of all those deaths on her conscience. She would not be the one to precipitate another Blue Water right here on this spot.

But there was something else gnawing at her, and that was her burning curiosity. She had thought her ties with the white world were forever severed with the massacre on Blue Water Creek three years ago, but now it seemed that one rusty link endured. Could she turn her back on it and pretend it did not exist? Could she spend the rest of her life wondering, always wondering? She hesitated. Once again she faced a painful and difficult decision. In the end there was only one thing she could do.

"Give me a few minutes," she told him.

Inside the lodge, surrounded by all that was familiar, she was seized by a sudden sense of panic. She thought fleetingly of lifting the skin and slipping out through the back, yet she knew what the consequences would be if she did. She quickly gathered a few things, stuffed them into a parfleche and headed for the entrance. On her way out, she passed Black Moon's buffalo-hide shield and lance, his things of war that she respectfully never touched. Just this once she reached out and ran a hand lovingly over the smoked skin.

When she emerged from the lodge carrying her bundle, her eyes darted around at the curious faces that poked out from corners and under lodge skins, no one daring to come outside. There was only one figure standing there unhidden, one pair of eyes that watched openly and unafraid. It was Pretty Shield.

In her mother-in-law's eyes Katie saw the same desperate questions she was asking herself. What about Black Moon? Would he understand?

She hurried over to Pretty Shield and placed a hand on her arm. "I am not taking much with me. I will not be gone for long. Tell him I will be back." Her fingers tightened for emphasis. "*Tell him.*"

Pretty Shield drew in an uncertain breath and nodded.

Turning away from the fearful look on her mother-in-law's face, Katie mounted her pony and followed the solders out of the village.

***

She tied her pony to a hitching post and followed one of the troopers up a flight of stairs and along the balcony to a room equipped with a rough bedstead and a tin pail filled with stagnant water. A brass crucifix hung on the wall over the bed. Placing her bundle down on the wafer-thin mattress, she stepped onto the balcony for a look around.

From her second-story vantage point she could see over the high adobe walls of the fort out onto the prairie. A wagon train appeared in the hazy distance, white tops bobbing up and down as if on a rolling sea. About a quarter of a mile out they stopped and wheeled into a circle to encamp. Within the hour the parade ground filled with awkward men in broad-brimmed hats and brown homespun and women with cadaverous faces lost in poke bonnets. And everywhere was sprinkled the regimental blue of the Untied States Army.

Katie grew restless. When several hours passed and no one called for her, she left the room and went downstairs where she melted into the stream of activity. Catching the arm of a passing soldier, she asked, "Who is in charge here, and where can I find him?" Aware of the sight she presented, a white woman dressed in Indian clothing, she nevertheless thought him rude for staring.

"That would be General Worth," he said. "You'll find him over yonder in Old Bedlam." He pointed toward a two-story pillared building that housed the officers' quarters.

"Welcome to Fort Laramie, Miss McCabe," Brigadier General Marcus Worth said without rising when Katie entered his quarters. His pale watery eyes washed over her. "I hope the accommodations are to your liking. But then, I suppose compared to what you're used to, this…" he spread his arms wide, gesturing around them, "…is elegant. Is there anything you would like?"

She disliked him instantly and completely, not only for his cruel humor but for his undisguised disdain. "I would like a bath."

"A bath?" he repeated with surprise.

"The ride was hot and dusty."

A slow smile spread across his lips. "I didn't know Indians take baths."

"I would say there are a lot of things about Indians you don't know, General," she replied with a touch of venom.

Katie had heard about the general from McCabe, who had complained that he knew nothing about Indians but imagined himself a great authority. As commander of the troops along the Overland Road on the Platte, he paid scant attention to their customs and had little real interest in preserving peace. His unsympathetic treatment of the Sioux made the atmosphere on the North Platte and the Laramie explosive.

"So?" Katie said. "What happens now?"

"I have a detachment leaving in the morning for Fort Randall. You'll be going with them. From there, passage has been booked for you aboard a steamboat bound for St. Louis."

She detested his brusque manner. "If that's all, I'll be going."

"That will not be all. There are some questions I would like to ask you. Why don't you have a seat?" He motioned toward the chair before his desk.

Katie remained standing. "I can't imagine what questions you would have to ask me."

"Oh, I think you can. Why don't you begin by telling me where I can find that renegade, Black Moon?"

"You knew where to find me, General," she reminded him.

"That's true. But when he returns to the village and learns that we were there, he will take his people into hiding. You can make our search for him easier if you tell me where he is apt to go. You must know his hiding places."

"Must I? And even if I did, it's not likely I would tell you. Why should I? So that you can hunt them down and kill them the way you killed my father and brother?"

"That was an unfortunate incident, but an example of

what happens when our orders are not obeyed. Now tell me where I can find Black Moon."

She remained tight-lipped.

"How many warriors does he have?"

Still no response.

"Where does he plan to strike next?"

With each question he fired at her, Katie's fury mounted. "You want to know these things so that you can flush them out and slaughter them the way you did those people on Blue Water Creek. I know all about the tactics you use. I've seen your atrocities. Women and children butchered. Homes destroyed. Lives shattered. I'll not have a hand in helping you. I'll not have my soul condemned to eternal hell for it, General."

"Are you mad?" he exclaimed. "Do you know what you are saying? Atrocities? How dare you speak to me of atrocities?"

He shuffled furiously through the papers on his desk. Finding the one he wanted, he pulled it out from the pile and swept the others away with an angry gesture. "Here it is. It's a field report. Let me read to you how they found the bodies of the men of C Company. Eyes torn out. Noses cut off. Ears cut off. Chins hewn off. Teeth chopped out. Ribs slashed to separation. Punctures on every part of the body. Mouths stuffed with grass. Private parts hacked off. Scalps taken. Shoulders wrenched from their sockets…"

"Stop!" Katie cried. She could not bear to hear another word. "I don't know if those things are true. If they are, it can only be the result of the terrible pressure brought to bear upon desperate and frightened people whose way of life is being ground into dust."

"Are you aware of the consequences of withholding evidence from the government during a time of war, Miss McCabe?"

She gave a brittle laugh. "Are you telling me that Congress has declared war on the entire Sioux nation?"

"Not officially, of course," he replied. "But that does not mean we are not in a state of increased hostilities. Look around you woman."

Katie's eyes flashed like bits of green glass. "I am," she

said with disgust. "And what I see makes me sick."

His face turned a mottled red. "I sent an entire company into hostile Indian territory to retrieve an errant white woman who doesn't seem to know where her rightful place is."

"I did not ask it," she shot back. "You could have left me there."

"The order came from Washington."

"Ah, there you see, General, that is just one of the many differences between us. You follow orders. I don't."

"But you will proceed to St. Louis," he said threateningly.

"Aye. I will. But only because I choose to." With that, she pivoted sharply and strode from the room.

She was relieved that he made no attempt to stop her, but if he had, she would have been ready for him, if not with words then with the knife she kept strapped to her calf beneath her dress, and damn the consequences.

Back in her squalid little room she lay atop the yellowed mattress, one arm crooked behind her head, staring at the cracks in the ceiling. Presently, there came a knock at the door. When she answered it, she was surprised to see a large wooden rub rolled in.

"Hot water'll be up in a minute, ma'am," panted the red-faced trooper who had hauled the tub up the flight of stairs. Could it be there was a trace of kindness in the General's grizzled old heart after all?

Daylight came upon the fort from over the ridge. With it came the ever-constant wind and a lone eagle circling the sky. Katie refused an offer to ride in the cook's wagon and was sitting astride her Indian pony waiting patiently along with the rest of the company for the commanding officer to take his place at the head of the column.

A figure emerged from Old Bedlam into the pale light of dawn and walked with long, easy strides to a waiting horse. His head was bent, his face concealed by the broad brim of his hat. He mounted, and with a flick of the hand set the column in motion.

The wooden gates of Fort Laramie opened and the regiment trotted out two by two. They had three hundred miles of the roughest country to cross on their way to Fort Randall.

They had not ridden more than a mile when a trooper reined his army mount alongside Katie's pony, and said, "You're wanted up front."

She urged her pony into a canter. At the front of the column she fell in beside the man whose uniform markings signaled his rank. His head was turned as he spoke to one of the men. She cleared her throat to make her presence known. When he turned to her, Katie found herself looking nto familiar gray eyes. It was the same young officer who had marched boldly into the Oglala village to find her.

He smiled, and said, "I never got the chance to introduce myself." His voice was smooth and friendly. "I'm Lieutenant Josh McIntyre. I want you to know that I will endeavor to make this journey as comfortable for you as possible."

"There's no need to worry about me, Lieutenant. I can take care of myself. But it seems to me that if you take as little precaution on this journey as you did when you rode into that Indian village, then it's you who should be worried. Are you aware that there are Indians out there right now who would like nothing better than to bring home the scalp of a bluecoat?" Making no attempt to mask her contempt for his uniform, she jerked on the reins, wheeled her pony about and galloped back to her place in the column, raising a trail of dust.

CHAPTER 18

After two weeks on the march Katie thought she would go crazy.

Every day the routine was the same. After reveille the rolls were called. The first bugle call signaled tents to be struck and everything packed up for the day's ride. At Boots and Saddles the horses were readied and the wagons loaded. At the call "To horse" each man led his mount into line and stood at its head. At the command, "Prepare to mount", each trooper placed his left foot in the stirrup. When the bugler sounded the Advance, the troops moved out in columns of four. The company that led the advance the day before rode at the rear.

For Katie, there was only one way to break the monotony. A shower of starlight illuminated the path to the remuda. Slipping beneath the ropes, she stood beside her spotted pony, stroking its muzzle, offering it the scraps she had saved from her dinner plate. The animal had been a gift from Black Moon to replace *Peta*. The thought of Black Moon brought a secret smile to her lips. Her hand went to her neck to caress the necklace of trade beads he had given her. He called them love beads. The warmth of the smooth glass beads against her skin made her feel closer to him despite the miles separating them.

The spotted pony gave a contented whinny. "Do you want to go for a gallop?" Katie crooned. "It's a fine night for it, and Lord knows, I can use it."

Thank goodness she was not compelled by military regulation to take part in the ridiculous regimen, although if that handsome Lieutenant McIntyre had his way, she'd be jumping to his orders along with the rest of them. He was polite enough to disguise his orders as requests, asking her to remain in her tent at night, but who was he to tell her she couldn't gallop her pony up and down the flats at night? Still, there was something about him that was almost...likable.

Maybe it was the habit he had of removing his hat and running a hand through his sandy brown hair, the way a man does when he is tired and confused and most of all disillusioned. Katie sensed he was struggling with something deep down inside, something that made him vulnerable and unlike the others who wore blue uniforms.

"Going somewhere?"

The sound of his voice startled her as he stepped from the shadows and threaded his way through the horses towards her.

"I was going for a ride," she said.

He cocked a brow at her. "Were you planning on coming back?"

"I don't blame you for being suspicious, Lieutenant," she said, "but if I wanted to leave, I'd have been gone long before tonight."

With equal candor he said, "I'm glad you didn't run away, because if you did, I would have come after you. My orders are to escort you to Fort Randall."

"And orders are orders."

He gave a slow, deliberate nod of the head.

"Well, you have nothing to worry about. I have no intention of running away. Now surely you wouldn't deny me a ride, would you?"

She peered up at him, green eyes sweet with seduction. The moonlight bathed her face. Her red hair hung in dark waves down her back. Starlight caressed each tress, making it seem on fire.

His throat tightened. "I can't let you go out there alone."

"Then why don't you come with me?"

Finding his horse in the herd, he jumped astride its bare back, and they rode out of camp.

When they had gone a distance, they urged their horses into a trot. The steady thud of hooves increased in tempo until they were thundering over the dark ground at a neck-and-neck gallop. They rode like that until the horses began to tire, and then they slowed to a walk.

The moon emerged from behind a cloud to sprinkle their path with pearly light. Bullfrogs croaked from a nearby stream, owls hooted in the branches of the pines, coyotes yipped and wolves howled. Katie inhaled deeply, filling her lungs with the cool, crisp scent of the night.

"There's nothing like a good ride to clear the cobwebs from your head," she said. "It's almost like a bath."

"Speaking of baths," said Josh, "I'm afraid that old wooden tub was all I could find. I hope it wasn't too uncomfortable."

"*You* sent that tub to my room?"

"Yes. I thought you might want a bath after the ride to the fort, so I…what's so funny about that?"

Her laughter was soft and genuine. "I thought the General sent it. You should have seen the look on his face when I told him I wanted a bath."

"I heard you gave him a rough time."

"It was no more than he deserved. I shudder to think that men like that are in charge of things."

"He's typical," said Josh. "For many officers service in the west amounts to something like social exile. Along comes an Indian war and they say goodbye to their families and set out to seek, what? Fame? Glory? Not likely out here. I don't know many military men who have reaped laurels from their Indian campaigns. At the end of each campaign an officer can feel confident that his fellow citizens will either cheer him if he has massacred enough Indians, or belittle him for any leniency he may have shown."

He shook his head. "The point is you can't have it both ways. Sooner or later you have to make a choice about which kind of soldier you want to be. There's a general cleavage of views when it comes to Indian policy. It's peaceful persuasion versus forcible control, and in case you haven't noticed, practically all the military men out here are committed to the latter. Any one of them has the ability to precipitate an Indian war."

There was no mistaking the disillusionment rifling his voice. Now Katie understood what was troubling him. Here was a soldier who'd been sent west by the country he believed in to deal with a problem by methods he did not personally endorse. His was one sane voice in a chorus of insanity. He was waging a battle not just against the Indians, but over the rightness of what he was doing. It was duty over conscience, loyalty against ethics, blind devotion to country versus a man's humanity toward his fellow man. Sensing these things about him made him seem less like an enemy.

"But you're an Army man," she said pointedly.

"Commander of the Eleventh Ohio Calvary along the North Platte. Bona fide graduate of West Point," he said. "Son and grandson of generals. When I came west three years ago, the only thing I knew about Indians was what I read as a boy in the penny novels of James Fennimore Cooper. But I learned quickly that Cooper's romantic portrayal of the Indian is far from the reality. I also learned a thing or two about my fellow officers."

"And I take it what you learned you don't like."

"I can't believe the eagerness with which they look forward to an Indian fight," he said. "The enlisted men are no better. They listen enviously to the tales the mountain men and the traders tell. Some even discard their uniforms for buckskin and buy Indian ponies with their pay. Although they've been sent west to maintain the peace, they break the monotony of garrison life by stirring up a little trouble with the Indians whenever they can. A skirmish here, a random killing there are usually sufficient to keep things interesting. That they haven't succeeded in bring on all-out war with the Sioux is a miracle."

The anguished look on his face confirmed that he spoke his true feelings.

"I do my best to keep my men under control," he went on. "Granted, life at a frontier post is a humdrum affair, but that's no excuse to have artillery practice on friendly Indians. I was sent to the Upper Platte to keep the Sioux quiet, and the only way I know how to do that is to treat them fairly. I've made it my business to make friends with all the principal chiefs. I've learned about the tribes, their numbers, and mostly their dispositions. I knew how dangerous it was to ride into that Oglala village to fetch you. If the information I was given proved wrong and the village was filled with fighting men, me and my men would have been massacred on the spot."

"And if I had refused to go with you?" Katie questioned. "Could you have fired on a defenseless village?"

He let out a long, low sigh. "Thankfully, I never had to find out."

"Things are getting bad," she said. "Soon it will be all-out war."

"And in the end victory will not be determined by who is right, but by who is left." There was no disguising the bitterness that riddled his tone. "And now, just when I feel equipped to do a real service in the name of the United States Government, I've been ordered back east. That's why I was assigned to lead this company to Fort Randall. From there I'll proceed to the capitol to answer a summons by those in the War Department who are questioning my fair treatment of the Indians."

Now that she understood the terrible turmoil with which he struggled, Katie asked, "Why have you told me all this?"

Josh shrugged. "I don't know. Maybe because in a way you're a lot like me, trying to find some peace amidst all the madness."

They rode in silence for a while, bathed in moonlight and the warm scent of the prairie, the silence broken only by the soft thud of their horses' hooves. After a while, Katie said, "Would you mind telling me how you knew where to find me? Surely, you didn't march into the first Indian village you came to."

"The army has its informants," he said. "In this case, I believe General Worth said it was an Indian named Yellow Hand who told him where your village would be camped and that the men would be off hunting. What's the matter?" he asked, when he saw the look on her face. "Do you know him?"

Black Moon should have killed Yellow Hand when he

had the chance, Katie thought bitterly. "No," she lied, "I don't know him."

Back at the sleeping camp they slipped past the sentries. Josh dismounted and went around to Katie's pony. Reaching up, he placed his hands about her waist and lifted her to the ground. It happened so swiftly that neither of them expected it. All of a sudden, he was pulling her up against him and his lips were closing over hers. He kissed her long and passionately.

Katie placed her hands up between them and pushed him away.

He was breathing hard when he stepped back. His emotions were plainly written on his face, and because she sensed that they were sincere, she said softly, "Don't let your life get tangled up in mine. You're a good man, Josh McIntyre. I can feel it in my heart. But there can never be anything between us. You're a soldier. It's your duty to fight for what you believe in. But it's also my duty to fight for what I believe in. We stand for different things. And besides," she added, her voice dropping to barely a whisper, fingers going up to caress the glass beads at her throat, "There's another man I love."

Josh emitted a sigh of frustration and forced an unconvincing laugh. "You can't blame a man for trying."

He looked past her, eyes searching the corners of the night. "He's out there, isn't he?"

A faint, knowing smile played at the corners of Katie's lips. "Aye, he's out there, somewhere. Maybe far from this place, but he's there."

"Do you think he'll come after you?"

Her smile faded. "You'd better hope he doesn't. If he does, I'm likely to forget all about St. Louis and return with him."

"I'd have to stop you."

"Aye. I know it. And then you'd have your own personal Indian war on your hands."

CHAPTER 19

Virginia Devlin Beauregard was as strong-willed and formidable as the mighty Mississippi. She had escaped the potato fields of Ireland and come to America thirty years ago. That the voyage had not killed her as it had so many others on that crossing was a sign of her tenacity. In America she made quick use of her resourcefulness by gaining a position as a kitchen maid for a wealthy Louisiana family. Her comely appearance caught the attention of the master of the house who took her as his mistress. Within a few years she had saved enough money to leave him and move to St. Louis where she opened a small millinery shop. In those days the city's population had been predominantly French, and with those French ladies having such a penchant for fashion, in no time the shop prospered.

One day a steamboat pulled in at the levee and off the gangplank stepped Colonel Abner Beauregard, the rich Mississippi gentleman who captured her heart. They were married in the spring of 1834 and resided in the house the Colonel built atop a hill overlooking the river where the romantic tradition of the south lingered in Greek porticoes and impressive Doric columns that took on a blue glow at sundown. Fifteen years later he made her a rich widow.

Her once-red hair was now a dull cinder gray. She wore it parted down the middle and pulled into an orderly chignon at the back of her head, over which she fastened a net of black silk spangled with bits of jet. Her face, although thin with age, still bore faint traces of the beauty that had once captured men's glances. Her Irish brogue had eroded since she'd left Ireland. It was only when she was angry that it infiltrated parts of her speech to remind her of her humble beginnings. It was something she cared not to remember.

The stroke she suffered two years ago had left one corner of her mouth in a permanent droop and hastened the formation of lines around her eyes, but more than that, it made her realize how afraid she was of living the rest of her life alone. The saddest part of growing old, she discovered, was the loneliness that pervaded the soul when one had outlived one's friends and family.

Then one day she read an article in the *St. Louis Herald* about an Indian massacre out west at a place called Blue Water Creek. Among the dead was a man named Tom McCabe, described as a well-known trader in the area. The article mentioned that McCabe's wife, Kathleen, had died of cholera some years earlier. Virginia's heart had convulsed with grief for the younger sister she had not seen in more than thirty years. But when she read about a daughter whose body was never found after the massacre, Virginia's pulse had quickened.

She had embarked on a three-year-long search to locate the girl. Her inquiries at the War Department and the Indian Department indicated that the girl was believed to be living with the Indians. It was a shocking thought indeed, but not enough to deter a strong willed woman intent on finding her last living relative. Using her influence in high places, she found out as much as she could about the girl's whereabouts. As it happened, the secretary of the War Department was an old friend of the Colonel's from his West Point days. She wrote to him and received his assurance that he would do whatever he could to help. She waited and waited for word to arrive.

Then, one day a telegraph arrived informing her that the girl had been found.

It there was any doubt in Virginia's mind as to whether or not the girl was really her niece, it was dispelled the instant Katie walked into the room. She was the exact duplicate of

Kathleen from the delicate structure of her face to the capricious slant of her emerald eyes.

After a long assessment from head to toe, Virginia announced, "It will take a while for your complexion to fade to a more respectful alabaster hue. And, of course, the wildness will have to be bred out of you. You appear to have a natural grace, and with your astonishing beauty it should not be difficult turning you into the talk of the town."

"There's no need to turn me into anything," Katie said. "I like myself just fine the way I am."

"I see you have your mother's knack for speaking your mind," Virginia said disapprovingly. "Well, never mind. Right now I'm sure you'd like a hot bath. " She walked to a small round table and shook the bell that rested on a silver tray.

In moments the maid appeared. "Jane, would you show my niece to her room and draw a bath for her? And ask cook to prepare something for her to eat." Turning back to Katie, she asked, "Where are your bags?"

"I have only this," she answered of the parfleche tucked under her arm.

Virginia cast a disparaging look at the rectangular envelope made of stiff, untanned leather that was crudely painted with geometric designs. "Jane, take that…that…thing."

When the maid moved to take it, Katie pulled it closer. "That's all right. I'll carry it."

Katie followed the maid up a curving staircase, along a hallway that was spread with a cinnabar runner atop wide wooden planks and lined with more doors than she'd seen in her life. The room they entered was bigger than the cabin on the Laramie, but it wasn't until the maid drew back the heavy drapery and the light poured in that its full splendor was revealed to Katie's astonished eyes.

As the maid heated pails of water over the fire to prepare the bath, Katie went to the open window and looked out.

The winds along the Mississippi were pungent with summer growth. Tatters of steamboat smoke smudged the blue sky. With long, windy shouts and the paddle wheel churning, a steamboat came to the levee and lowered its gangplank. Katie watched workers unload barrels of molasses and bales of cotton. At another spot along the levee a steamboat was leaving, white plumes jetting from its whistle valves, sounding short, crisp toots of goodbye.

She left the window and turned her attention to the room. The walls were papered floor to ceiling with panoramic landscapes and decorated with framed prints of winter scenes of teams of well-groomed horses pulling sleighs and summer scenes of men fishing. The bed was a massive structure of mahogany with turned bedposts and carved medallions on the headboard and a mattress amply stuffed with feathers and covered in the finest linen. In one corner of the room was a chamber set consisting of a basin and a large-mouthed pitcher for washing, and a chamber pot. Whale-oil lamps of brass hung about the walls. An upholstered armchair with its projecting arms on either side of the headrest was a far cry from the old slat-backed rocker her father used to relax in. A serpentine-back sofa sat before an elaborate stone hearth.

"Madam had that shipped over from France," the maid said when she saw Katie starting at the French Portico clock on the mantle.

Katie shrugged. "Such a fancy thing to tell time, when all you really need is the sun. But then, I don't suppose Aunt Virginia has ever had to rely on the sun for time, has she?"

The maid stifled a giggle. "No indeed. Come on now, your bath is ready. Let me help you out of your dress."

"You're very kind to call it that," said Katie as the maid slipped the hide dress up over her head. "I'm sure it's quite heathen to my aunt."

"She's a right proper lady with her own ideas of how things should be. You'll get used to her in time, and to all of this."

"Oh, I don't think I'll be here long enough for that," Katie said as she stepped into the tub.

The aroma of the softly-scented water filled the room, and the heat soothed her weary bones and muscles and lulled her overwhelmed senses. She closed her eyes as the maid sponged her back and arms with the warm, soapy water.

When she rose from the tub, she allowed the maid to pat her body dry. Never in her life had she been so pampered and petted, and she was beginning to think that her journey east was worth it just for this.

From the wardrobe the maid withdrew some garments and laid them out on the bed.

"What's that?" Katie asked, pointing to one ruffled garment.

"Why, those are your pantalettes, miss. Here, let me help you into them."

It was all happening so fast, like a whirlwind. One minute she was clad in buckskin, and the next she was clothed in a dress of blue taffeta, with a fitted bodice and a full skirt made to stand out all around by starched and flounced petticoats and yards of crinoline.

Katie tugged at the weight of it. "You can't be serious. It's an intolerable burden to walk around like this."

"Fashion must be obeyed, Madam says."

"I don't know," Katie objected. "I've never—" The words froze upon her tongue when the maid turned her around toward the cheval glass and she saw herself transformed. All her daydreams had come true. "Well, maybe it's not so bad, after all."

Katie ran her hands over the lustrous fabric that fit her slender body like a glove, and asked, "How did she know what size I would be?"

"You're about her size, so I expect she just assumed it runs in the family."

Family. To Katie the word had taken on a completely different meaning since the day Josh McIntyre had ridden into the village and she learned that she still had a tie to the white world. Once again, she was plunged into a well of confusion. To which family did she rightfully belong, the blood family consisting of one old woman she didn't know, or the adopted family that consisted of an entire tribe of people she had come to know and love?

"Where did all these clothes come from?" she asked.

"Madam bought them for you when she heard you were coming home."

Home. No, she wanted to say, this is not home.

"Come, miss, sit down at the dressing table and let me fix your hair. And such beautiful hair it is."

Katie sat motionless as the maid brushed her hair to shining and then swept it up off her shoulders and into a knot at the back of her head, with ringlets about her ears and a few wispy red tendrils cascading at her temples. From a drawer in the dressing table the maid withdrew a comb of black jet and fastened it in her hair.

When the maid was finished fussing over her, Katie observed, "I kind of look like my aunt."

McCabe always told her she looked like her mother, which was why, she supposed, he would sometimes turn away with a teary look in his eyes, as if looking at his daughter brought back too many memories of the woman he had loved. Without the benefit of photographs or paintings, Katie's only memory of her mother's face was the one she treasured in her mind. But now, sitting here in this opulent room, wearing a dress straight out of her daydreams, she had only to look at her own reflection in the mirror to see the resemblance. It made her feel closer to the mother she lost to the cholera, while at the same time it made her feel like a stranger to herself.

"Why, you're a bloomin' beauty, miss. Madam will be very pleased."

Katie tucked her thoughts away and looked at the maid through the mirror. She judged the young woman to be not that much older than herself. Her features were plain but pleasant, her demeanor calm and solicitous. "You like her, don't you?"

"She can be a little ornery at times, but beneath that tough old shell is a good heart. She was very happy when she found out you were alive. You being here means a lot to her."

"I understand. And I'm sure you being here means a lot to her, as well."

"Oh miss, I'm just a maid."

"Please call me Katie."

"I couldn't. It wouldn't be proper."

Katie smiled mischievously through the mirror. "Do I seem like a proper kind of person to you?"

The woman hesitated. "Well, since you put it that way. But not in front of Madam."

"Very well. And Jane, you shouldn't underestimate yourself. You're going to be here with her after I'm gone. Because, like I said, I don't plan on staying very long."

In the weeks that followed Katie's prophecy was all but forgotten. Her transformation was nothing less than astounding. To see herself dressed in a gown of silk, it was difficult to believe she had shown up just a few short weeks ago wearing the skin of an animal. Instead of thick braids, her hair was done up in the fashionable mode of the day with a mass of ringlets framing her delicate face and the back gathered up and held in place with a silk net spangled with jet.

At first, Katie was overwhelmed by the grandeur all around her. At her disposal was a wardrobe filled with dresses of smooth, crisp taffeta and lustrous silk, parasols fringed in lace, a pelisse lined in crimson silk, mantles trimmed in fur, shoes and hats and under things—more clothes than she'd seen in her entire life.

The days passed in a kaleidoscope of color and excitement in which the very texture of her life had changed. She met enough people to fill the pages of a social register. Every day someone new called at the house to meet the long-lost niece of Virginia Devlin Beauregard. For a little while Katie even forgot that at one time it had taken none of these things to make her happy, only the simple exuberance of living. It all came crashing down one day with a single glance in the mirror.

She had just come in from shopping, still marveling at the eagerness with which the merchants extended her credit based solely upon her name. As she unclasped the cloak from her neck, she spotted a stranger in the vestibule. In a naked instant she realized that the stranger she saw was her own reflection in the mirror.

The young woman looking back at her bore no resemblance to the person she had been. The clothes were stunning, but they looked all wrong. Why wasn't her hair hanging long and loose the way she liked it? Where was the rosy glow on her cheeks from a gallop across the prairie? Where was the healthy brown color of her skin from lots of good sunshine? Where was the laughter in her eyes? Why wasn't she smiling?

Inside of her was a dark and lonely place where her heart had once resided. She had come to St. Louis with all good intentions, but she knew now as she stood staring at herself in the mirror that she left her heart in that wild country around the North Platte.

In truth, she hated the socials and bridge parties and sewing bees and matinees that her aunt pressed her to attend. Often, she would find herself gazing at the lily-white hands of the other women, wondering how long any of them would last if they had to do the work of a Lakota woman. They were a frivolous lot, carefree and indulgent in their easy lives. Yet, in spite of all they had, Katie was certain that not one of them had ever known the kind of freedom she had known.

She would be eternally grateful to her aunt for everything she had done for her, but she had a desperate longing for the country of her birth, where the land was as wide as the soul and the sky as high as the heart dared to reach. Where a dark-eyed warrior was waiting for her. It was time to go home.

Virginia was sipping tea in the parlor while penning correspondence at her desk when Katie entered. "Did you have a pleasant outing, my dear?"

Katie walked to the window and gazed wistfully at the meandering river sparkling in the afternoon sunshine. "Yes, Aunt," she said dully, searching for a way to break the news that she would soon be leaving.

"Really, Kathleen," Virginia said in a tone of sharp annoyance, "if you spent as much time answering your invitations as you do staring out that window, you would be the most popular girl in St. Louis. Goodness knows I have worked hard enough to introduce you to all the right people."

Katie let the isinglass curtain slip from her fingers and turned away from the window. "I have no desire to be the most popular girl in St. Louis, Aunt Virginia. If the truth be known, I've been thinking of going home."

Virginia placed the quill-tipped pen down and looked at her intently. "But I thought you liked it here."

"I do. It's just that I miss my home."

"You must think of this as your home now."

"But it isn't." She came forward to make her point. "I'm

a stranger here. I don't fit in. Don't you think I see the way they all look at me? It makes me feel like I'm an exhibit in a museum."

Virginia waved Katie's complaint away with a sweep of her bejeweled hand. "That is perfectly natural. They are curious about you. Things are bound to be difficult for a while considering your...er...background. But that will change. You'll see. You must give it a chance."

"Why do you make such a point of evading my past as if it does not exist?" Katie said. "I wasn't born the day I arrived on your doorstep. I've got nearly twenty-one years of living behind me. More living in these past three years than anyone deserves in a lifetime," she added with a touch of bitterness. "I think that gives me the right to say what I will or will not do with my life. Why must I give this a chance when it's not what I want?"

"You owe it to yourself to give it a try," Virginia argued.

"And I have. But I also owe it to myself to do what makes me happy."

Virginia's frown deepened. "You're just like your mother. Strong-willed and defiant." Her tone hardened. "But so am I. And I went through a great deal of trouble to find you and bring you here."

"I didn't ask you to."

"But you came, didn't you?"

"Aye, I came. Because I was curious. And because..." She paused, suddenly no longer sure of her motives in coming east.

"Because you knew that I am the last link with your family," Virginia said. "We all need those ties no matter how strongly we deny them, Kathleen. Without our families we are solitary creatures in a vast sea of humanity. Believe me, my dear, you are much better off here with me. Some day you will thank me for this."

With a sigh, Katie conceded, "It's true what you say about families. But that doesn't mean I should give up the life I love in exchange for one that doesn't fit. Don't you see, Aunt Virginia? I feel trapped here, like I'm strangling. Everywhere I look I see smoking chimneys and steam and soot. And people everywhere, more people than I've seen in my whole life. I miss the freedom of the plains, and unless you've known the kind of freedom I'm talking about, then you mustn't be telling me where I'd be better off."

"Think of your mother," Virginia implored. "How would she feel knowing you are living among savages? When she and I were children in Ireland, she used to talk of growing up one day to be a great lady. Think how happy it would have made her to know that her daughter has fulfilled that dream."

A whistle rose in the air, prolonged and mournful, as one of the big steamboats pulled out of the levee to follow the river to the vast untouched northern wilderness.

Katie sighed, wishing she could follow. "My mother had the love of a good man," she uttered. "It was enough."

In the hidden corners of her heart Katie was remembering what it was like to have the love of a good man, and when loving him was enough. She knew now what a dreadful mistake she made in leaving him. She had come east looking for...what? The fulfillment of a fantasy? A dream? What a fool she'd been not to realize that every fantasy, every dream that dwelled within her was about Black Moon.

"We could write to each other," she suggested. "I could come east to visit once in a while. It's not like we would never see each other again. We could— Aunt Virginia, are you all right?"

Virginia's hand clutched at her chest. The blood rushed violently to her face, flooding it with too much color before receding sharply and leaving her complexion as white as milk. The pen fell from her hand. With a strangled groan she slipped from the chair. Katie caught her just as she collapsed onto the carpet.

That night the house atop the hill was dark and still. Long, hazy streamers of moonlight wandered negligently through the window to fall upon a slender figure pacing back and forth across the floor.

"What's taking so long?" Katie groaned, wringing her hands before her.

"Don't worry, miss," said Jane, who came to stand vigil with her. "She's a tough old bird. She'll make it."

"Oh, Jane, I hope you're right."

Katie was feeling a black load of guilt for having brought on her aunt's attack with her thoughtless and selfish behavior. She'd been so consumed with her own feelings that she hadn't stopped to consider how her aunt would feel over the prospect of losing the niece she'd only recently found.

The minutes seemed to stretch to eternity until at last the door to Virginia's bedroom opened and the doctor emerged.

Katie rushed forward. "How is she?"

Gravely, he said, "She's had a heart attack. She needs complete rest and quiet."

"Will she be all right?" she asked anxiously.

"I'm afraid there is nothing more I can do for her. Only time will tell. This one did not kill her, but the next one will."

Jane was weeping softly behind her. A lump formed in Katie's throat. "May I see her now?"

He nodded. "But do not say or do anything that would cause her stress. I'll call again in the morning."

The room was enveloped in an eerie stillness when Katie entered. The smell of alcohol and laudanum permeated the air. The shadow of death lurked close at hand. She could feel its anger and could almost imagine it shaking a hooked finger at the woman on the bed, as if to say, "I'll get you next time."

She tiptoed to the bed and looked down at her aunt's face, tiny, pale and lost in the goose down pillow. She felt a rush of pity for her aunt and was about to leave, when those thin, veined eyelids fluttered open and the pale lips moved imperceptibly. Katie bent her head close to listen.

"Kathleen…" The voice that emerged was a mere rasp of breath. "Don't leave…promise."

It seemed irrelevant for now, for Katie had already decided to stay in St. Louis a few more weeks until her aunt was stronger. She smiled tenderly and patted the woman's frail white hand. "Yes, Aunt. I promise."

Virginia's voice emerged a scratchy, pleading whisper. "A year. Promise. A year."

Katie practically choked on her own gasp.

"Promise, Kathleen…promise."

Virginia's face was stamped with fear, and Katie carried the power to turn that fear into reality. She dreaded the burden of that responsibility. Inwardly, she railed against the unfairness of it. If she acquiesced to her aunt's request, it would be at the cost of her own happiness. But she had learned a long time ago that life was not always fair, no matter how hard she believed in what was right. Her own life was proof enough of that.

For one terrible, agonizing moment she stood poised on the brink of indecision. Once again, Providence held her in its massive grip, tossing her back and forth from one hand to another, like the bones in Chatillon's game of hands. In the next moment it was decided when Katie heard her own voice, expressionless and detached, utter, "Yes, Aunt Virginia, a year. I promise."

She walked numbly from the room and somehow found her way downstairs. At the sideboard she took out the crystal decanter of brandy her aunt kept there. Pouring the amber liquid into a glass, she swallowed it quickly and winced as it burned its way down her throat. The brandy did nothing to ease the pain and despair she was suffering, but it gave her legs the strength to carry her to the window.

Katie pressed her fevered cheek against the pane. Silent tears wet the smooth, cool glass. The river below was dark and silent and moving, the air outside softly scented with summer blossoms. Far beyond these walls lay the promise of life. Within them only the gloom of sickness and the despair of loneliness. Katie's heart felt like a caged bird, thrusting itself over and over again against the bars only to weaken a little more with each failed attempt to break free. Her conscience was her jailer. How could she leave a sick and fearful woman? She had given her word, and now her honor had locked the door to her freedom.

Yet she had also given her word to another. It was the message she left with Pretty Shield for Black Moon. What must he be thinking? She recalled his deep-throated words the night he came to her lodge to claim her as his wife. "I will not lose you to another. You must know that I will do whatever I can to stop that from happening." And what could he do now, when he had lost her not to another man but to her own foolish heart? In coming east, she had placed before him something he could not fight. If he loved her, all he could do was let her go and hope, *know*, that she would come back to him. And she would have…if only…

McCabe used to say that all the if-only's in the world meant nothing in the face of what was. And what was, was that she was thousands of miles away from the place where she wanted to be and the man she loved. Where was he? What was he doing? Did he think of her at all as she was thinking of him?

CHAPTER 20

When Pretty Shield's lungs, weakened from the harsh winter, drew their last breath, Black Moon carried his mother outside so that she could die in the arms of her mother, the Earth.

He stood by in taut silence while the women prepared Pretty Shield's body for the scaffold, dressing her in her finest attire, placing on her feet the spirit moccasins with beaded soles, painting her face with the marks of honor to which she was entitled, and tucking her awl case and sewing kit beside her. As the burial bundle was hoisted atop a scaffold, Black Moon took one long last look and turned his scowling face away. One more thing he loved was lost.

When he had returned from the hunt and heard that Katie had ridden off with the bluecoats, he had walked around the village like a loaded gun about to go off. His heart was black over it, and he blamed everyone for not stopping her. People learned to stay out of his way. Only Good Deeds seemed to want anything to do with him, trying hard to catch his eye whenever he rode by.

Black Moon felt sorry for her. He would never have willingly given up the woman he loved the way his brother had given up Good Deeds. She had been betrayed, not maliciously, nor out of ignorance, but out of his brother's love for the people and a misguided notion of the best way to show it. And now she walked around like one who was dead inside, as he himself was.

On a crisp day in the Moon of Frost on the Tipis, when it was obvious to everyone that the red-haired woman was not coming back, Black Moon was approached by Good Deeds.

"If Black Moon cannot have the woman he wants, would he be willing to settle for someone else?" she asked.

"There is no one else," he said flatly.

Good Deeds drew in a deep breath, and said, "There is me."

Black Moon eyed the thin, frail girl. Clutched in her arms was a cradleboard in which an infant was laced. "You do not want me," he said. "I can give you nothing."

"I do not ask for myself. I do not love you and you do not love me, and I know this thing with my brother stands between us. I ask only for the sake of the child." She held the cradleboard up for him to see the baby's face. "This is your nephew. Some day he will need someone to teach him how to be a strong warrior."

"There are others who can teach him."

"Perhaps. But who will protect him when Gray Wolf sees his resemblance to your brother?"

Black Moon looked down into the face of his nephew, then back up into Good Deeds' beseeching eyes. "What kind of life would you have with me?"

"What kind of life will we have without you? You are our only hope."

CHAPTER 21

Katie gazed out on a day coated in pale pewter light. Dark, dusky clouds were painted on the sky. The river was clogged with ice and strong winter winds lashed the landings. People by the thousands had succumbed to the lure of the steamboats and left the frozen city for the land of sunshine and cotton. The only things preventing Katie from leaving were the promise she made to a dying woman and her father's haunting voice reminding her that only dishonest men and cowards broke their word.

"Katie?"

Her name called softly from behind scattered her dreary thoughts. "I'm sorry, Jane," she mumbled. "I didn't hear you come in. Did you want something?"

"Madam would like to see you upstairs."

Virginia was seated on a chaise lounge pulled up before the fire when Katie entered her bedroom. A quilt of goose down was tucked in all around her. On the bed tray straddling her legs was a cup of tea and the morning mail that Jane had brought up to her.

"Sit down, dear," she said in a weakened voice. "There are some matters I wish to discuss with you."

Katie spread her skirts over the tufted hassock beside the chaise and looked at her aunt. The left corner of Virginia's mouth sagged so low now that when viewed full-face, she appeared to be half-smiling, half-frowning, as though she could not make up her mind whether to laugh or to cry.

In a slow, measured tone, Virginia said, "I'm glad you have finally come to your senses and talk no more of leaving. In time you will realize it's all for the best. Now I can tell you that after the unfortunate incident last spring I had my attorney draw up a new will. I am leaving this house to you. You look so surprised, Kathleen. Did you think I would leave it to those silly old vultures at the bank? There is one small codicil, however, a provision which will be revealed to you upon my demise. I can see you hardly know what to say. Well, never mind. And then there is this."

It was then Katie noticed the letter in the old woman's pale hand.

"I have received a letter from an old and dear friend. She writes that her son will be arriving in St. Louis and asks if I will permit him to call at the house. Since I am somewhat indisposed, I shall naturally expect you to make him feel at home."

"I'll try to act civilized, Aunt, but I can't promise anything. You know how unpredictable we savages can be."

The unaffected side of Virginia's mouth frowned at the saucy reply. "Oh, for heaven's sake, Kathleen, be serious," she scolded. "And I would advise against mentioning anything to him about your background."

"Half of St. Louis already knows about it. It's hardly a secret."

"All the same, this young man is not from St. Louis, so perhaps he hasn't heard. Besides, we all know you were abducted against your will. We read about things like that in the newspapers all the time. The poor, innocent white women who are taken against their wills and forced to become the squaws of those savages."

They had never discussed the subject of Katie's upbringing nor the circumstances surrounding her living with the Indians. What would Aunt Virginia think if she knew she'd gone willingly to live among the Oglalas? Or that the savage her aunt referred to was nothing more than a man, with the same primitive hungers as any man? Or that her love for him had not been forced out of her or coerced, but given freely and openly?

"All I'm asking," Virginia said, "is that you refrain from bringing it up."

"And what if he asks?"

"I'm certain you will think of something suitable to tell him. Whatever it is, make sure it's respectable. We wouldn't want to offend a prospective husband."

"Husband!" Katie's green eyes went wide with disbelief. "But I don't want a husband"

"Nonsense," her aunt said flatly. "It's high time you were thinking of marriage. It's nothing to be afraid of, provided you marry the right man. Admittedly, there are certain obligations a wife must perform for her husband, if you take my meaning, but that's a small price to pay for financial security. Look around you, child," she urged in answer to the look of horror on Katie's face. "The pretty dresses you wear, this house, the fine things in it, all cost a great deal of money. I might add that my friend inherited a sizeable sum when her husband died several years ago, and her son is her only heir."

Katie wrinkled her nose with distaste. "You make it sound like a business transaction."

"Which it is."

"And love? Does love not even enter the picture?"

Virginia shrugged her frail shoulders, and replied, "Love comes in time, if you are lucky."

"And when he learns that he is not the first?"

Virginia waved her hand as if to shoo the unsettling thought away like a pesky fly.

"Nonsense. You are beautiful, child. Men have been known to overlook a woman's shortcomings when she is beautiful. Now run along and pick out something very pretty to wear. He'll be calling tonight."

The lit tapers of the candelabra sent soft, reflective shadows skimming over the walls of Katie's bedroom later that evening as she prepared for the visitor. At the dressing table she ran a hairbrush through her long red hair and plaited the shining tresses into a thick braid that she wound around her head like a coronet, leaving a few crimson tendrils to cascade over her forehead and at her temples.

She selected a dress of green silk that matched the color of her eyes. The skirt was flounced and embroidered in black lace rosettes and made to stand out all around by a crisp crinoline over a hoop of reeds and muslin. The ungainly contraption brought a mild oath to Katie's lips but she could just hear her aunt proclaiming, "Fashion must be obeyed".

She fastened a black velvet ribbon around her neck and wondered if this young man would be like all the others she met, dull and unimaginative. She had half a mind to appear downstairs wearing the elk skin dress she had hidden in a cedar trunk at the foot the bed. That should shock him out of his sensible wits.

On her way downstairs she heard the brass knocker at the front door and called to the maid, "I'll get it, Jane."

A blast of chill wind rushed in when Katie answered the door. The first thing she noticed was the uniform. The dark blue of his coat was instantly familiar. She recoiled at the sight of it, for blue uniforms still haunted her dreams. But when her eyes traveled upwards, they flared with instant relief and recognition.

"Lieutenant McIntyre!" she exclaimed. "What in the world are you doing here?"

He smiled, and said, "I believe I was invited."

The swish of petticoats accompanied the sway of her hips as she led the way into the parlor and took his coat. "You don't appear at all surprised to see me," she noted. She went with him to stand before the fire so that he could warm his hands over the flames.

"When my mother heard I was coming to St. Louis on official business, she asked me to call on a friend of hers. When I heard the name, I recognized it immediately. I wasn't certain you would be here, but I'd be lying if I said I wasn't hoping you would be. In case you're not aware of it, the whole town is talking about the beautiful woman with the flaming red hair and green eyes rescued from the Indians. As soon as I heard it, I knew it had to be you."

Her skin was a translucent hue reflecting the fire's glow. "Rescued," she huffed. "That's a laugh."

"You can't expect them to accept something they don't understand," he said.

With the uncomfortable weight of his eyes upon her, Katie went to the pink damask sofa and sat down. He sat down next to her, maintaining a respectable distance between them, but close enough for her to smell the wool of his uniform.

Jane appeared with a tray of tea and biscuits and word that Madam did not feel well enough to join them.

"Just set it down over there, Jane. I'll take care of it." She was grateful for the opportunity to do something more than just sit there with his gaze upon her. "So, tell me, Lieutenant," she said as she poured the tea, "what brings you to St. Louis. You mentioned something about official business. When last I saw you, you were on your way to Washington."

"I was ordered to Washington for review by the Indian Office," he said. "There are some who feel I have not exerted enough forcible pressure on the Indians. Apparently, their voices carried enough weight to have me summoned for an accounting of my actions. That's where I've been these past few months, trying to convince the top brass and President Buchanan that there are other ways to deal with the Indians besides using force."

He sipped his tea. "They're talking of disbanding the Eleventh. I won't know for some weeks yet what the decision will be. Meanwhile, they've put me to work carrying dispatches from Washington. This trip took me to St. Louis. Who knows where it will be next?"

"And you do it?"

He put his cup down and spread his hands wide in a gesture of helplessness. "What else can I do? I'm an army man, Katie. And orders are orders. As much as I may resent the Army's treatment of me, and as strongly as I question its dealings with the Indians, there's too much regimental blue in my blood for me to do much about it."

"Every day I read the newspapers for word of what's happening out west," she said. "It seems pretty quiet for now."

"A little too quiet, if you ask me," Josh responded gravely.

"How so?"

His tone dropped to one of confidentiality. "The Indian

Office has reason to suspect that some of the agents may be falsifying their reports when they claim that the Indians are peaceful. The agent at the Upper Platte Agency in particular."

"Major Twiss? My father always spoke well of him."

"It seems he never makes any mention in his reports of the fact that the Sioux in his charge are constantly warring on the Crow. Yet I know the Oglalas at the Twiss agency hunt and camp in Crow country and go clear up to the Yellowstone to attack the Crow in their own villages."

"What's so unusual about that? The Sioux have been warring on the Crow for generations." She suppressed a shudder over her own experience at the hands of the Crow and said, "Perhaps Major Twiss doesn't think something as natural as that is worth reporting."

"He's always suggesting new plans to the Indian Office that have no purpose other than to benefit himself and his trader friends. He even proposed establishing new agencies so that the Indians would settle down and become self-supporting farmers. Did you ever hear of such a thing? Those Indians on the Upper Platte are as wild as wolves. You and I both know they would never settle down to farm. He also abandoned the existing agency at Fort Laramie in favor of a new one on Deer Creek on the Overland Road about a hundred miles to the west. They say he lives there now with his Oglala wife and pet bear."

"Stories about the old major are as common as the scenery," Katie said. "He seems to prefer the company of the traders and the wild Sioux. His dealings may be shady, but he's always been a friend to the Sioux. My father used to say he was one of the few white men they trusted."

"Well, they're hollering for his resignation," said Josh.

"I've a good mind to go to Washington and tell them what fools they are."

"I wouldn't do that if I were you," he warned. "You're not still out in the wild where you can speak your mind and anything goes. You're in a civilized society now, where people live by strict rules."

Her green eyes flashed defiantly. "Three years you were out there and you learned nothing?"

"What's that supposed to Mean?" His own gray eyes

brightened with annoyance.

"It's hardly a free-for-all out there. Those Indians live by a strict code where everyone knows their place. They're not the indiscriminate, wanton savages everyone thinks they are. I would expect such presumptions from the others, but not from you, Josh McIntyre. And I'll tell you something I told someone else once. I'm here because I choose to be, and if I feel like leaving, I'll do that too. Your rules don't apply to me, so I'll thank you not to try to impose them on me."

He sat back and folded his arms across his chest.

"What are you grinning at?" she asked.

"I guess I'm just glad that underneath all that silk and lace you haven't changed."

"And I'm not likely to," Katie replied, succumbing to a smile of her own.

"I wouldn't have you any other way."

The hour passed in small talk, with Josh stealing glimpses of her from the corners of his eyes and Katie blushing appropriately. When the floor clock struck the hour, he rose from the sofa. "I should be leaving."

Katie fetched his coat and walked him to the door. As he shrugged into his coat, he said, "I'll be in St. Louis until I get new orders. I'd like to call on you again."

"I would be glad for the company. Aside from Jane, yours is the friendliest face I've seen in all these long, lonely months I've been here. But Josh," she began.

"I understand, Katie. No promises. No guarantees." He smiled tenderly. "I know it's been rough for you, coming to a strange, new place, meeting new people, your aunt's illness. It's been kind of rough for me, too, and I can use the company myself. So, what do you say, will you join me for dinner, say, tomorrow evening?"

She looked into his gray eyes that tried so hard to hide their eagerness. "Yes, Josh, I'll have dinner with you tomorrow."

Later that night Katie stood at her bedroom window gazing down at the gas-lit streets below, thinking about Josh McIntyre. What would happen if he were ever confronted with a real Indian war, the kind she knew in her heart was coming? Would the blind devotion for country that had been bred into him since boyhood overwhelm his emotions? For his sake, she hoped he never found out.

She was flattered by Josh's attention. What woman wouldn't be? He was handsome and kind, and as much as she mistrusted the blue uniform, she had to admit he cut a dashing figure in it. Yet she could not pretend to feel something for him that she did not feel, not when there was another man who owned her heart.

Not a day went by that she did not think of Black Moon. Not a single night without dreaming of him. Did he think of her? Did he miss her as desperately as she missed him?

The only answer she received was the violent slap of the shutter against the window as a gust of wind blew up from the river.

Her thoughts turned to winter, not the bleak, miserable winter of St. Louis, but winter on the plains. The way her breath turned to crystals upon mingling with the cold, clean air. The sky that blinded with searing intensity. The gale-force blizzards that swept in from the north. Would she ever see that frightening and beautiful place again? At times it seemed she would not. A year was a painfully long time to be away. And if she ever did go back, what made her think Black Moon would still want her? Black Moon. His handsome, fierce face invaded her thoughts, and the memory of his voice, strong and defiant, filled her with such intense longing. She whispered his name like a prayer against the frosty pane. "Black Moon."

CHAPTER 22

*T*he two warriors traveled in single file through the deep snow along the Tongue River below Hanging Woman Creek, taking turns to break the trail. On their feet they wore bear paws, wide, flat shoes made of willow rods, to keep from sinking into the snow. The old snow was dry and crunchy, the new snow as soft as a marsh. The whining in the branches of the big pines sang of yet another blizzard to come.

They stopped to rest on the frozen ground and pulled their buffalo robes up over their heads. With the aid of a strike-a-light they made a small fire and over it roasted a long-ears. Two more lay nearby. They were lucky to find game today. Most days when they went out to hunt, they returned empty-handed.

"Life is easy for those Lakota who live near the agent on Deer Creek," Lone Horn said. With soot grease streaked over his cheeks to protect against the frozen blasts of wind, he looked painted for a different kind of war. "There are no hungry bellies in those camps."

Black Moon sliced off a chunk of meat with his knife, offered a bit to the Four Winds, the Earth and the Sky. Features knit in a tangle of worry, his voice spliced the icy solitude. "Our nation is melting away like snow on the hillside where the warm sun shines, while the *wasichus* are like the blades of grass in the spring moon."

Lone Horn stirred in his robe. "There is talk in the village of riding south in the spring to camp near the soldier town."

"They will go south to become like those lazy Lakota loafers who live off the handouts of the white?" Black Moon said with a sneer.

"Each year the buffalo herds grow less. It takes much traveling to find them. Who knows? Maybe in the spring I will ride south with them."

Black Moon's ebony eyes flashed above the ashes he had rubbed beneath them to shield against the blinding glare of the vast white wilderness. "What you are suggesting is surrender, and that is the same as giving up."

The Minniconjou's features sagged, making him look older than his thirty-five winters. He spoke in a quiet, disillusioned voice. "Often I ride alone on the prairie or I go into the hills for a vision to show me the way. The answers do not come easy. Nor is it easy to fulfill the vows I took when I was made shirt-wearer."

Through the thin wintry air Black Moon stiffened at the mention of the shirt, but Lone Horn went on, undaunted. "I promised to protect the people," he said. "To have them follow me, a hunted man, is not protecting them. To lead them to safety is. Do you think I want to see them surrounded by whites? Depending on the enemy for stringy beef? Deprived of the free life? But that is where the food is. How many can I ask to starve because I refuse to give up my freedom? I ask myself if I am not being too selfish. What you call surrender I call living."

Surrender. The word ricocheted off the walls of Black Moon's mind like a gunshot. It made no sense to him. It had no meaning. It ran contrary to everything he felt, all that he was. His features grew taut and a hard line formed over his mouth. "Surrender? Never! They will have to hunt me down like prey and drag me in chains to their iron house."

Black Moon shared a similar fate with his friend. The only difference between them was that Lone Horn did not have something tearing him down the middle like Black Moon did. For him, it was the green-eyed woman who continued to haunt him. He had fought for her...killed for her. His insane jealousy had driven a lance of misunderstanding between himself and his brother. She had a way of doing that, of turning men against each other, of turning a man against himself. He could fight the whites who came to steal his land, the Crow who stole Lakota women, the Pawnee who stole their horses, but how could he fight this torment of the heart? This was an invisible enemy whose lance was as sharp, whose arrow struck as deep, and who would not be satisfied with merely counting coup. This enemy would not stop its pursuit until it had killed his heart.

Black Moon hunkered down in his buffalo robe. With the warm fur against his skin, he remembered another time when he had sat like this wrapped in a robe on a snowy day, when the heat had come not from the robe but from the warm, female body next to his. It was the day they had taken the shirt from him. He had ridden out of the village feeling ashamed and angry and suddenly no longer certain that he was following the right path. Only she had the courage to come after him that day, to challenge him to be unashamed of what he had done, to love him even without the shirt. Only she had the power to quell his furious emotions and tame his savage heart.

Up here in the ice-encrusted hills there were no exploding guns, no cries of hunger, moans of pain or keenings of grief. There was only a deep, abiding hush in which to sing a silent song to *Wakan Tanka* for the strength to endure this misery of the heart.

He would have given up a hundred shirts and more just to have his red-haired woman back in his arms. To feel her warm breath fanning his cheek, her lips on his, her smooth white hands touching him, stoking his desire into flame, her beautiful eyes, as green as the *Paha Sapa* in springtime, shining with courage, would have given him everything he needed to survive.

If she were here right now, the word *surrender* would never have passed her lips. But she was not here to encourage him to remain steadfast in his beliefs. She was far away, in a place he could not reach. It drove him to irrational fury to think that he would never know the truth of her leaving. He hated her for it. A day did not go by that he did not vow revenge against her. Yet even now as he sat on the frozen ground in his buffalo robe deploring her, even now he longed for her.

CHAPTER 23

A black wreath hung on the door of the house overlooking the river.

In the parlor, Katie gazed down into the coffin lined with cotton batting and lace at the ashen face of death. She was numb with disbelief and trying hard to come to terms with the frightening speed with which events were taking place. Just three days ago her aunt had been alive. Handicapped and frail, but mentally alert and as strong-willed as ever. Now an eerie silence gripped the rooms. An incommunicable emptiness hung over the place like a fog. It was as if every timber and brick, each corner and crevice of the old house was acutely aware of the passing of Virginia Devlin Beauregard.

The funeral was a private affair. In accordance with Virginia's wishes only a few close friends attended. There was an elderly gentleman whom Katie had never seen before. From the way he wept like a baby, she imagined that somewhere in their lost youth he and her aunt must have been lovers. Feeling sorry for him, she offered him the same words once offered to her when she was grieving. "In death there is life. We all return to our place of beginning." He just looked at her with a blank expression on his tear-stained face as though she were speaking a foreign language. She told herself she should have known better.

It seemed there were many things she should have known yet somehow didn't. She should have known, for instance, that something was afoot when her aunt's attorney summoned her to town to meet with him several days after the funeral.

Her reaction to the news that greeted her was swift and genuine.

"What? Everything? She left everything to me? You're joking, to be sure."

The attorney looked at her from beneath bushy white eyebrows across a massive rosewood desk, laced his fingers over his portly belly, and replied, "I assure you, Miss McCabe, it's no joke. It's all yours. The house, the money, the bonds, the land, the jewels. You need only sign this." He pushed a piece of paper across the desk toward her.

Katie's head swam with the news. All the things she used to daydream about were now hers. For one dizzying moment it was the most thrilling and incredible thing she'd ever heard. She picked up the paper awaiting her signature.

"There is, however, one proviso," he went on. "A codicil signed only weeks before your aunt's death. In order to inherit a single penny of her estate, you must remain in St. Louis permanently."

The air went out of her like a burst bubble. Her aunt was dictating her wishes even from the grave.

Katie was only dimly aware of folding the paper and thrusting it into her reticule. She rose on unsteady legs. "Thank you, sir," she mumbled.

"Shall I begin the arrangements to have everything transferred to your name?" he asked.

"Yes...no. I don't know. I'll be in touch."

She hastened from the room. Air, she needed air to clear her head and sort out the tangle of confusion surrounding her.

She walked back to the house as if in a trance, oblivious to the people who passed her on the street and the street vendors' cries of "Charcoal by the bushel!" "Scissors to grind." "Porgies at five cents a pound."

Oh, Aunt Virginia, she wailed inside, *what have you done?*

Later, as she sat in her room staring at the flames in the hearth, Katie realized that she should have known her aunt would not depart from this world without having a final word as to how she spent the rest of her life. It was a tempting offer, to be sure, but what good were pretty dresses and fancy jewels and all the money in the world if there was no happiness to go with it?

McCabe's lusty voice broke through the web of despair. "Tis what ye are inside, Katie m'darlin."

God, how she missed him. He always had the right words to say. She wished he was here right now to guide her through uncertain times. He would know what to do, not just about the inheritance, but about Josh McIntyre, as well.

Since the night when Josh appeared at the front door, he came to call on her whenever he was in town. There was no denying that she was flattered by his attention, but she'd been honest with him from the start. Hadn't she told him that her heart belonged to another? She hadn't meant for him to fall in love with her. The kisses she placed on his cheek were meant to show affection, but no more than that. Why couldn't it be enough for him? Fortunately, Josh was a patient man, but Katie knew that even a patient man would not wait forever.

She closed her eyes and tried to imagine what it would be like loving Josh. She could imagine the fire spreading through her, the nerve-tingling sensation caused by a warm breath at her ear. Yet try as she might, she could not envision his face. All she could see were the jet-black eyes of an Indian.

They were so different, the Sioux warrior and the white soldier. Josh talked of ambitions and goals, of the future and his place in it. He was forever questioning who he was and redefining his purpose in life to coincide with his shifting and expanding ideals.

Black Moon, on the other hand, lived only for the present. He was not concerned with being any different or better than he already was. Once, when she had asked him if he did not ever ask himself who he was, he had looked at her guilelessly, and said, "The river flows, the sun rises, the grass grows. I am just a small stone on a giant path. Who am I to ask who am I? Isn't it enough simply to be?"

Josh was a good man, but he was a soldier, and like it

or not, he was committed to destroying something that was as much a part of her as the air she breathed. Wasn't he, in his way, as much her enemy as he was Black Moon's?

Katie's disquieting thoughts forced her to her feet. Picking up a candle from the rosewood dresser, she slipped the hurricane shade over it and left the room. Downstairs, she lit a whale oil lamp in the parlor and went to revive the cold hearth. April nights along the river were chilly, and she shivered as she waited for the flames to flare to life and warm her.

When the fire was crackling and sending pitches of orange flame up the flue, there came a rapping at the door. Katie glanced at the clock on the mantle. It was ten-thirty; late for anyone to be calling.

"I had to come," Josh said as he strode in past her.

"Come into the parlor where it's warm and tell me what you're doing here at this hour."

"I've received my orders," he said. "They've decided not to disband the Eleventh after all. I'm back in command."

"Oh Josh, I'm so happy for you," she said warmly. "I guess that means you'll be going back out west."

"Yes. But not for a week or so. It will take that long for the papers to go through all the usual channels."

"I envy you. You must be very happy."

"Only one thing would make me happier."

Katie tensed. She'd been half-expecting this. "Can I get you something to drink? Tea? Coffee? Brandy to toast your good news?"

"Don't you see, Katie?" he said, ignoring her offer. "This changes everything."

Weakly, she ventured, "It does?"

"Before, my future was uncertain. Now, it's in the bag. How about it, Katie, will you marry me?"

The words all bunched up in her throat and she could not answer.

"You wouldn't have to come with me," he went on. "You could stay right here in St. Louis while I go west."

"To do what?" she asked tersely, finding her voice. "Kill Indians?"

"Are we back to that?" he said with a groan. "I'm a soldier, Katie. I'm bound by duty. You know that."

"Aye, I know it. And I told you once before, Josh, that I'm bound by duty, too."

"What are you talking about? Your duty is right here. Who else is going to run Virginia's estate?"

Her face registered surprise. "How did you know?"

"The news is all over town. Your aunt was one of the wealthiest women in St. Louis. Heck, on the whole eastern seaboard. It's no secret that she left a sizeable estate."

"But that's just it. It's Virginia's estate. Not mine."

"Of course it's yours. She had no other heirs."

"Yes, yes," she said, growing impatient. "It's not *me*. All right? Does that make better sense to you? It's not me."

"But this is where you belong, Katie."

"No. This is where you and Virginia want me to belong."

"Is that why you look like that?" His eyes swept over the peignoir of pink cashmere trimmed with a Persian border that opened over a white embroidered petticoat. "The servants are asleep. It's late and no one was expected, yet you answered the door wearing an elegant dressing gown. Not the style of a wild Indian, if you ask me. Maybe there's more civilized blood in you than you realize."

"There's not a drop of Indian blood in me," she said, "yet I feel a kinship with them as strong as blood. How do you explain that?"

"You feel beholden to them. It's understandable."

She shook her head. "It's more than that. They're my family. I belong with them."

Josh's eyes went wide with disbelief. "Don't tell me you're thinking of going back!"

She turned away from him and confessed in a whisper, "Sometimes I don't know what I'm thinking."

"Katie, listen to me." He placed his hands on her shoulders and turned her around to face him. With the tip of his finger he lifted her chin, guiding her gaze to his. "We could have a good life together."

"Oh Josh, don't you see? Life and living are too different things. Life is the mere act of being alive, of being born and dying. Living is everything in between. Yes, I suppose we could have a good life, but what about all the rest?" She broke away from him and went to stand before the fire. The flames burned red along the silken shafts of her hair and the amber light played across her face like the glow of sunset.

"Aren't you forgetting something?" she said. "How do you think it will look for a commissioned officer to have a wife who has lived among the Sioux? What you've seen out west is nothing compared to what is coming. We both know it. It might be five years or twenty, but the real war is coming. And when it does, you'll be passed over for a command in it. I believe they call it a conflict of interests."

"I'm willing to take that chance. Are you?"

Katie hesitated.

"Are you telling me you don't love me?"

"No, I..."

"Don't tell me you're still in love with that Indian."

When she didn't answer, he rushed forward and exclaimed, "He's a renegade, for Christ sake. They'll hunt him down and kill him, if they haven't already done so." The color drained from her face, but he pressed on. "What kind of life would that be for you, always on the run? Are you prepared to watch him die? Are you prepared to die yourself? How much sympathy do you think they'll have for you if they capture you? All the money in the world won't buy your freedom from the prison they'll throw you in. Katie, think! Think what you'd be throwing away. And for what? For a man who may not even be alive, and if he is, who has probably forgotten all about you?"

His voice rose as he spoke, until it filled the room with desperate indignation. "I know that what I'm saying hurts you, but what about me? What about my feelings?"

She whirled to face him, green eyes bright with tears and fury. "I was honest with you from the start."

"That's true," he said grudgingly. "But it's been more than a year. All those dinners together, the nights at the opera, the evenings we spent here in this room, the way you flirt with me and tease me and give me reason to hope. Excuse me if I thought your feelings for me were genuine."

"They are."

He laughed bitterly. "Right. Only what you feel for me isn't love, is that it?" Her silence was all the answer he needed. "I've been patient, Katie," he said, his voice hardening. "I've given you all the time you need to get over him. But he's not here, and I am, and I'm offering you a good life. As for love, I can only hope that in time you'll come to feel for me what you feel for him."

Katie moved away from him. She could never feel for any man what she felt for Black Moon. But she could not wound Josh any more than she had already done by saying so. "You must give me time to think about it. I'm confused."

"Oh gosh, Katie, I'm ashamed of myself for putting pressure on you after all you've been through. What was I thinking? It's just that..." He paused to draw in an unsteady breath. "You are, without question, the most beautiful woman I've ever seen, and the most intriguing. Only someone as unconventional as you could have made the transformation from half-wild Indian to an elegant lady so dramatically. You're like lightning in a bottle. You stir me in ways I never thought possible. I thought, with the news I brought, maybe things would be different. Heck, Katie, I'm a soldier, not a poet. I have trouble putting into words what I feel for you."

But there was no mistaking what he felt when he reached for her and pulled her into his arms with unexpected force. He pressed his lean body so tightly against hers that the wool of his uniform scratched her and the cold, round buttons bit into her flesh. He kissed her long and thoroughly and was breathing hard when he finally released her and took a step back.

"I'm not going to apologize for that," he said. He reached for his coat and put it on. "I'll be leaving at the end of the week. I want you to marry me before I leave. I'll call on you tomorrow evening for your answer."

When he was gone, Katie went back to her room. Picking up the poker, she stirred the dying embers and placed another log on the fire. She sat staring into the flames, contemplating the mass of contradictions her life had become.

The fabrics she wore were softer and finer, yet there was something indescribable about the feel of deerskin tanned to white suppleness to which not even the costliest silk could compare. The food she ate was rich and creamy, yet her mouth still watered for the succulence of ripe choke cherries right off the bush and buffalo ribs roasted over an open flame.

In St. Louis the sky was choked with soot and barely visible between the buildings, the air filled with the ghostly whistles of the steamboats, the clattering of carriage wheels and the pandemonium of the riverfront. Out on the plains the sky was blue and infinite, the air so silent one could almost hear the snow falling. Here, she was confined like a canary to a cage. There, she was free to soar like the eagles. Here, when she gazed into the flames she saw only despair and loneliness. There, she saw hope and promise.

Katie's heart was torn. Could she live without the glorious sunrises and sunsets of the plains? Without the Black Hills to inspire her? Without the reckless thrill of galloping her horse through an ocean of grass as high as her knees? Could she live the rest of her life without the touch of one special man? With only this raw burning hunger to gnaw at her for the rest of her days?

Josh promised her a good life, and yes, she believed he would do his best to keep that promise. He was a good and honorable man, and he clearly adored her. But was his love for her so blind that he would settle for a woman who did not...could not...return his love? Her mind pitched to and fro as she wrestled with her thoughts. Why, oh why couldn't she love Josh? It would have made everything so much simpler.

Suddenly, something McCabe had said to her what seem a lifetime ago pierced her consciousness.

"Ah, Katie m'darlin', the man who tries to tame that wild heart o' yers is in for one helluva fight."

And there was her answer. Josh McIntyre wanted to subdue her untamed spirit and squeeze her into the mold of a proper wife. For that reason she could never truly love him.

Black Moon had never tried to tame her wild heart, but had embraced it. He had not sought to turn her into something she was not, and despite his hatred of the whites, had come to love her for herself. With him she felt no restraint. Living with him had not been like living in captivity. It had been a blending of two similar souls, two wild hearts beating as one. And for that reason she loved him in a way that was as deep and as true as love could be.

Maybe Josh was right when he said Black Moon had forgotten all about her. But he'd been wrong to suggest that Black Moon might not be alive. If that were true, she would have felt it deep down in that place where such things are known without actually knowing. No, he was as alive as her love for him was alive.

Katie's hand went up to her neck to caress the strand of beads around her neck. Gently, she lifted them up over her head and carried them from the room.

Downstairs, she knocked softly on Jane's door in the maid's quarters, rousing the sleeping woman who answered the knock in a homespun chemise, her plaited hair disheveled.

"Yes, Miss?" she said, stifling a yawn.

"Jane, in the morning I want you to go into town and deliver this to the attorney." She handed her an envelope on which she'd written the attorney's name and address. Inside, contained the unexecuted document to transfer the estate to her name. After wrestling with the prospect of all that wealth, she realized she wanted none of it for herself.

"And Jane, when Lieutenant McIntyre calls tomorrow evening, you are to give this to him." Into her palm Katie pressed the strand of love beads and closed her fingers over them.

Jane looked at the necklace, then back up at Katie questioningly.

"I won't be here when he comes," Katie explained.

"What if he asks where you went? What should I say?"

"He won't ask. He'll know. Now, Jane, after I leave I want you to go to my room and help yourself to anything you want."

"Oh, miss...Katie...I couldn't."

"It's my way of thanking you for being such a good friend to me. I don't know how I would have gotten through this past year without you."

Jane's expression turned faintly suspicious. "Are you going on a trip?"

"No, Jane," she answered softly. "I'm going home."

CHAPTER 24

*B*lack Moon led his people down out of the hills and toward the agency on Deer Creek. Astride his red pony, the jaw rope grasped loosely in his hand, dressed unassumingly in plain buckskin and fur-wrapped braids, his dark eyes were focused straight ahead looking at no one. Behind him came the old chiefs and the warriors followed by the women, the old ones, the pony drags and finally the herd of thin-ribbed ponies.

The decision to bring his people in had not come easy. Starvation and the white man's sickness had taken a sharp toll on them over the winter. Many had not lived to see the new spring moon. Even Good Deeds was sick, every day growing paler and thinner.

He had been reluctant to accept Good Deeds when she came to him, but he supposed it was just as well that he had. Her spirit was too tender and her health too frail for her to resist Gray Wolf's brutality. But it was more than her health that persuaded him to take her in. Her child had seen almost one winter and was looking more like his brother every day. There was no need for the boy to suffer at Gray Wolf's hand.

In return for his protection, Good Deeds cooked his food, tanned his robes, sewed his moccasins and kept the lodge clean. In time, he might even bestow upon her the privilege accorded a wife of carrying the scalps her husband took on a pole during the dance. She was his wife in all ways but one. She offered him that, as well, but he refused. He could not bring himself to love her, not when she would always belong to his brother and when his own heart was dead to love.

Still, he could not help but feel tenderness toward Good Deeds. At twenty, she had already seen too much. The warpath was a good thing for warriors, but he wanted to make it so that those like Good Deeds never again had to see the people on the ground like animals butchered in the hunt. So he made the decision to lead the people to the agency at Deer Creek where they would have food to fill their hungry bellies and the white man's medicine to make the sick ones well again. When they were strong again, he would lead them back to the wild country. In his mind it was as simple as that. He was compromising nothing.

The Indian agent held the far-seeing glasses to his eyes and watched the procession approach. This was his first glimpse of the infamous warrior whose name spread panic among the white population of the whole upper Platte country

Standing grim-faced beside him was Yellow Hand. When the procession passed by them, Black Moon's dark eyes shifted stealthily toward him and a silent look radiated from them that said "You will pay for what you did."

Several days after Black Moon was established in his own camp a few miles from the agency, a company of bluecoats rode over from Fort Laramie. Speaking through a half-breed interpreter they said, "The big soldier chief at the fort welcomes you and asks if there is anything you would like."

Black Moon stood before them, his disdain evident in the hard, unflinching line of his jaw. "I would like to be left alone."

Back at Old Bedlam, when Brigadier General Marcus Worth heard of Black Moon's response, he flew into a rage.

"Damn him," he stormed. "I sent detachments west to Horseshoe Creek, east to the Sand Hills, north to the Black Hills and south to Lodgepole Creek, scouring Sioux country for more than a year looking for that renegade. My orders are to convince him to go to Washington to meet with President Buchanan and the War Department. If they can't get him to give up his war, then maybe the sheer number of people he sees back east will be enough to convince him of the futility of his fight. Go back and tell him that if he will go to Washington, we will allow him to take his people on a buffalo hunt on the Powder River."

When Black Moon heard the offer, he spat with contempt. "Allow! Who are you to say what I can and cannot do?"

The General's patience was wearing dangerously thin. "Tell him I want to have a council with him."

Black Moon responded flatly, "If the three-star wants to council with me, he knows where to find me."

Furious, but undaunted, the General seethed, "Fine. If I can't get that damn Indian to come to a council with me, then I'll bring the council to him."

A warm May sun glinted off the dew drops that clung to the early-morning grass as the entourage made its way from Fort Laramie to Black Moon's camp. Half-way there they were stopped by a familiar face.

Yellow Hand drew the general aside, and whispered, "Black Moon is planning to kill you."

The general's mouth fell open.

Yellow Hand pressed on with his lie. "He is desperate. He will involve us all in war. Believe me, I know him."

Worth eyed the hawk-nosed Indian suspiciously. Through the interpreter he asked, "How do I know what you are telling me is true?"

"Did I not tell you where to find the red-haired woman?"

The general nodded and drew his officers into a hasty conference.

"Black Moon should be put under arrest," one suggested.

"And how do you propose we do that?" the General asked sharply. "We can't just walk up to him and lead him away."

Yellow Hand stepped forward. "I know a way."

The next day when Yellow Hand spied Black Moon leave camp for a morning ride, he waited for Good Deeds to emerge from the lodge and intercepted her.

"Black Moon has been in a fight!" he cried out. "He is hurt bad. He is at the agent's house. He asks for you. You must come quick."

Good Deeds ran back inside, scooped up her son and hurried after her brother.

When Black Moon returned from his ride, Yellow Hand was there to greet him. "My sister has been taken to the fort," he lied. "The white doctor there will give her the medicine she needs to get well."

Black Moon's gaze slid over him like ice. "If Good Deeds went to the soldier fort, it was against her will."

"She is in poor health and too weak to make such a decision for herself. As her brother, I made it for her."

"When did you ever think of anyone but yourself?" Black Moon sneered.

"The boy went with her."

For several furious moments Black Moon's look ripped into Yellow Hand before he turned away with disgust and stalked into the lodge.

That night a pale moon hung in the sky. Far out on the plains the wolves sent their plaintive howls to the sky. A few miles away in the army camp, while the cooks were preparing the evening meal, General Worth greeted a visitor who came secretly to his tent.

"Black Moon slipped out of camp alone on horseback," Yellow Hand reported through the interpreter. "He is headed for the fort."

The general sat back in his chair and folded his hands over his chest in a self-satisfied manner. "Good. I have sent word ahead to expect him. When he arrives, my men will be waiting. And the woman and the child?"

Yellow Hand replied with a laugh, "Won't my old friend be surprised to learn they were right here at the agency all along?"

Black Moon rode hard to get to the fort. Daylight was breaking over the hills when he arrived. He waited until he spied a group of Indians making their way to the big gates and fell in among them. With his blanket of blue trade cloth pulled up around himself, he was indistinguishable from the others.

Inside the walled compound he saw bluecoats everywhere. He located the doctor's quarters and entered.

The doctor tensed upon seeing him and aimed a shaking finger at a small adobe building across the way.

Black Moon crossed the parade ground and approached the building with caution. His eyes swept over the place. He could not dispel the feeling that all was not as it seemed. He sensed danger and was gripped by an instinct to flee. But he knew that if he did not take Good Deeds away from this place, she would become like the other Indian women who lived in a special camp outside the fort who carried half-breed babies on their backs. Worse was the thought of his nephew growing up never knowing real freedom.

With a guarded look around, he opened the door. The scent inside hit him like an explosion, and he recoiled at the dankness and gloom of the place. His eyes lit up with wild disbelief when he saw the bars on the cell doors and window. It forced a quick revulsion into his stomach and immediate indignity into his mind.

He whirled to flee, but several dark shapes sprang out of the shadows to surround him. He glanced around frantically at the bayonets pointed at him from all directions.

Trapped! The thought staggered him and set his reflexes into action. Breaking free of the cordon, he struck out against his captors. Whipping a knife from his sleeve, he made a dash for the door, slashing at anyone who would get in the way of his freedom.

Pandemonium broke loose in the guard house. In the melee, the butt of a rifle struck Black Moon at the back of his head. The pain seared through his brain. The last thing he saw before falling unconscious were the bars on the window. Beyond them a lone eagle was circling in the blue sky.

CHAPTER 25

*T*he tiny prairie peas were in bloom when Katie returned to the wild country around the North Platte. The river was at full rise, and the winds that blew across the basin from October to April bringing cold out of the northwest flowed warm over the valley on this spring day in the Moon of Shedding Ponies.

Katie's breath caught in her throat when she gazed out the stagecoach window once again upon the beautiful, shifting panorama. Oh, what a fool she had been to think that her dreams of happiness could be found anywhere else on earth. It was more than the changeable beauty of the land, though, that made her heart thump with anticipation. It was the uncertainty of what she would find. Never before had the hills seemed so high, the valley so wide, the shallow Platte so deep. Somewhere within this vast realm of wilderness was the man she had come all this way to find.

What would he do when he learned that she had returned? Would his heart grow furious against her as perhaps was its right? Would he laugh contemptuously in her face? Or would he enfold her in his arms and press urgent kisses to her lips and whisper, "Welcome home, *mitawin*" in that strong, deep voice that sent chills down her spine? He was such a victim of his own turbulent emotions that it was difficult to tell just what his reaction would be. One thing, however, was certain. If Black Moon did not want to be found, he would elude her forever.

She had to find him, to explain what happened to make her stay away so long. He had to understand the promise she made to a dying woman. He was a man of his word, after all. But would he forgive?

As the stagecoach rumbled along the rutted road, jostling Katie on the hard planked seat, she tried to keep her mind off the dust churned up by the massive spoked wheels by making a mental a list of the things she needed for her journey into the hills. A sturdy pony, of course. A rifle, ammunition, provisions, and some proper clothes.

The taffeta dress she was wearing, although fine for travel by steamboat from St. Louis to Fort Randall, was proving to be warm and confining in the heat within the enclosed coach, and even though she had left that ridiculous willow-reed hoop behind, it would be much too cumbersome for the days and maybe weeks ahead on horseback. A dress of tanned elk skin or calico cloth was what she needed. The most important item on her list was the services of an Indian scout or one of the traders to accompany her north. The battle-scarred plains were no place for a woman alone, not even one who was as familiar with them as she was.

It wasn't the natural elements that frightened her. She'd been through winters with blizzards that dumped ten feet of snow over the ground, spring thunder storms with zigzagged streaks of lightning that struck trees and set them aflame, and summers that turned the land as dry as a tinderbox and scorched her lungs with each breath she took. She had seen what the animals could do—wolves bringing down prey, buffalo stampeding and trampling hunters who got in the way. No, it wasn't anything in the natural world that frightened her. It was the human element that made her flesh crawl.

Fresh in her mind was the memory of the two soldiers who had tried to rape her, callous men like Big Belly and Watchful Fox, schemers like Corn Woman, heartless men like Henri Chatillon, men without souls like Baptiste and without conscience like General Marcus Worth, and murdering traitors like Yellow Hand.

The stagecoach pulled in at the Deer Creek mail station and jolted to a stop. Katie climbed down, swatted the dust from her skirts and looked around. By-passing the Indian agent she went straight to the trading post of Jasper Gillette, a fur trapper turned trader her father had always spoken of with grudging respect.

The toll bridge Gillette had built across the river for the emigrant trade had made him a rich man. These days, he had an Indian trading house, a dry goods store, a post office, and an Overland stage station. The Sioux were his people. He had married into them and raised a passel of sons and daughters who were more Indian than white. Katie knew that if anyone could lead her to Black Moon, it was Jasper Gillette.

She found him and his half-Oglala progeny at his Indian store about a mile up the road. The bell atop the door jingled when she entered. Her face was flushed from the walk and she was fanning herself with her hand when a man emerged from the back room holding a Hudson's Bay blanket and stepped to the front of the counter.

"Can I help you, miss?"

He was a fine-looking old man, with a snowy beard and mustache and eyebrows to match. He was dressed in a buckskin tunic over a plaid woolen shirt. Like most of the old-time traders the fringes on his pants were longer than usual, a throw-back to the early fur-trapping days when they drained off rain and were a steady source of binding-thongs. On his feet he wore moccasins that were beaded in the colorful Lakota designs.

"Mister Gillette?"

He folded the blanket, and said, "I'm Gillette."

Katie came forward in a swish of taffeta. "My name is Katie McCabe."

"I know who you are."

She looked at him curiously. "Have we met before?"

"No, we ain't never met. But you're Tom McCabe's girl. I can see that plain as day."

With a smile, she said, "My father always spoke well of you."

He shook his head. "Was a damn shame what happened to him."

Her smile faded. "Aye. A shame."

"He was a good man. 'Course, he was my main competition among the Indians. Beat me to some good trades.

But he wasn't like the others. He never traded liquor. Most of the traders had pure alcohol, the kind that'd make a jackrabbit spit in a rattlesnake's eye. It's kinda sad watching those Indians lose all control when they drink that stuff, rolling around in the dirt and crowing like roosters. The Pawnee, now, they know better. They refuse to trade in whiskey. The Crow call it fool's water. I heard they don't allow it in their villages."

Katie's thoughts jolted back to the game of hands in the Crow village and the sight of Big Belly rendered unconscious from too much whiskey. "You heard wrong," she said.

He went behind the counter and placed the folded blanket on a splintered shelf. "Now, how would you know that?"

"It doesn't matter." She had no wish to share with him an episode from her life that she would rather forget. "As for my father, you're right. He didn't trade in whiskey. He used to say that many a trader's life became part of the bargain."

"Ain't that the truth," he said. "I knew a trader once who was dealing out liquor at an Assiniboine village on the upper Missouri when one of them got so drunk he up and killed him."

"My father had more respect for the Indians than to deal in liquor. Although he told me that a Brulè chief once offered him his daughter for a jug."

"Offering a wife or a daughter ain't so uncommon, especially when they know a man ain't got no wife of his own. I hear tell your pap never took another woman after your mama up and died."

"Aye. That's true. He raised me and my brother by himself."

"There was some speculation going around about what happened to you after Blue Water."

"Providence was kinder to me," she said, without bothering to elaborate.

"Well, I'd say. Course, we all knew you'd taken up with the Indians, but look at you now, all fancied up like that. We don't get many ladies in here wearing such fine clothes."

Katie glanced at the inquisitive faces pressing against window for a better look at her, and laughed. "I must be a sight for sore eyes."

"You sure are that, girl," he agreed.

"Mister Gillette, I'd like to do a little trading with you."

He nodded with approval. "What can I do for you?"

As Katie ticked off the supplies she needed, he began to withdraw things from shelves behind and beneath the counter.

"And I'll trade you this dress I'm wearing for something else," she said.

Gillette sized her up with his eyes. "That fancy dress looks like it was ordered right out of a catalog. I could get a pretty penny for it from one of the officer's wives at the fort. The emigrant women who come in don't have the money to buy such frivolous items, or the figures to wear them. You appear to have both. But I ain't got nothing in calico."

"Hide will do."

"It seems a shame," he said, "to hide such beauty beneath heavy buckskin." He bent down behind the counter and withdrew something from the bottom shelf. "I got here this Arapaho dress."

Katie smiled with appreciation when she saw it. It was of deer skin, tanned to whiteness and as soft as velvet, decorated with cowrie shells along the yoke and cut in fringes at the bottom. "This will do just fine."

"I'll throw these in, too." He tossed onto the counter a pair of women's high-top moccasins that were made from the smoked top of a tipi. "And this." It was a belt made of harness leather studded with brass tacks. "Got this from a Sioux over at Deer Creek a few weeks back."

"If you don't mind," Katie said, scooping up the bundle, "I'd like to change into these things right now."

"Right through there, little lady." He pointed toward a muslin curtain that led to the back room.

"You said you wanted a good mount," he called out to her. "I got a sturdy Army horse out in the corral.

Her voice issued from the back room. "I noticed that brown Indian pony. How about that one?"

"Yup, you're your pap's daughter, all right. McCabe had an eye for good horseflesh, too. Okay, the Indian pony it is. But I have to tell you, he don't come cheap. I had to trade some buck a helluva lot for him."

"I'll pay whatever he's worth."

"You got yourself a deal." He bundled up her other items in brown paper and tied it with a string. "I'll throw in a decent saddle, too."

The woman who emerged from the back room was just as beautiful as the one who had walked into his store, but in a very different way. Gone was the costly dress with its flounced skirt and frilly sleeves, replaced by one of tanned hide that fit her body like a second skin, the leather belt cinched at her waist accentuating her slenderness. She had unbound her hair from the knot at the back of her head to let it spill past her shoulders and down her back in red waves.

"Well, I'll be," he said with appreciation. "You make a fine-looking Indian."

Katie loved the feel of the tanned hide next to her skin. It had been long, too long, since she'd been unhampered by frilly undergarments and starched crinolines.

"You've been very fair to me, Mister Gillette," she said. "If I may, I'd like now to ask something else of you."

"You just name it, little lady," said the old trader. "If I ain't got it here, I can get it."

"What I need is of a different nature." In answer to the way his white bushy brows knit with a question, she said, "I need information."

"And what information would that be?"

In a voice that remained calm and level in spite of the anxiety that was growing within her, she said, "You can tell me where I can find the Oglala, Black Moon."

He gave slow, understanding nod of the head. "Yeah, word had it you'd taken up with that renegade. I seem to recall hearing a rumor that you disappeared a while back, gone east or something. I guess that would explain why you showed up here today in those fine clothes. Don't get me wrong. I ain't judging you for any of it. But what makes you think I know where to find Black Moon?"

"I may be a lot of things, Mister Gillette," she said, "but I'm no fool. If anyone knows where to find him, it's you."

"What do you want with him?"

"It's a personal matter."

"I see."

"No, you don't. But that doesn't matter. What matters is that I find him. Which I will do with or without your help. My guess is he's somewhere up north. Now, I could go on up there myself and try to find him, but it could take weeks, maybe months. You'd be saving me a lot of time if you just tell me where to look."

"I ain't the only one who knows where Black Moon is," he said. "Most everybody in these parts knows."

Katie did not fail to notice that he had grown uncomfortable under her stare. "What are you saying?"

"What I'm saying is that he ain't up north. You'll find him locked up in a cell over at Fort Laramie where he's waiting for an order from Washington to ship him off to some place back east called the Dry Tortugas. I hear they got an army prison there."

The color drained from Katie's face. Her legs turned rubbery and threatened to give out from under her. Somehow, she managed to remain standing. Her voice eked from her lips in a choked whisper. "Wh—what happened?"

"Well now, it ain't a pretty story."

"Not a whole lot about my life has been pretty," she said weakly. "Tell me."

"It was a bad winter, real bad. Come spring he brought his people to the agency at Deer Creek. They were a starving mess. Some of them had the coughing sickness."

"Pneumonia," she muttered.

"Yup. They got set up with their own camp. Then all hell broke loose. Black Moon wound up at the fort." He hesitated. "They got him locked up over there."

At first she remained very still, her face pale and expressionless except for the near imperceptible wince in her eyes. Slowly, as her shock turned to outrage, the green in her eyes changed from a dull, lifeless color to stark, raging emerald.

"Where are his people?" she demanded in an angry, defiant tone. "Has no one tried to help him?"

Gillette shrugged. "His people picked themselves up one day and left the agency. I hear they've gone north to meet up with the Hunkpapa Sioux on Box Elder Creek."

"Why would they go there?"

"There's a brave up there who's been gaining some influence. Name's Sitting Bull. My guess is they've gone where the power is now that Black Moon's gone." He gave a dismal shake of his head. "You know, I used to think that if any Indian could unite his people against the whites it'd be Black Moon. That sonofabitch knows how to fight the whites and beat them at their own game. Now it looks like he'll never have the chance to finish what he started."

Katie's heart was breaking. Black Moon had always soared as free as an eagle, now he was caged like an animal. He did not belong in a cell. He belonged to himself and himself alone.

"What was he doing at the fort?" she questioned. "He would never have gone there willingly."

"It had something to do with the woman," Gillette said.

"What woman?"

"The one he took into his lodge. They say she had his brother's baby."

She drew in her breath. "Good Deeds?"

Gillette shrugged. "I guess."

Katie's shock was complete. Without uttering another word, indeed, unable to speak, she walked slowly, numbly toward the door, her body seeming to move of its own volition.

It was a warm, sunshiny day, but as she emerged from the trader's shop she shivered. The injustice of Black Moon's capture and incarceration was nothing compared to this.

She followed her aimless footsteps to the top of a grassy knoll from whose rise she had an unobstructed view of the land. Squinting against the sunlight she gazed out over the plains. As she stood there looking at the country of her birth, she was oblivious to the rawhide fringes rustling at the hem of her dress, the birds that flew overhead, the breeze that blew up the tips of her hair to tangle in her lashes, the children who were attacking each other with the mud balls they threw from the tips of sticks, screaming and hollering with each well-aimed shot.

A terribly tremble seized her and shook her hard. She was angry. Angry at Black Moon for placing so little faith in her love that he had taken another woman for his wife. Damn him and his heathen heart! All those long, lonely nights when she had lain awake in bed in St. Louis thinking only of him, apparently he hadn't been thinking of her.

But mostly, Katie was angry at herself for having fallen in love with him against all odds. She had only herself to blame for the heartache she was feeling now. Why? She raged. Why had she fallen in love with him? The answer was simple, really. It was because he was a part of this place she loved so much. His existence, although just a tiny beat in the pulse of all that was, was a thundering vibration in her own small world. Like the eagle that is marshal over the air, Black Moon was master over her heart. She lived a lifetime in every minute she was with him. He was every breath she took. In the end, no matter how dreadfully his unfaithfulness hurt her, the simple fact of the matter was, she still loved him, and she could not stand by and watch him led away like a lamb to the slaughter.

Living in a cage was not living at all. That was something she had learned for herself in St. Louis. Sending Black Moon off to a prison in the east may have been the Army's way of getting rid of him, but Katie knew down to the depths of her being that he would never make it there alive. He would make every attempt to escape and probably die trying.

She didn't know if Black Moon ever wanted to see her again. Was Josh right? Had he forgotten all about her? It would seem so, judging from what Jasper Gillette told her about Good Deeds. She couldn't blame the girl, not really. A woman out here needed a man to hunt and bring back food for the kettle and skins to make new lodge covers. And everyone knew that Gray Wolf was a foul-tempered man. There was no telling what he would have done when he found out that she had given birth to Fire Cloud's child. But why couldn't she have gone to someone else? Couldn't her family have found another man for her? Why did it have to be Black Moon? And why, oh why, did he have to accept?

The more Katie thought about it, the more outraged she became. Damn him. She had half a mind to leave him to Good Deeds. But she knew if she did that, Black Moon was as good as dead. Good Deeds was not a bad woman. She'd done what she had to do to look after herself and her child. But she did not have the courage to do what now needed to be done.

Jasper Gillette looked up when Katie came charging back into his store. "Is there something else I can do for you?"

"Aye," she responded, defiance burning strongly in her green eyes. "You can accompany me to Fort Laramie."

CHAPTER 26

Katie gazed out the second-floor window to the plains beyond the walls of Fort Laramie. Silhouetted against the twilight was a cluster of Lakota lodges, all facing east, smoke-browned at the tops. Some bravely flew horsehair banners, but most were plain and unadorned.

The sight of them brought back memories of the nights she had lain awake inside an Indian tipi listening to the fire crackle and watching the shadows flicker across the hide walls, while overhead the stars peered down through the poles. Some nights the moon climbed right up over the poles to look inside.

Her thoughts drifted back even further, to cold winter nights sleeping warm and sound beneath a buffalo robe in her father's cabin on the Laramie. To mid-summer gooseberries picked from the bush, dried and packed in a parfleche to later make gooseberry mush, and the wild onions, sweeter than turnips, dug up when the prairie grass was thickest. To autumn rose berries and acorns she collected and turned into little pies that McCabe loved even more than rabbit stew.

Her attention was caught by a band of horses being herded back in by armed guards. The gates of the fort swung open and the horses streamed in. A pale yellow one stood out among the others. With a pang, she thought of *Peta*, the beautiful, sleek palomino Black Moon had given her. She wondered what had become of him.

Pressing her cheek to the window, Katie sighed against the pane. Why was it that the things she cared for most in the world were always the things that were taken away? First, her mother, victim of the cholera that raged up the Platte, brought by the emigrant parties that came by steamboat. Then her father and brother in one fell swoop, victims of a different kind of plague that turned men into monsters in their lust for land. Then Fire Cloud, whom she had cared for in a tender way, killed by one of his own. Then *Peta*, Black Moon's special gift. And now, Black Moon himself.

Voices coming from Soapsuds Row interrupted her dismal thoughts. Turning her attention toward the line of cabins where the laundresses and seamstresses were quartered, she saw an enlisted man duck into a room with one of the immigrant women. His slurred speech and her lusty laughter were a sure sign that they were already drunk on the whiskey they had bought at the sutler's store.

Soon it would be dark, and the unfortunate soldier who had drawn guard duty would march along the sentry paths with his musket on his shoulder, calling out "All's Well" at regular intervals. Up and down, up and down, he would march until he was relieved by the next unfortunate soldier who would, in turn, march along the sentry paths while fighting to stay awake. If Katie was going to do something, she had to do it before night fell. She inhaled deeply, and leaving the past behind, screwed up her courage and left the room.

At Old Bedlam she balled her fist and knocked on the door.

"Well, well, so we meet again." If the hard-bitten military man was surprised to see her, he made no show of it. "And to what do I owe this pleasure?"

Katie faced her old nemesis, and said, "I think you know why I'm here, General Worth."

"Yes, I suppose I do," he replied in a bored tone that made her bristle.

"What are you going to do with him?"

"What I should have done a long time ago."

Katie got right to the point. "I am prepared to use every bit of influence and wealth at my disposal to stop you from doing that."

It was not an idle threat. If it would secure Black Moon's freedom, she was prepared to return to St. Louis, where a sizeable inheritance waited, and remain there forever in accordance with her aunt's wishes. With money came power and influence. She'd seen her aunt wield both like a sword. Although it would break her heart, she was willing to give up the man she loved in exchange for his life.

"Your wealth and influence carry no weight with me, Miss McCabe," he coolly informed her. "By the time you got a message to whomever you have all this influence with, it would be too late, anyway. He's being shipped out tomorrow. At first light, he'll be gone, and he won't be my problem any more. And in case you're thinking of doing something foolish, like attacking the company escorting him, you should know that their orders are to shoot first and ask questions later."

Her gaze stuck bravely to his. "I am only one person, General. I could hardly attack an entire army regiment all by myself, now could I?"

He laughed, but it was a sound without mirth. "Frankly, Miss McCabe, I wouldn't put anything past you. I'm sure you're already concocting some wild scheme to save that renegade."

"You give me too much credit," she replied. "I have no intention of attacking the troops, and I don't have some wild scheme planned. I am merely a woman standing before you and asking you to have mercy. He's only a man, General. He's not this larger-than-life creature you've made him out to be. His heart beats just like yours. He bleeds just like you. He loves those dear to him, just as you surely love those dear to you. He hurts when they hurt. He grieves when they die. He protects them by whatever means he can, just as you protect yours. When they are in danger, he fights. Can you blame him for doing the only thing he knows how to do? No, General, you and he are not so very different, after all."

With each word his outrage grew, until it burst from him like cannon fire. "No different? How dare you compare that heathen to a civilized man like me! Your impudence is too much. If it's mercy you want, you should look to a higher power. I have none for that renegade."

"I regret my attempt to appeal to you as one human being to another," she said with undisguised disgust. "You pay no attention to their customs and make no attempt to understand them. You have no interest in preserving peace. You'd be happy for all-out war so that you could eradicate them down to the last one, just to satisfy your self-righteous misconception that only you and your kind have the right to live. You're a disgrace to your uniform!"

Feeling sick with anger, she stormed out of his quarters, slamming the door behind her.

Outside, the sinking sun painted the sky red. The parade ground was still bustling with the traffic of horses and buckboards. She cut across it on her way from the general's quarters. She was so wrapped up in her furious thoughts that she did not see the big gates swing open, nor hear the guard on duty in the blockhouse shout the arrival of a company of soldiers. She was oblivious to the dust the horses kicked up as they entered and trotted past her. Raging privately to herself, she walked smack into a horse that stood motionless blocking her path.

She was about to voice a strenuous objection to the rider, but upon looking up, the words froze on her tongue. The soldier looking down at her was Josh McIntyre.

He sat rigid in the saddle without speaking. She wanted to say something, *anything*, but he pulled sharply on his horse's reins and trotted off. She stifled a sob as she watched him ride away. Drawing in a supportive breath, she continued on her way to back to her room.

***

Josh answered a knock upon his door and blinked hard at what he saw. An Indian woman was standing there wearing a dress with cowrie shells dangling from the yolk and long fringes that brushed the tops of her leggings. On her feet she wore hide moccasins. Her hair was plaited in two long red braids into which she had laced an eagle feather. His eyes raked over her, not failing to notice the way the supple hide hugged her hips and how her braids fell over her softly heaving breasts. Despite the transformation and the look of apprehension on her face, she was magnificent.

Her green eyes were large and beautiful and brimming with vulnerability. It was that look which prevented him from slamming the door in her face. It took an iron will to step aside and allow her to enter.

"Come in." Each word was cold, separate, crystalline. He closed the door behind her, saying, "I have to hand it to you, Katie. I didn't expect to find you here. Nor did I think you would have the nerve to face me again. You just keep proving me wrong, don't you?"

"Josh," she began, "please..."

He put a hand up quickly. "Save it, Katie. He cast a disapproving look over her. "Judging from the way you're dressed, I'd say you're not here to apologize."

"Apologize for what? Not falling in love with you?" she responded defiantly. "Besides, I had some hard riding to do and couldn't very well do it in silk or taffeta. And I thought I would attract less attention this way with all the Indians about."

Was she really so naïve to think her beauty would not shine through even if she were wearing a flour sack? The fact that her dress was not made of silk and did not plunge at the neckline did not make her any less alluring. Any man would have noticed.

Damn, Josh swore to himself, there he went again, allowing his masculine hunger to interfere with his common sense. He forced himself to remember the night he went to her house only to be informed by the maid that she had left early that morning. In her place she left a string of worthless trade beads. It was as if she had committed treason, betraying his love like a common traitor. Yet the sorry truth of it was that she had made him no promises. If there was a traitor at work, then it was his own heart for misleading him into thinking she could be trusted.

The initial onslaught of pain had subsided to a dull ache. He was only just now beginning to function again as a human being when he saw her on the parade ground and the old feelings of anger and resentment came rushing back.

He stood before her now stiff and unyielding. In a tone similar to the one he used when addressing a recalcitrant subordinate, he said, "Just tell me why you've come."

Katie hesitated.

"Well? I'm waiting."

Katie licked her lips nervously, and said, "He's here. In the guardhouse."

"That's where they usually put men who have broken the law."

"As far as I know, the government has not declared war against the Sioux nation," she said. "He hasn't broken any laws, and you know it. Unless it has suddenly become a crime to protect your people and your land."

"Don't be a fool, Katie. You know very well why he had to be put under arrest."

"Had to be? Or because men like General Worth are too afraid to fight a superior opponent?"

"Bows and arrows are no match against the army's guns," he responded.

"I wasn't talking about weapons."

His gray eyes flared, and then darkened when her meaning became clear. "It doesn't matter how smart he is. He's just another Indian in the Army's way."

Katie bit back a gasp. "I expect that kind of callousness from General Worth, not from you."

"Maybe you don't know me as well as you thought you did."

"And maybe you don't know me as well as you thought you did if you think I'm going to stand by and watch this happen."

Behind her indignation Josh saw the vulnerability in her eyes, and although he fought to remain impervious to it, a deeper part of him was moved by the sight of it. He drew in an uncertain breath and let it out between pursed lips, showing softness beneath the steely demeanor. "Look, Katie, it's not my intention to hurt you by what I'm saying. I think there's been enough hurt between us already."

"Josh," she said, "I never meant to hurt you. I have feelings for you. You know I do."

He turned away in anguish, but she pressed on, her voice softly pleading. "But I cannot help what I feel for him. You don't choose who to love. You should know that. It comes on you like a sickness, claiming a piece of your heart every day until your heart is no longer your own. You fight it with everything you have, but in the end it wins. Even when you know it's wrong it becomes something you cannot survive without, like the air you breathe. If I could wipe him from my heart, don't you think I would? God knows, I've tried."

It was as though she were speaking his thoughts, his feelings, his desperation. If they shared nothing else, at least they shared the heartache of loving the wrong person. He felt suddenly tired. His muscles ached from days in the saddle. His emotions were on the brink of exhaustion. He could not hate her, not when he felt sorry for her. Not when he was still in love with her.

He ran a hand through his hair, sweeping the sandy locks from his brow with the wearied gesture of a man who is fighting a battle he knows he cannot win. In a worn-out voice, he said, "There's nothing you can do for him. They're taking him out of here in the morning."

"I know. That's why I have to do something tonight."

Josh shook his head. He looked defeated and vulnerable. "What do you think you can do? He's under lock and key with a twenty-four hour guard."

"I want you to help me help him escape."

Josh's eyes grew large and incredulous even as his face paled. "What?" he gasped.

"I have nowhere else to turn."

"You want me to help you save that renegade? My God, this is too much! Even for you!"

Katie rushed up to him, pleading, "You have to help me."

He looked at her as if she'd gone stark raving mad, his voice echoing his disbelief. "*Have* to?"

"What I mean is—"

"What you mean," he cut in angrily, "is that you want me to forget what you did to me, ignore the law, and jeopardize my commission, is that it?" His voice grew stronger with emotion. "Do you know what you're asking me to do?"

Her voice was a mere whisper next to his. "Yes."

"And still you would ask it"

She nodded.

"Do you think you have the right to ask it?" He turned away and walked to the window, making it obvious that he was not interested in her answer.

The events of recent months had taken their toll on him. He was glad to be back in command of the Eleventh and was hoping that after a few weeks on the frontier he would be his old self again. Well, not quite as before, for there was the matter of his broken heart. But the prairie sun was like a tonic, and he was looking forward to the long march north that the Eleventh would be making in a few days. Days in the saddle and nights beneath the stars were just what the doctor ordered for his weary heart, and while he did not relish his orders to search out and destroy an Indian village, he nevertheless welcomed the chance to throw himself into something and forget his own personal torment for a while.

Lights out had been sounded over an hour ago. The parade ground was vacant and still beneath the light of the moon. Along the sentry paths the cry of "All's well" echoed through the night. He felt Katie come up behind him and every muscle in his body went rigid.

With his back to her, he muttered, "Why should I help you? There's nothing in it for me except possibly getting booted out of the army or court-martialed and hanged."

She put her hand out to touch him, but drew it back. "Josh." She spoke his name softly, plaintively. "How can I make you understand that there's more at stake here than a woman's love? He cannot help being what he is. To keep him locked up is the coward's way out. He is a threat only because he is capable of resisting. Without him, the way is clear for you to march against his people. But what honor can there be in it for you to fight people who are clearly no match? Old ones too weak to lift rifles. Women. Children. Without him they are defenseless. If you don't do it for them, and you won't do it for me, then in God's name, Josh, do it for yourself. Aye, you're a soldier, and you'll do what you must. But at least do it in the honorable way."

His body tensed and his breathing deepened. Honor was something about which he felt strongly. His upbringing had been predicated upon it. His military training was focused on it. Live with honor. Fight for it. Die for it. But Katie was right, damn her. Where was the honor in destroying innocent people? The answer seemed to be lodged somewhere in that shady gray area that lay between love and duty and to which are ascribed all the decisions he made that were not entirely justified in his mind.

"It will take a lot more than honor to convince me to help you," he spoke at last. "You have a hell of a nerve asking me to risk everything when you offer nothing in return." He felt her hand on his arm then and his muscles tightened involuntarily at her touch.

Katie's voice scarcely rose above her breath. "You said once that you love me."

Josh whirled around to face her. "My God!" he cried. "Is nothing sacred to you? Will you stop at nothing to save that goddamn Indian?"

"I know what you're thinking," she said. "And I don't blame you for feeling this way. But you did love me once, and I thought…that is…if you still do…"

Josh's voice tore from his throat in an agonized groan. "If I still do? Damn you! Here's how much I still do."

He tore at his shirt, snapping the button from the collar and sending it arcing across the room. With a savage gesture he pulled his shirt aside to reveal the string of beads he was wearing around his neck. With tortured emotion, he confessed, "I haven't taken them off since that night."

She was standing so close to him he could smell the sweetness of her breath when she said, "You asked me once to marry you."

She was offering herself to him on a silver platter. He had only to reach out and take that for which he hungered. My God, he thought, aghast, was she so in love with that Indian that she would sacrifice herself for him? He should have hated her. He should have told her to go straight to hell. But the longer he looked into those green eyes all shiny with tears and at that full bottom lip that trembled, the more hopelessly entrapped he became. If this was the only way to have her then, God help him, he would do it.

He straightened up and his manner turned official. "We'll go over to the church first thing in the morning and get married. Then I want you to return to St. Louis. As soon as I finish up with this campaign, I'll join you there."

Katie nodded her head stiffly to seal the agreement.

"So, I suppose you have some sort of crazy plan concocted," he said humorously.

She swallowed hard and cleared her throat. "I thought you could divert the guard while I slip to the guardhouse from behind."

"And do what? Blow a hole through the wall with dynamite?"

She ignored his sharp sarcasm. "They won't let me inside, but I managed to get close enough to see that there is no glass in the rear window. Only bars. I could pass a weapon through to him. A gun or a knife."

"A lot of good a weapon will do if he can't get out of the cell," he pointed out.

"Then I'll have to think of a way to get the guard into the cell. If Black Moon can overpower him…"

"Forget it," he said flatly. "Orders are for no one to go into that cell. They don't even go in to give him his food. They pass it in to him through the bars. Why do you think his hands were never manacled? As I hear it, in the confusion they were glad just to get him behind bars. They shoved him in and locked the door behind him so quick that no one thought to put the chains on. Now no one wants to go in there to do it. To his credit, I'll say he's got them scared out of their wits. They can't wait to get him out of here."

"There has to be a way to get the guard into the cell," Katie insisted. "Suppose I slip him a length of rope? He could tie it to one of the crossbeams and—"

Josh knew instantly what she was thinking. "Are you crazy? What if something goes wrong? Are you willing to take that chance?"

"Nothing will go wrong if you do your part. All you have to do is detain the guard outside long enough for Black Moon to get one end of the rope tied around the beam and the other end around his neck. When the guard comes back in and finds him, that would get him into the cell, wouldn't it? "

He let out a stunned breath. "I guess so."

"But if you detain the guard any longer than necessary, it will mean Black Moon's death."

"And what makes you think I won't use this opportunity to permanently remove him as a rival?"

Katie smiled. It was genuine and warm, and it disarmed him. "I know in my heart you won't betray me, Josh. You're far too honorable a man for that." She turned and started for the door.

His voice, low and shaking, stopped her. "Tell him..." His voice cracked and he began again. "Tell him we'll be riding out in a week to attack a Sioux village on Box Elder Creek. Our informant tells us it's Black Moon's band."

She tensed. "Was it the same informant who told you where to find me?"

"Yes."

She paused with her hand on the door latch and looked back at Josh. He looked torn and desperate. Her voice choked with emotion. "Thank you."

A gust of wind blew up the ends of Katie's braids when she stepped out into the night. She gulped in a huge breath of air and let it out slowly. The easy part, if she dared call it that, was over. The hard part was about to begin.

She made her way along the parade ground, keeping to the shadows, eyes scanning the darkness to make sure no one spotted her coming from Lieutenant McIntyre's quarters. Josh was right, of course. It was a crazy plan. If it failed, it would mean Black Moon's death. Could she live with that for the rest of her life?

She asked herself what Black Moon would do. She could just imagine the way those dark eyes would flash with defiance when faced with a heart-wrenching dilemma such as the one she now confronted. She knew him well enough to know that the streak of unbridled courage running through him would never shrink from what had to be done.

Hadn't leading his starving people to the Deer Creek agency been proof of that? Always he placed the welfare of others ahead of his own. He was the kind of man who raced headlong into danger, blind to the consequences when the end result was all that mattered.

He had saved her from the brutality of the soldiers after Blue Water when he could just as easily have let her perish. What was the life of one white woman to him? And yet, he had seen the wrong in the vicious attack and had acted against it. He had risked his own life by going to the Crow village to find her even though she had been another man's wife. He had rescued her from the lust of Chatillon and Baptiste. Never once had he second-guessed himself over whether it was the right thing to do. To him, it was the *only* thing to do.

And therein lay the answer to Katie's dilemma. For all he had done for her, this was the least she could for him. And if helping Black Moon escape resulted in his death, she knew he would have it no other way. And if all went according to plan, what then? The promise she made to Josh to become his wife stuck like an arrowhead in her heart. Would Black Moon understand if he knew? Would he even care? With freedom in sight, would he jump astride his pony and escape without a second look back, never bothering to question the circumstances that had set him free or the broken heart he was leaving behind?

How ironic it was that the marriage proposal she had turned down in St. Louis would come again, and this time she would accept, knowing full well that in doing so she was losing the only man she loved beyond all rationality.

Overcome with confusion, only one thing was certain. Whether her plan succeeded or failed, after a year's absence, tonight she would see Black Moon again. The anticipation of it filled her with a wild hope and was almost more than she could bear. Yet it also meant that tonight would be the last time she would gaze upon that proud, handsome face.

With that agonizing thought in mind, she went in search of a rope.

CHAPTER 27

Black Moon paced the cell like a restless creature, muscles bristling and nerves on edge. He had lost count of how many suns had risen and fallen since his confinement. Day after day he forced himself to eat the white man's food, the stringy beef and the bread made from wormy flour, in order to keep his strength alive. He knew not how or when, but he knew he would escape. Or he would die trying.

Everything he loved lay on the other side of the bars. The flat-water, the river the whites called the North Platte, so close he could almost smell the cattails growing along its banks that were marshy from melted snow. The sacred *Paha Sapa*, fragrant with new spring growth. The yellow hollow-stem flowers that grew as tall as a man out on the prairie. The earth, moist and clean-smelling beneath the shaggy-leaf trees. The painted winged ones fluttering from flower to flower. The warrior bird that swooped over the land.

He went to the barred window and stared up at the moon, three days past full and as white as frost in the western sky. Every night he sang to her, like the true dog that howls at the moon, his anger and bitterness echoed in every note of his voice. But unlike the dominant-tail, the leader among wolves, he had no pack to lead. A great lonesomeness gnawed at him. Lifting his face toward the sky, he sang for an end to the misery of his people and to the despair raging in his heart caused by his relentless longing for a green-eyed woman.

He recalled with a pang how it used to feel to hold her while she slept, the way her nose wrinkled when she laughed and her eyes sparkled like the traders' green glass when she was happy. If he closed his eyes, he could imagine himself getting lost in her exuberant passion. There had been a time when the only place he wanted to die was in her arms, but he knew now he had been foolish to think that a warrior's death could be anywhere but on the battlefield.

He knew how to fight his age-old enemies and win. The Crow, the Pawnee, they were real. He could touch them and count coup on them. He could capture their horses and take their scalps and feel the pride of being a Lakota warrior swelling in his breast.

He could fight this newest menace, the whites, and drive them back with his fierceness and cunning.

But how could he fight this enemy living inside of him that had no name and no shape, and yet which threatened to destroy him as surely as any Crow arrow or bluecoat's gun? Against this enemy his own arrows were useless. His war cries went unheard. It was a battle he fought every day, and lost. It was the red-haired woman who threatened to destroy him, and where was the pride in that?

He vilified her and vowed revenge against her, all the while wanting her with a desperation that went beyond all reason. And then, all of a sudden, as if stepping out of one of his dreams, she was there.

Starlight softer than a whisper fell upon her when she stepped out of the shadows. The dress she wore was cut in the Arapaho style and molded itself to her slender body. A white eagle plume tied in her hair floated with the motion of each step she took as she came closer. Who but she would have the courage to wear the feather of the warrior bird, a distinction reserved for warriors like himself? She was more beautiful than he had ever seen her. Like a blade of grass that has no choice but to bend beneath the breath of the wind, Black Moon was powerless to fight the surge of desire that flooded his being. His eyes swept over her, consuming her in one mad, desperate rush.

She approached the barred window and said in a

guarded whisper, "There is a horse waiting for you among the trees below the fort."

Black Moon's guard went up around him. His look turned coldly inquisitive.

"There is no time to explain," she said. "Take this." From beneath her dress she slipped the knife she kept strapped to her thigh and slid it between the bars. It disappeared quickly into his palm. "And this." In her hand she held a deerskin pouch. "There is enough food to last for a day."

He hesitated, looking at the pouch with disdain.

"It is not the white man's food," she said. 'Just some pemmican I traded for with one of the Lakotas who loafs around the fort."

His fingers touched hers as he accepted the pouch, and a bolt of lightning strong enough to split the trunk of a tree shot through him.

"And this," she said.

Black Moon looked questioningly at the rope she passed through the bars.

In a hurried whisper, she said, "You must stand on the chair and tie one end around the beam in the ceiling and one end around your neck. When you hear the guard come back in…" She hesitated, choking on the words. "You must kick the chair away. That will bring the guard into the cell."

Suspicion deepened in Black Moon's eyes as he grappled with uncertainty. He had learned the hard way not to trust her with his emotions. Could he trust her now with his life?

In the moonlight her white skin was paler than he had ever seen it. It reminded him of the colorless faces of the emigrant women who came through his country in the wagons with with the big covers that were pulled by oxen and mules and left ruts in the Holy Road. The look on their faces when they saw Indians was pure fear. He saw fear on Katie's face through the bars, but this was a different kind of fear, not of him, nor of what she did not understand, but of something much deeper than her words could ever express. It told him there was no other way. He stifled a bitter laugh. Who but she would be crazy enough to suggest such a stunt? And who but he would be desperate enough to try it? Looking into her beautiful green eyes, he nodded his understanding of what she was saying, and all that it meant.

"The bluecoats plan to attack a Lakota village on Box Elder Creek," she said in a whispered warning. "Your people are there. There is something else you must know. It was Yellow Hand who told the soldiers where to find them."

Through the shadows that played across Black Moon's face his muscles tightened and a murderous rage leapt into his eyes. A look of pure hatred twisted his features. He looked into her pallid face and asked, "Will you be waiting at the horse?"

Tears formed in her eyes. "I am not going with you." Without another word, she turned and hurried away and was swallowed up by the shadows.

At the front of the guardhouse, the trooper assigned to guard the prisoner snapped to attention when the lieutenant approached.

"At ease, soldier," Josh said. "Nice night."

"That it is, sir."

"Are you keeping a good eye on the prisoner?"

"Yes sir," the trooper replied. "Not that that evil-eyed Indian needs much guarding. All he does is stand at the window singing at the moon."

Josh lit a cigarette and offered one to the trooper.

The man hesitated. "I'm on duty, sir."

"Go on," he said, "Take it. At a lousy wage of thirteen dollars a month that doesn't leave extra money for smokes." A woman's giggles and a man's drunken laughter come from the direction of Soapsuds Row. "Or that," Josh added.

"Ain't that the truth," the trooper said with a laugh.

"When does your watch end?"

"Not for a couple of hours."

They smoked for a while in silence.

A sound from the shadows snapped them both alert.

"Who goes there?" the guard demanded.

The tame antelope one of the men kept for a pet trotted into view. Josh laughed, a little too nervously. "Antelope stew would be a sight better than the usual army fare of jerked beef and dried vegetables," he said. "That no one has put a bullet through that animal's skull and cooked it is a miracle." He ground the stub of his cigarette into the ground with the heel of his boot. "Well, goodnight." He walked off and disappeared across the parade ground.

The trooper hoisted his rifle back up to his shoulder to resume his watch, when a sound from inside the guardhouse caught his attention. He stomped inside.

"What the—!"

The prisoner was hanging from a rope in the cell.

The key ring jangled furiously as the frantic guard fumbled to get the cell door unlocked. He ran to the chair, righted it, and jumped up on it and began to slice through the rope with his knife, cursing out loud at what seemed like an eternity before the rope finally snapped and the prisoner fell to the floor.

Black Moon lay motionless face down on the dirt floor of the cell, his skin red and raw from the burn of the rope still tied around his neck, his breathing shallow by sheer force of will. He opened his eyes just a slit. The bluecoat's boots were close, the toes pointed toward him as the man leaned in for a better look. Then the boots pivoted and started to hurry away.

In that moment Black Moon pounced. He sprang up and whipped the knife from his belt in one swift motion. Grabbing the bluecoat beneath the arms from behind, he lifted him off the floor and brought the blade across his neck in a sweeping motion. A gurgling sound issued from the white man's throat. His legs thrashed about violently, and then went still. In less than a heartbeat the struggle was over. The guard was dead, a crescent of blood spilling from his throat into the earthen floor.

Breathing heavily, Black Moon glanced down at the white man laying dead at his feet. He felt no remorse over what he had done, only the cold certainty that if the situation were reversed, it would have been him laying there in a puddle of blood.

With a savage gesture, he pulled the coarse rope from around his neck. It had been close, much closer than he cared to think about. He could still feel the air being choked out of him as he hung there for what had felt like a lifetime. Even now the mere act of swallowing was a painful reminder of how close he had come to death.

Grabbing the rope, not daring to leave it behind for fear of it being linked to Katie, he crept to the door of the guardhouse and pressed his ear against the grainy surface, listening for sounds from outside. Hearing nothing, he opened it cautiously and looked around. His sharp senses were tuned to the slightest hint of danger in the air. Seeing no one about, he darted into the shadows.

He moved like a wolf through the compound, his fingers gripped tight around the hilt of the knife whose blade was stained with the white man's blood, prepared to use it again if need be. He made it across the parade ground without being seen. In front of him a fifteen foot high adobe wall blocked his path to freedom. There was only way to go and that was over it.

Spotting a trader's wagon close by, he tucked the knife into his belt and used his formidable strength to push the wagon up against the wall and climb onto it. From there he hoisted himself to the top of the wall. For several seconds he crouched there, casting a hateful sneer down at the soldier town. Then he jumped to the ground, rolling upon impact.

Springing to his feet, he darted off into the darkness. His keen sense of smell led him to the waiting pony concealed among the shaggy-leaf trees. He was about to mount when a noise from behind spun him around.

"When the red-haired woman returned, I knew she was up to something."

Yellow Hand's voice spliced the night with venom. The razor-sharp blade of his knife glistened in the moonlight.

Black Moon's hand went for his blade as he jumped away from the pony.

The two warriors circled one another, bodies crouched, knives brandished menacingly, blades glinting. Yellow Hand was taller and huskier, but Black Moon was quick, darting this way and that to avoid the deadly blade that slashed at him.

Yellow Hand fought with vicious intent, to obliterate Black Moon and wipe away all traces of his crimes.

Black Moon fought with the desperate fury of an animal that has been caged and will fight to the death never to relive the experience. But it was more than that which drove Black Moon. He fought to avenge his brother's death, and the deaths of all those people that were sure to ccme if the bluecoats attacked the village on Box Elder Creek. Yellow Hand's duplicity and falseness of heart could not go unpunished.

Beneath an array of midnight stars the two Oglalas engaged in a deadly hand-to-hand combat. Both warriors were skilled with knives. Each knew how to gouge and slice and draw blood. Yellow Hand backed Black Moon against a tree, and with swelling pride launched his attack, his face contorted with rage, eyes bulging in anticipation of the kill. Lashing out with his knife, he caught Black Moon on the chest with its tip, drawing first blood.

A hot pain ripped through Black Moon. His fury exploded, blinding him to everything now except his thirst for revenge. He was all motion, instinct and impulse, reflex and action. He lunged and felt a surge of triumph when his blade ripped through buckskin and struck flesh.

Yellow Hand let out a howl of pain. His gaze flew to the ripped sleeve revealing the gaping gash on his forearm. It was deep, to the bone. The surrounding muscle was spread wide, all white inside, not yet begun to bleed. It was the chance Black Moon was waiting for. With a cry, he hurled himself at Yellow Hand, hitting him with the impact cf a boulder.

Together they toppled to the ground, arms grappling, fists flying. The blood from their wounds mingled as it smeared over their bodies until it was impossible to tell whose blood was whose.

The strength seeped from Yellow Hand's mangled arm. With one powerful sweep, Black Moon snapped the knife from his hand and sent it flying off into the darkness. His own knife was still gripped firmly in his fist. He landed on top of Yellow Hand and glared down at him. His hand drew back, the blade glinting threateningly as it poised above his head in readiness for the fateful plunge.

Yellow Hand's eyes were large with terror and filled with pleading. There was an eerie expression, part fright, part resignation, stamped on his face. It was useless to beg. From his trembling lips issued his death song, just a few short words of it, and then…silence.

Black Moon staggered to his feet, panting heavily. It was done. His brother's death was avenged. Freedom was so close now he could almost touch it. Yet he lingered over Yellow Hand's lifeless body. His gaze strayed back to the walls of the fort. Everything he despised lay within those high adobe walls. He should have jumped astride the pony's back and fled to freedom. Yet what was freedom without the one thing that gave him reason to live? The one thing that kept his hopes alive all during the devastating winter that killed so many of his people and fed his spirit during his time in the white man's cage. The flat-water, the *Paha Sapa*, all the four-legged ones and the winged ones could never fill that place inside of him the way a certain pair of green eyes could do.

When he saw her tonight, he had been seized by an impulse to reach through the bars and grab her by the throat and squeeze until there was no more life left in her, the way her leaving had strangled the life out of him. But as she had stood beneath the window, all he saw was her face, pale and beautiful in the moonlight, the curve of her mouth, the glorious green of her eyes. And all he heard was the sound of her soft woman's voice, the same voice that called to him night after lonely night in his dreams. She had to know how much he hated her, and still she and only she had come to his rescue. And because of it, the hatred melted like snow in the sun, leaving in its place a dark hunger that had grown ever more urgent with each day she'd been gone and culminated with her appearance in the moonlight.

Black Moon turned his face toward the trees. Beyond them lay the hills and freedom…and emptiness. A savage frown marred his features. For many long moments he felt nowhere, alone and adrift. He squeezed his eyes shut and tried to concentrate on his breathing, pulling the sweetly-scented night air into his lungs as he thought of all the things he loved and of those he had lost. He called to them now for guidance.

He heard his mother calling from the spirit world, urging him to listen to his inner voice. He heard his brother telling him to follow his heart's path. He heard his father asking how many would suffer because he desired something that would never be his. To which he heard his own heated response. "Never? We will see about that." And with that memory, Black Moon knew exactly what he had to do.

CHAPTER 28

Katie lay on the cot, tears streaming unchecked down her cheeks, wetting the pillow. In setting Black Moon free she had lost him forever. An awful loneliness crept into her being. Now she was truly alone in the world. Yes, she thought unhappily, she had Josh, who proved tonight just how much he loved her. Come morning, they would be husband and wife. But what kind of marriage would it be predicated not on love, but on a bargain?

The thought of a loveless marriage to Josh McIntyre distressed her. The prospect of never seeing Black Moon again was almost more than she could bear. But to leave the country of her birth, to never again see the prairie at sunset or the Black Hills in springtime, never to breathe the sweet, fragrant air of summer along the Laramie or the crisp cold air of winter in a secluded valley along the Platte, that was perhaps the cruelest fate of all.

She had experienced the crowded streets of St. Louis, breathed in the soot-filled air, cringed at the cacophony of noise from steamboat whistles and clattering carriages. She had slept in a bed piled high with goose-down pillows and donned dresses of silk and satin like the ones she used to dream about. It had taken all that for her realize that her home was right here in the heart of Indian country. And now, to save the man she loved, she was going back to a place that was sure to suck the life out of her. How ironic. How unfair. But she had seen enough of life to know how unfair it could be.

Through the turmoil and confusion pounding in her brain, her father's lusty Irish brogue drifted back to her. "Katie, m'darlin', there're no guarantees in life." But McCabe was wrong. There was but one guarantee in life, and that was that she would lose everything and everyone she loved.

She had been unprepared to see Black Moon again after all this time. It wasn't that she had forgotten what a handsome, proud-looking man he was; it was just that she had underestimated the impact it would have on her. The face that had looked back at her through the bars was beginning to show faint lines etched around the eyes as he approached the age of thirty. But age only lent a raw, rugged appeal to his otherwise unblemished features.

There were so many things she had wanted to say to him, like how desperately she had missed him, and how very much she still loved him, and what a rotten scoundrel he was for betraying her with another woman, but there had been no time. And now she would never have the chance to tell him what was in her heart. With that bleak thought in mind, she rolled over and wept inconsolably into the pillow.

Through the tears a scent wafted into her nostrils, of the earth and sweet grass and a masculine ambrosia she would recognize anywhere. She bolted upright.

A figure stood by the window bathed in pearly moonlight. He was wearing plain buckskin leggings and a breech cloth. A familiar armband of red-dyed porcupine quills spanned his upper arm. His body was taut with aggression, the muscles of his naked chest expanding with every breath he took. Droplets of blood were visible from the gash in his flesh.

Katie's heart thumped wildly at the sight of him, the proud, arrogant stance and the midnight eyes that cut through the darkness. More than anything she wanted to run to him and throw her arms around him and hug him close. Her fingers ached to touch his brown skin, but something in the way he stood there prevented her from acting on her impulse.

Slowly, she rose from the bed, her eyes never leaving his. Through the darkness she whispered, "What are you doing here? Why haven't you gone? They will find you. You must…"

He took a menacing step toward her, cutting short her words.

There was something different about him. His face bore no smile to see her, only a tight, hard line across his mouth. His eyes held no welcome, only a dark threat. She had seen that look before, the very first night in the cave, when she had awakened to find him sitting across the fire looking back at her with bristling hostility and hatred. At the time she had been too traumatized by her experience to feel any fear. But now, standing an arm's length away from him, she felt the peril.

A quick glance down at the knife in his hand revealed a dark stain upon its blade. She had given him the chance to escape knowing it could mean someone else's life, so why was the proof of it suddenly so shocking to her?

He moved slowly toward her, danger and aggression in his step. She could see him clearly now and grimaced at the ugly bruise at his neck where blood welled just beneath the surface. For the first time she was afraid of him. She backed away from the stranger he had become.

For several tense moments he said and did nothing. There was an unreadable look in his eyes. Then, without warning, he reached forward and yanked her around by her arm.

Katie felt the bite of the rope around her wrists and knew instantly what he was up to.

"No!" she cried. "You don't understand."

But from his actions, it was clear to her that Black Moon was beyond understanding or caring. He worked swiftly to overpower her, tying her wrists with the same rope that had nearly choked the life out of him. He bound her mouth with strips he ripped from the bed sheet with his teeth. With an unceremonious jolt he slung her over his shoulder and headed for the window. He was about to climb out the same way he had climbed in when her rifle leaning against the wall caught his eyes. He grabbed it on his way out.

Katie struggled to no avail. She was plunked none too gently onto the waiting pony she had gotten from Jasper Gillette. Black Moon jumped up behind her, his strong arms going around her to grasp the coarse mane. With a sharp kick to the horse's flanks, they were galloping away from Fort Laramie.

They rode like the wind, with only the light of the moon to guide them across the dark, flat land. When it seemed they'd been riding forever, Black Moon finally pulled up and brought the tired, frothing horse to a halt.

He chose a spot well concealed among the trees. Without speaking a word to her, he sliced the rope that bound her wrists and used it to hobble the horse. Then he set about making a small fire.

The evening lay before them, cool and sweet. Katie sat on the ground before the fire, her knees pulled up to her chest and her arms wrapped around them, thinking about the first time they met. It had been across flames such as these that she had first looked into those ominous black eyes. Now, as then, she felt the menace of him, the uncompromising hostility, the ancient pride of the Sioux radiating around him like a halo of light.

Look at him, she huffed to herself, *sitting there like he owns the world*. She would never forgive him for carrying her off like a sack of potatoes and giving her absolutely no say in the matter. She had always made her own decisions, and right or wrong, had abided by them. Her decision to marry Josh McIntyre, albeit made under extreme pressure, was one she had intended to live up to. How dare this arrogant Indian take that decision out of her hands by sheer brute force?

She also did not care for the way he was looking at her, as if he had not seen a woman in God knew how long. If he wanted her at all, it could only be her body he craved. Hadn't he already proved that he did not want her love?

She sat there growing more indignant by the minute. At last, unable to contain her turbulent emotions, she jumped to her feet. "What are you looking at?" she exclaimed. She began to pace before the fire, shooting angry glances at him. "You look at me as if you have not been with a woman in years, but we both know better than that." Her tone turned scornful. "No doubt, Good Deeds knows."

Black Moon rose fluidly from his spot before the fire and blocked her path, halting her pacing. Bringing himself up to his full height, he towered over her and glared down at her with suppressed rage. "How would you know what I have been doing?" he spoke. His voice sounded like an animal growl from deep in his throat. "You have not been here for a long time."

Katie stood her ground before him, just as she did that first night in the cave, refusing to be cowed by him. "All right!" she cried. "I left. But I had to. I had to find out who I am…what I am. That is something you will never understand. All you know is that you are. I did not know. I had to find out."

"You are no better than a Crow thief who sneaks into the village to steal ponies and leaves without a trace."

The contempt in his voice felt like a backhanded slap. "I told your mother I would be back. Did she not tell you so? Ask her why—"

"My mother's bones are scattered across the prairie," he interrupted savagely. "Whatever words you said to her died with her."

Katie stifled a gasp. "I…I did not know." She pressed a hand to her mouth, willing herself not to cry, and looked away, torn by pain and confusion. "Why did she not tell you?"

"Perhaps because she knew you would not return."

"No, it is not that. Your mother never approved of our marriage. Maybe it was her way of getting you to forget about me in the hope that you would find another, which is just what you did."

He met her gaze with a dark smile.

"Only cowards turn from the truth," Katie said, "no matter how ruthless it is."

Neither confirming nor denying her accusation, he said, "We will never know the truth about what you told my mother."

Her green eyes flared wide at that. "First you call me a Crow thief, and now you call me a liar?"

He did not answer, but instead questioned bitterly, "And did you find what you were looking for when you went away?"

He was mocking her, driving her into irrational fury. All the long months suddenly converged upon her like rushing water, overwhelming the banks of her emotions. She threw herself at him, small balled fists beating at his chest as her voice rose to a pitch bordering on hysteria.

"You arrogant, insufferable man! Do you know what I discovered?" Her beautiful face was flushed with rage and her green eyes blazed. "I discovered that I am nothing without you. Do you hear me? Nothing!"

His hands went out to catch hers. He brought her arms to a stiff halt and silenced her with the sheer force of his eyes.

Katie trembled. Even now he had the power to reduce her to a shiver with his glance alone. Her throat went dry at the thought of what just one caress could do. She was trying hard to remember how much his unfaithfulness had wounded her, but with the meeting of their eyes came a familiar heart-throb. All of a sudden none of it mattered any more. All she saw was his eyes burning into hers with desire written in their ebony depths. All she could think of was the heart-stopping passion she knew waited in his arms. She closed her eyes in anticipation of the inevitable.

But the passionate give and take that had always been a part of their lovemaking was not forthcoming on this night. Instead of a tender caress, she received a harsh yank on her arm with a pain that burned clear to her shoulder as he pulled her forward and crushed her fiercely to his chest. One arm snaked around her waist and pinned her there with such force that she could scarcely draw breath, while his other hand grasped the hair at the back of her head and roughly pulled her head back.

For several moments his gaze seared into hers and his mouth stretched into a cruel smile before it covered hers in a hard and angry kiss.

There was no gentleness in his kiss, no softness in the lips that raked over hers. His tongue filled her mouth, plundering the deep, sweet recesses, claiming it all over again. This was not the careful lover she knew, but a stranger intent on having his way at the expense of her pride.

Tearing his mouth from hers, he swept her up into his arms and carried her with long, wolf-like strides to a spot beneath the trees, where he forced her to the ground and covered her body with the lean length of his. She struggled beneath him, trying to push him away with her strength that was no match for his, while a distant part of herself welcomed his touch even if it was rough and forceful. He seized her wrists in a cruel grip and held them above her head as his mouth came down over hers in a kiss filled with hunger and rage.

There was something untamed and savage about him. With no care to her feelings or pleasure, he pushed her dress up past her thighs, forced himself between her legs and took her in a heated rush. A guttural claim of possession tore from his throat when he drove himself into her, pumping harder and faster, as if nothing in the world mattered to him except the satisfaction of his pent-up lust.

In the heat of his assault, Katie's legs wrapped around him, drawing him in deeper as she matched him thrust for thrust in a desperate attempt to be a part of him in any way she could. With one final thrust her body convulsed in great waves that were neither pleasure nor satisfaction, but the desperate throes of a need that went beyond anything sexual to the deepest core of her being.

CHAPTER 29

Black Moon's breathing was erratic and he was sweating despite the cool night air. There was no fulfillment in what he had just done, no triumph to be had in overpowering a woman who had not the strength to fight back. There was just a surge of self-disgust accompanying the sating of his lust.

He looked up at the moon surrounded by stars in the sky. One of his Cheyenne friends had told him once that the white people were like the stars, so many they could never be counted. Of all the stars in the sky, why did his fate have to be entwined with this particular one that had the power to hurt him and reduce him to nothing more than a rutting stallion?

He thought about the way she had rained her fury on him and how the long waiting and wanting had melted into nothingness. It had been worth it, every agonizing moment, each tormented longing, just to see her again like that, her beautiful face flushed with rage and her green eyes blazing up at him.

He turned his head to look at her now. Her eyes were closed, but a single starlit teardrop glistened on her cheek. As much as he tried to hate her for the way she had hurt him, he hated himself even more for having inflicted his brutal lust upon her. He had not meant for it to happen that way. One moment he'd been glaring into those glorious green eyes, ever so aware of the rise and fall of her breasts beneath the supple skin of her dress, breathing in the fragrance of her hair, and remembering what it was like to be moving inside of her. In the next moment he had been tearing at her like a man gone mad, driven by want and need in a way he could never have imagined himself capable of doing. If she thought the worst of him before, what must she think of him now?

The moon climbed higher in the sky as he lay awake listening to the sounds of the night and the gentle breathing of the woman asleep beside him. A familiar, predictable longing welled up inside of him. Rolling onto his side, he slipped his hand beneath her dress to caress the contour of her hip.

Her body tensed as she came awake in anticipation of another assault of his merciless lust, but he put a hand on her shoulder and gently pulled her onto her back. He could smell the grass, its midnight dampness crushed beneath their bodies as he rolled on top of her. From a nearby creek the croaking of bullfrogs and the chirping of crickets mingled with the beating of his heart.

His gaze caressed her face, from the smooth skin of her forehead, to the long sweeping lashes framing her magnificent eyes, to the mouth whose bottom lip quivered partly in fear, but mostly with anticipation. This time when he brought his mouth to hers, it was with a gentleness that lingered over the soft, generous curve of her lips. And when his tongue filled her mouth, it was with the sweet searching of a lover discovering its secrets all over again.

He took his time undressing her, slipping the hide dress up over her head, the pitch of his breathing increasing as her delicate white skin was revealed to his eager eyes. A strangled groan escaped his throat when he gazed upon her naked body in the moonlight. One day her breasts would belong to the child she would bear, but tonight they belonged only to him. He cupped each one in turn in his warm hand, running his palm across the nipples that felt like ripe berries beneath his touch, squeezing them, rolling them between his fingers, bringing his face to the rosy points thrusting upwards to meet his hungry mouth and tasting their succulent sweetness like a boy discovering such things for the first time.

The movements of her body beneath his charged Black Moon with a desire that was wilder than any that had come before. The sheer force of it blinded him to the pain she had caused him. His passion burned hot and unchecked. He wanted to savor every single moment of this encounter, to experience each nerve-tingling sensation to the fullest. He wanted to fill her up with himself, but he held back. He would take her again, but this time he would wait until she was ready for him, until his fingers had probed her soft woman places and made her wet.

Her hands were all over him, exploring, feeling, touching, teasing, discovering all over again the softness of his skin and the hardness of his desire. Wrapping her fingers around the hard vibrant part of him that strained beneath his breech cloth, she stroked softly, then faster and faster, until it throbbed between her fingers and deep guttural moans came from his throat.

Black Moon thought he would explode with hard, driving pleasure. It was only his desperate determination to bring her with him that gave him the will to capture her hands and pin them above her head where they could work no more of their maddening magic on his heated body.

This time when he wedged his knees between her legs, she was ready for him, responding with a breathless cry and a willing acquiescence in the way they opened wide to receive him and then wound around him, pulling him closer, swallowing him up in her warm, wet passion.

Her body was fuller and richer than when she had come to him four winters past. Deep into her womanly wetness he thrust, harder, faster, creating a rhythm that resounded like a drumbeat throughout his entire being. There was an undercurrent of animal-like desire in the insistent way their bodies merged. In velvet words of love their bodies did the talking, becoming a single writhing thing until the passion that burned strong and hot converged into one awesome pitch that shot high into the darkness, up through the veil of night to meet the brilliance of the stars.

Afterwards, Katie tried hard not to think. A midnight breeze cooled her fevered brow. Her body ached from the way he had pressed his lust upon her. Her muscles felt torn and bruised, her legs were sore from the way he had forced them apart. But it was more than the physical pain of his forceful possession that had brought the tears to her eyes after it.

More than the thought that he cared so little for her that he would use her in such a manner. To her shock and dismay, it was the shameful, humiliating way her body had responded, for in the heat of his assault, her legs had wrapped themselves around him, drawing him in deeper, and she had matched him thrust for thrust in a desperate attempt to be a part of him in any way she could.

But now, as she lay in his arms, the midnight air evaporated the sheen of perspiration from her naked body, and in his touch was the welcome home she had longed for. Now when she rolled onto her side to face him, she saw the face of the man she loved, the one she remembered from her dreams, the one she had sacrificed everything to save.

He lay on his back without moving, one arm crooked behind his head, staring straight up at the sky, the scent of sweat and rawhide on his skin. By the light of the moon she could see the rope burn that smudged his neck, and she shivered to think that but for seconds it would have been too late and she would not be here with him like this.

The thought of his narrow escape forced an unwanted memory, that of the promise she had made to another man. Her mind cried *tell him*, while her heart pleaded, *no, not now. Don't break the spell of this moment.* She would ride with him to Box Elder Creek so that he could warn his people of the impending attack, and then she would do the hardest thing she'd ever had to do—explain to him why she could not stay. Then she would ride out of the village, and his life, forever.

Black Moon's voice drew her away from her thoughts. "I did not mean to hurt you," he said. "If there is anything I can do that would make up for what I have done, ask it of me."

She raised herself onto an elbow and placed a hand over his lips to silence him. Her voice was low and husky with the weight of satisfied desire. "I am hurt, but the pain comes from within. From all the months I stayed away, knowing that my place was here with you. And from your taking Good Deeds as your wife."

He grasped her hand in his and drew it away so that he might speak. "I should not have let you think that Good Deeds is my wife."

She looked at him with starlight in her eyes. "But you share a lodge with her."

"I did it for the child, my brother's son, to protect him from Gray Wolf. And, yes," he admitted, "I did it also for Good Deeds. She was alone and had no one. A woman alone cannot survive. But Good Deeds was never my wife.' His gaze burned strongly into hers. "I have only one wife."

Katie's heart soared even as a part of her was ashamed for having thought him guilty of betrayal. "We have both made mistakes," she said. "Mine was in thinking that my place could be anywhere but here, and for the jealousy that let me think you had taken Good Deeds as your wife. And yours was in not trusting me to return to you. Even if you did not hear it from your mother, your heart should have told you that I would come back."

She nestled against him, kissing his bare shoulder and tasting the salt of his flesh on her lips. There was so much more she wanted to say, like why she was going to leave him again, but she could not summon the courage to do so, not when there were other words that had never been spoken between them and which suddenly seemed so necessary to say. For all the nights she had lain in his arms, before she was his wife, and after, for all the love that raged between them, she longed to hear the words that had never been uttered.

"What are you thinking?" she asked.

"I was remembering what it was like to hold you like this, before you went away, before the sickness took so many of my people and they were hunted like prey, before the agency at Deer Creek and the soldiers' iron house. Nothing will ever be the same. The only thing that has not changed is what I feel for you which has only grown stronger since the day I brought you to live among my people."

Katie moved out of his embrace and turned her body toward him. Looking into his eyes, she said, "I love you and only you."

"My heart rejoices," he said. "And I–"

"No," she cut in. "Not in Lakota. You asked what you could do to make up for what you did. It is this. You can say it in my language."

Black Moon hesitated. In all his life he had never spoken the white man's language except to speak her name. The expression on her face, of love and expectation, told him that it was something she needed to hear.

He asked, "How is it said?"

She spoke the words slowly, deliberately. "I love you."

For several long moments he gazed into the eyes of the woman who had brought him such incredible joy and such deep sorrow, the one he had fought his attraction to as if fighting an enemy. She was the one star in the heavens that *Wakan Tanka* had singled out only for him. He brought his hand to her face and caressed her cheek with the back of his finger, and said softly, "I love you."

Katie knew how difficult it was for him to speak the white man's language and that he would never do so again. She favored him with a long luminous smile and settled back into his arms.

The red glow of dawn was peeking over the treetops when Black Moon slipped his arm from beneath Katie's head and rose. The cool morning air nipped at his naked flesh as he pulled on his buckskin leggings and slipped his breech cloth in place.

Without his warm body beside her, Katie shivered. Reaching her arms up over her head, she stretched in the grass like a contented kitten. She smiled up at him, a teasing, inviting little smile that left little doubt as to what she was thinking. He felt the rising of his desire and was tempted to take her again right then and there in the damp grass, but instead, he retrieved her dress from the grass and tossed it to her.

"How long will it be before the bluecoats begin their march?" he asked.

The reality of the situation chased away Katie's mischievous thoughts. "Seven suns. Maybe a little more."

Holding out his hand to her, he said, "There is no time to waste. If we ride fast, we will have time to warn the people, strike the lodges and flee." He pulled her to her feet.

"You are not going to stay and fight them?" she asked as she dressed.

He knelt to untie the pony's hobbles. "I will fight, but first I must get the old ones and the little ones to safety. We have seen that the guns of the bluecoats make no distinction."

She came to stand beside him at the pony's side. "Will you have enough warriors to fight them?"

"I will fight them alone if I must."

He placed his hands at her waist and lifted her onto the pony's back. Then he jumped up behind her, reached forward to grasp a handful of mane, and putting his heels to the pony's flanks, they took off at a gallop.

Black hair and red whipped out behind them as they rode. Every pounding hoof beat carried them further away from Fort Laramie and closer to Box Elder Creek. Each breath Katie took brought her closer to saying goodbye to her one true love.

CHAPTER 30

Claw untied the stiff rawhide container that held the winter count and unrolled the hide. He had begun this winter count when he was a young man. More than seventy snows had fallen on his shoulders, fifty since he had begun his drawings. Each year he had taken his paints from the small hide bag and drawn something to commemorate that year. There were drawings of sun-gazings, of warriors returning victorious, of the year the Pawnee attacked, of deep-snow winters, of the time the banks of the Big Muddy flooded its banks and several people drowned.

As his gaze moved reverently over the hide, it came to rest upon the drawing of a fiery cloud that appeared the day his first son was born, the tender-hearted son gone now many winters.

With a beleaguered sigh, Claw's gaze moved to the drawing of the darkened moon that had appeared in the sky the night his second son was born. So different they were, one born under a fiery sky, the other born in darkness. And now, only one remained, trapped somewhere in the soldiers' cage, perhaps never to be seen or heard from again.

Claw ceased drawing on the hide when his first son died. But now, looking at the hide unfurled before him, he felt the need to draw again. But what picture could he draw that would depict what was happening now?

A voice tugged gently at his ear.

You know what picture to draw.

It was the voice of his wife, gone back to their mother, the Earth.

He does not deserve it, he answered in his mind.

He, more than anyone else, deserves it.

He has torn the people apart. Broken the sacred circle.

He gives them reason to unite against a common enemy.

His ways lead to death and destruction.

His ways lead to salvation.

Claw sat motionless, thinking on this for a long time. But how would he know what picture to draw that would best tell his son's story?

His woman's voice was soft and cool in his mind. *You already know what picture to draw.*

Yes, he knew.

He preferred cottonwoods buds because the paint made from those brown, gum-covered buds lasted a long time, and this was one drawing he wanted to last long after his time on earth was finished. Dipping his quill into the paint, he began to draw. When he was finished, he waited for the paint to dry, then rolled up the hide and set it aside. Tired, he leaned against his reed backrest and closed his eyes to contemplate what he had drawn.

***

Turning Hawk sat in the center of the lodge, his nose like a claw jutting from a thin face weathered by age. In a voice hollow with disillusionment, he said to the men seated in a circle around the fire, "When the kind-hearted son of Claw was murdered, although I knew which name was whispered behind the lodge skins as the killer, I did not call for vengeance. When the fierce-hearted son of Claw was captured and put into the white man's cage, though that one has always been a thorn in my side, I did not rejoice. Even now, with the people scattered and the bluecoats angry and looking for a fight, even now I say peace is the only way."

The pipe with the red polished bowl and stem wrapped in red flannel moved around the circle from east to west. Turning Hawk was beginning to lose his hold over the people. When the pipe reached him, he dropped an ember into the bowl and puffed four smokes, letting the smoke curl out slowly through pursed lips.

"The coming of the white men is no different from any other bad thing," he said calmly. "We learn from it all."

Lone Horn shifted in his cross-legged position. His lips curled over white teeth when he opened his mouth to speak. "A very long time ago you earned the right to wear the feather of the warrior bird in your hair," he said to Turning Hawk. "But that was before you put away the war lance and took up the pipe of peace. My own feather stands upright in my hair for having counted many coup, and not so many winters past that it is beyond anyone's memory," he added scornfully.

He turned his attention to the others. "What we have learned from the coming of the white men is that it divides us. There are those who put their lodges by the soldier fort and live on the handouts of the white men. There are those who choose to live the free life and bring down their food in the old way. There are those who call for peace at every turn, even when we are hunted like prey by the white men who want not only our land but our lives. There are those who would fight to keep our lands and our lives."

His voice rose when he turned back to Turning Hawk, filling the lodge with vehemence. "When the Lakota are divided, they are weakened. You talk of peace, but there is no peace here. The women sleep in their moccasins and are afraid of any unfamiliar sound. The children are warned not to laugh or to cry too loudly. People are quarreling with each other. And all are afraid. Is that peace? I am finished speaking. Now I will listen."

A disturbing silence infiltrated the lodge. Some men shifted uncomfortably in their spots. Others cast their eyes downward to avoid Lone Horn's stare.

Turning Hawk lifted the stem upwards. "This pipe is a sacred thing. It knows when you speak the truth." He offered the stem to Lone Horn, saying as he did, "I give you this pipe, for you do speak truly." He looked at the gaunt faces around him, adding, "But this is why we must strive for peace with the white men. Only then will they see that we mean them no harm. Their fear of us is like wood thrown on the fire. The old way—"

"The old way is dying!"

The entrance flap was jerked aside and Black Moon stormed into the lodge, startling the others and obliterating the rest of Turning Hawk's words with his strong voice. He tossed to the ground the rifle he had taken from Katie's room at the fort, and pointed to it. "Here is the new way. The new power. It can bring more food into our lodges than we can get with bows and arrows. It can kill our enemies from a greater distance."

As he spoke, he circled them, his fierce eyes moving from one face to another. "The white men are only men. Just as we are. It is this thunder iron that makes them so powerful. With it we can fight them on the battlefield and kill them."

"Kill, kill, kill. Is that all you can think of?" Turning Hawk said with disgust. "Gone are the days when all we took was a man's braids. Now it is his life." Appealing to the others, he argued, "What happened to the old teachings that say a greater man is the one who merely touches an enemy and shames him instead of killing him? Any animal can kill. Only man has the power to make the decision not to."

"Man is no different from any other animal," Black Moon countered. "Two-legged creatures learn from the four-legged ones and the winged ones to do what they must to survive. What do the buffalo do when a pack of true-dogs goes after one of their young ones? Does the old bull tell the others to remain peaceful? No! They surround the little yellow hair to protect it. How can we protect our young ones, our old ones, our women, if we do not fight? We have seen it happen over and over again. When the white man comes into our country, he takes what he wants, the buffalo, the beaver, the land, Lakota lives. These things are nothing to him. Do you think he makes any distinction between warriors and holy men? Between men who talk of war and men who cry for peace?"

"Black Moon is right," Lone Horn said. "Gone are the days when we fought our enemies for honor. Now we fight for our lives."

Silence spread in every direction, none daring to refute what they all knew in their hearts to be true.

Turning Hawk leveled a look at Black Moon, contempt rifling his dark eyes. "I know that when you leave here, you will take many with you. Some will follow because their hatred of the whites is as great as yours. Others will follow for personal gain and glory. But I will stay behind because I choose peace. I, Turning Hawk, chief among the Oglalas, have spoken."

"You are a fool," Black Moon spat. "The old way has been dying for years and you know it, just as my brother knew it." He saw the wince in Turning Hawk's eyes, but pressed on ruthlessly. "You hide behind your ceremonies and words of peace because you are afraid to fight. But do not worry, old grandfather, it is not you I have come for."

Riveting his attention now on the others, Black Moon said, "Do you believe the words of a leader who would deny his warriors a war? We did not ask for this war, but it is here. I have come for all those who call themselves Lakota warriors. The ones who are taught to lay down their lives for the people. There is a dangerous long-claws coming here to destroy us. But this is not the four-legged warrior we know. It is the white man. The one who wears a blue coat instead of a shaggy brown one. I have come for all those who will fight the bear." He cast a sulfurous look at Turning Hawk and said with a sneer, "I, Black Moon, Oglala warrior, have spoken."

With that he reached down, scooped the rifle from the ground and strode from the lodge.

Outside, he squinted against the sun. His long, angry strides had not taken him far when a voice called out to him from behind. Lone Horn fell into place beside his friend. "It is good to see you, *kola.*"

Without breaking stride, Black Moon scoffed, "You look like you are talking to a ghost."

"How did you get out of the white man's jail?"

"My woman helped me escape. You remember her, do you not? She is the one you once said would never be mine."

"Yes, I remember. I did not think any good would come from wanting another man's woman. I only wish..." A guilty look washed across the Minniconjou's face. "I wish it had been me who helped you escape."

"There was nothing you could have done. They would have killed you and made your children fatherless. Besides, the people needed you to lead them away from that place."

"How did she do it?"

Black Moon told him how Katie helped him escape, brushing his hair aside to show him the bruise at his neck.

Lone Horn's eyes widened and his mouth fell open. But when he heard the part about Yellow Hand's duplicity, his expression hardened like rock. "That one paid well for his crimes." He glanced away, his eyes ashamed to meet his friend's. "The woman," he began. "I was wrong about her. She has much courage. She is right for you."

"She told me the bluecoats are planning to attack us here."

"How does she know this?"

"I do not know, but I intend to find out."

"What will she do now?" Lone Horn asked.

Black Moon's brow furrowed questioningly. "What do you mean?"

"She is white. The whites are coming here to kill us. She has already seen her white family killed. She has no family left. Why should she stay?"

"She stays because I am her family," Black Moon curtly replied.

"If we survive this, it will mean always being on the run."

"She is free to go any time, but she will not." Yet even as he said it, Black Moon was not so sure. It was the way she had fought him back at the fort, as if she had already made up her mind to remain there. Something was not right with her. He sensed it.

"Do you think the others will follow?" Lone Horn asked. The sunlight glanced off Black Moon's lean shoulders when he pushed his doubt about Katie aside and shrugged. "I made a vow to protect the people. With them or without them, I will hold to that vow."

"You no longer wear the shirt," the other noted.

Black Moon would have tolerated the painful reminder from no one other than this trusted friend. He stopped in his tracks and aimed a hard look at the Minniconjou. "Do you think I need the bighorn shirt to be loyal to myself? When Turning

Hawk talks of peace, he is really talking about loyalty. Above all, a man must be loyal to himself, or he has nothing. I look to war as a way of keeping true to myself."

"Is there no way to compromise?"

Black Moon smiled grimly. "I am surprised to hear you talk like this."

"It is only because I fear what will happen to the people if we are divided. Remember, my friend, I, too, took the vow of shirt wearer to protect the people."

"There is no such thing as compromise," Black Moon said. "All it means is that there is a contradiction. One for this, one for that. When faced with a contradiction, remember that only one side can be truthfully right. I follow the voice I arrived on earth with."

"And what does that voice tell you to do about the other woman?"

Black Moon looked away at the reminder of Good Deeds. What would he do with her now that Katie had returned? There may have been room for the two of them in the lodge, but not in his heart. He would have to find another husband for Good Deeds. But who? The answer seemed suddenly so clear.

He turned back to his friend, and said slyly, "She is pleasing to look at, is she not?"

Lone Horn guessed at once what he was suggesting and opened his mouth to protest.

But Black Moon spoke up quickly, staunching any objection. "She is a hard worker. Your wife might welcome another pair of hands to help with the cooking and scraping the hides. Your children might like a young one to play with."

"Why me?" the other man groaned.

"Because you are the only one I would trust with my nephew. And with Good Deeds. She is a good woman and deserves better than what I can give her."

Lone Horn's expression turned thoughtful. "I will do it," he said. "But she must come to me willingly. I do not force myself on women. And I must speak with my wife. If she agrees, then I will take her."

Black Moon laughed and jabbed an elbow into his

friend's ribs. "Ho! So this brave Lakota warrior answers to a woman."

"No more than you do."

The smile faded from Black Moon's face. "It is true," he admitted. "Ever since she came into my life everything I have done is for her."

Lone Horn looked at his friend with poignant understanding. "All the time she was gone, I could see how much it weighed upon your heart. Yet now that she has returned, you seem much troubled."

"The bluecoats," Black Moon reminded him.

"Yes, the bluecoats. But it is more than that. Something in your look speaks of things unsettled between you and the woman. Where is she now, this woman you do all these things for?"

"Since the death of my mother, my father has been living in his sister's lodge. I sent her to find him when we rode in. Do you know where my aunt's lodge is pitched?"

"It is at the end of the tribal crescent," Lone Horn answered.

Black Moon turned in that direction. It was time to ask Katie the questions that had been preying on his mind since he returned to the village that fateful day more than a year ago to find her gone. Time to find out just how she knew the bluecoats were going to attack. Time to ask why she put up such a struggle back at the soldier town. He was not sure he wanted to hear the answers, but there were two things he had never run from. One was a fight. The other was the truth.

***

Black Moon swept aside the entrance to the lodge and bent to enter. When he saw his father sleeping, he hesitated, uncertain of what Claw's reaction would be to see him. But whatever apprehension he felt was quickly dispelled when Claw awakened and Black Moon recognized the welcome-home look in his father's eyes.

Claw set about emptying his pipe of ashes and stoking a new ember. "When I heard you were captured, for the first time I was glad that your mother was not still among us, for I do not think her heart already broken could have sustained such a blow. My own heart is glad that you have returned to us." He puffed on his long-stemmed pipe, then offered it to his son, but Black Moon held back, making no move to take it.

"I understand your hesitation," Claw said, "but you have earned the right to smoke the long-stem."

Black Moon sat down beside his father. His fine-shaped fingers closed around the pipe stem and drew it to his lips. He took four puffs and handed the pipe back to Claw.

"When I was a boy my own father told me that I was destined to be *Wicasa Wakan*," Claw said. "As a holy man I know that the Sun is the all-powerful chief of the spirit world and the Sky is the source from which each man derives his personality. I understand the beginning of things. I am keeper of our tribal memories. This pipe we smoke comes from my father and his father before him. It is unadorned. There is nothing to distract from the truth it holds and what it sees. And what this pipe sees now is a son whose face still looks much like the boy I remember, yet it also sees a troubled heart."

"It is summer," Black Moon said. "When I was a boy, summer was a season of fat moons and juicy berries. A season for giving thanks. But the world is turned upside down."

Claw placed a hand on his son's lean, brown shoulder, and asked, "What troubles you?"

"The bluecoats are coming here to kill us."

"Is there time to strike the lodges and flee?"

"Yes, if we hurry."

"Do you have enough warriors to fight them?"

Black Moon nodded. "I have sent riders to our Cheyenne friends to join the fight. There will be enough to defeat them...this time."

"Then what is it? What is wrong?"

"It is my woman. I lost her once to my brother, then to a Crow thief and then to the white world. Now I fear I am going to lose her again, and I do not know why or how to stop it."

"Ah, the woman." Claw heaved an understanding sigh. "You have fought long and hard for her, but have you considered that she was never meant to stay with us?"

Black Moon jumped to his feet. "Then why was she brought to me in the first place?"

"Perhaps to test you."

"At what?"

Claw shook his head. "Who am I to question the workings of the Great Spirit?"

"Oh, what she does to me!"

"The seasons ahead will be difficult. She can only distract you from what you must do."

"I am not talking about what she does to me beneath the robes. I am talking about the clarity she brings me. She helps me see what it is I must do and gives me the strength to do it."

Claw nodded thoughtfully and puffed on the pipe.

"Tell me what you are thinking," his son said.

"I am remembering the time I went to the sons of Turning Hawk to ask for the woman for you and was denied. When I told you the woman would never be yours, your temper was as explosive as the soldiers' big wagon guns. I am thinking about how wrong I was. You defied all the odds for the right to claim her as your own, and for the first time I see it for what it truly is. Your love for her goes beyond all reason or logic to the deepest part of your being. If there is anything that can bring a mighty Oglala warrior such as yourself to your knees, it is not a broken vow and a stripped honor. It is not war or imprisonment. It is a woman with hair the color of the setting sun. A love so strong can carry a man to the highest pinnacle or to the deepest depth. If you fear you are going to lose her again, there is only one way to find out what is in her heart. You must ask her. I sent her to the water with the paunch. Go to her. But before you go..."

He reached for the buffalo hide upon which he kept the winter count. Unfurling the hide, he spread it on the ground and beckoned for his son to come close.

Black Moon knelt on one knee, his black hair cascading across his shoulders as he leaned forward. There, on the hide was the history of his people, the yearly happenings told in his father's drawings. The count went back to when his father was younger than he was now. He smiled when he recognized some of the events from his boyhood. But the smile froze upon his face when he came to the final drawing. All the others were done in dark paint. Only this one bore a splash of color.

It was of two people astride a sorrel pony, their hair whipping about in the wild wind, the one in front with hair as black as night, that of the one behind as red as the setting sun.

CHAPTER 31

*H*e found her sitting beneath the sticky-wood trees by the creek. Her face was tilted upwards toward the yellow warmth of the sun. The delicate profile etched against the panorama caught the breath in his throat with its stark beauty—the small, straight nose, the clear, unfurrowed brow, the long, sweeping lashes, the full lips, the unblemished cheek, the smooth line of the jaw. Her long red hair hung loose about her shoulders and flowed down her back with scarcely a ripple, like the calm water in which her breath-stopping face was reflected.

For an instant Black Moon was transported back to the night in the cave when he had sat by the fire watching her sleeping across the flames. Like smoke from a distant fire, a strange, unwelcome sensation had crept into his being that night, signaling the start of a hunger unlike any he had ever known, a craving not for food or water but for something dangerous that haunted him to this day. Little could he have known then that the desire stirring in his loins for the beautiful, outspoken white woman who should have been his enemy would grow into the kind of love that comes only once in a man's lifetime. Only she could make him want her with the primal force of an animal and yet need her as only a man could need.

They had traveled a long and difficult path since that night. He had fought hard for her, not only against those who would harm her, but against his bitterness toward the whites, defying his own nature to win her, only to lose her. Although he had told no one, not even his good friend Lone Horn, all that long, cold winter she'd been gone he thought he would die from the loneliness. The silence of her absence had haunted him, following him deep into the wilderness, where every moan of the wind called her name and each snowflake that fell blanketed his heart with despair. And now, that same sense of anguish was creeping into his being, starting as a little warning whisper and growing into a thunderous roar, telling him there was the chance that she would leave him again, this time never to return.

He inhaled the ripe summer air into his lungs, hoping to find the strength he needed to ask her the question and to hear her answer. He knew how to fight his enemies, but how could he fight his own heart that robbed him of all logic? He should never have brought her to live among his people. He should have sent her back to her own people, and then questions like the one nagging at him now would never have to be asked, and answers like the one he was reluctant to hear would never have to be spoken. Yet even as he stood there watching her, Black Moon had no regrets, for he knew he would have done it all over again.

She was the most contrary woman he had ever known, the kind of woman a man dreams of and hopes to find. She was courageous and resilient and beautiful, so very beautiful that each time he looked at her he felt the hardening of his desire pressing at his loincloth. But it was more than the smoothness of her skin, her splendid green eyes and slender body that thrilled him. It was the way she and only she had encouraged him to follow his warrior's heart. It was the way she and only she had not looked upon him with shame when he had been stripped of the bighorn shirt. It was her stubborn pride that was an equal match for his own. It was the way she challenged him, defied him, and dared him to be all that he was.

She would never be like the other women. She may have understood a warrior's need to take a scalp, but she would never carry the hair trophy atop a pole in the dance. She did not cut her hair or gash her arms when loved ones died, nor paint her face when the war party returned victorious. The brief time they lived together as husband and wife she had cooked his favorite things—hump ribs, berry sauce, turnip soup—just the way he liked them, yet he suspected it was only because they were her favorite things, as well. She did not dance to the beat of the drums, yet he sometimes heard her singing to herself in the white man's language. When other women would have succumbed to the tragedies and cruelties she had endured, she only grew stronger. No, she was not like the other woman.

Turning Hawk and the others were right when they said she carried a great power, but they were fools not to recognize where her power really lay. She did not carry the power to find the buffalo herds that were dwindling in the northern country. Her power could not summon the rains during the harsh summer moons when the grasses were so dry they burned up and sent the game scattering. She could not chase away the coughing sickness any more than all the medicine man's chanting and rattling could do. Her power lay not in what could be seen but in what could be felt. She had the power to tame the savage heart of a fierce Lakota warrior such as himself, to quell the turmoil that raged within him over the rightness or wrongness of the path he followed, to go against everything he knew about the white people by wanting this one special white woman, to fill him with her courage when his own wavered, to lift his head in pride when others looked upon him in shame, and to instill in his being a love so potent and deep it could only have been a gift from *Wakan Tanka*.

Coming to terms with his hatred of the white people and his love for this white woman had been the most difficult battle he had ever waged. And now, after winning her for himself and feeling his pride swell with triumph, was he going to lose her? He reminded himself that he was an Oglala warrior. This was one more battle to fight. He had never run from a battle before, and he would not start now. His own war cry pierced his tortured thoughts. "Strong hearts, brave hearts to the front! Cowards to the rear!"

***

Katie turned her face from the sun and toward the still water. A small turtle emerged from the creek and hoisted itself onto the grassy bank to drink the dew that lingered beneath the shade.

When Bone Bracelet had given birth, she had placed the infant's umbilical cord inside a fetish she had fashioned out of hide in the form of a turtle, explaining to Katie that with their hard shells those little creatures were difficult to kill. She heaved a sigh and wished her own heart were as tough as the turtle's shell, capable of withstanding all the pain and sorrow that had come her way. Instead, it had been open and vulnerable, like an unsuspecting field mouse at the jaws of the wolf.

Black Moon had taught her that the wolf was a misunderstood predator. He himself was like a wild wolf prowling the high grounds, stalking her even into her dreams. Like the wolf, hunter and predator, beautiful and dangerous. The wolf was, after all, the patron of warriors. She recalled the summer when a wolf pup raised by one of the families to act like a camp dog, even carrying its moccasin pack on its back whenever the camp moved to another place, killed a dog that snarled at one of the children, following the age-old instinct of its kind to protect its pack. Such was the nature of the Oglala warrior she had come to love. He, too, followed an ancient instinct, acting on fierce impulses, killing without mercy, but like the wolf, never indiscriminately or without reason.

He had explained about Good Deeds, and though a part of her was relieved to know that his leanly muscled legs had not been between another woman's thighs and that he had not spilled his hot seed into anyone but her, still she could not banish this palpable ache within. For if Good Deeds was living with him in the same lodge, there was no room for her. She could never settle for sharing her man with another woman. And yet, Good Deeds had born his brother's child, and Katie knew that despite Black Moon's anger toward his brother, his love went deeper than anger and he would do anything to protect his brother's son. She would never ask Black Moon to choose between his nephew and herself, so perhaps it was best for everyone if she went back to Josh.

The promise she made to Josh McIntyre kept resurfacing in her mind, tearing her apart with guilt. Because of him Black Moon was alive and well. What must he think of her for having given him her word that she would marry him only to disappear yet again? He deserved so much better than that. He deserved a woman who loved him as much as she loved Black Moon, a woman to share his soldier's life, bear his children and grow old with him. She had tried to tell him that she wasn't for him, but loving a man like Black Moon made her realize how useless it was to turn back the tide of love.

And now, Josh was coming to this place to attack the village and no doubt take her back with him to the white world where she did not belong. And she would go, for she had given her word that she would be his wife. Black Moon would never understand her reason for leaving, but in the end, it would not matter. She would sacrifice her own happiness so that he could live wild and free. That was all that mattered.

High above the dusty plain an eagle-pair soared with wings spread on currents of warm summer air, calling to each other amidst glides and turns. Katie watched their aerial acrobatics, their parting and coming together again, imagining herself and Black Moon as such a pair, unbound by the white or the Indian world, soaring together on wings of love. Suddenly, the eagles separated, one swooping behind a distant peak, the other flapping off into a low-hanging cloud. Just as she and Black Moon were destined to part, each to follow a path that led away from the other.

The air all around her suddenly filled with a perilous presence. She turned her gaze away from the water and the sluggish little turtle and looked over her shoulder.

He was standing on a small rise in the earth, legs braced apart in that arrogant stance she knew so well, the sunshine reflecting off his shoulders and smooth-skinned chest. Dressed only in breech cloth and moccasins, in his near nakedness, with strength bristling in his lean muscles and pride radiating in his obsidian eyes, he was a magnificent sight to behold. The mouth that she knew to be capable of the softest, most sensual kisses was set in a scowl. His expression was unfriendly, his demeanor intimidating. If she did not know better, it would have been easy to imagine that this was the same hostile Indian she had awakened to that fateful night four years ago.

Her heart skipped a beat when he began to walk toward her, moving like the wind with fluid, noiseless steps. Now, as then, she had no fear of him, yet only now did she comprehend why. It was because of the desire she saw burning in his dark eyes as he came forward, the same look she had seen across the flames that night while she was locked in the grip of shock and sorrow. It was a look that went beyond his fierce demeanor to the tender, vulnerable core of a man who sees something he craves and knows he cannot have.

It was his all-too-human desire that kept Katie's fear at bay then and now as Black Moon dropped to the ground beside her and sat quietly, legs crossed. The sweet fragrance of sage lingered in his hair that was unbound and flowing past his shoulders, the dark ends flicking about his face, teased by the breeze. Reaching forward, he picked up a smooth stone in his long, lean fingers and skimmed it across the water, watching it skip along the surface.

When at length he spoke, his voice came from a place deep within him, low and steady and filled with emotion. "It is the time when our mother, the Earth, rejoices. When the trees are heavy with leaves and sage covers the plain. When the birds that knock on wood can be heard tapping the tree trunks and all the winged ones are happy in their nests. It is the time to gaze at the sun and give thanks for all that lives." His tone hardened. "But there will be no sun dance during this Moon of Ripe Plums, no sun lodge erected, no ceremony to choose the pole around which the warriors will dance and give pieces of their flesh to *Wakan Tanka*. The air is filled with a distant rumbling, not of thunder, but of war."

He turned to her then, and she saw in his eyes the ancient belligerence of his kind simmering in their depths. "I can accept only that which I understand," he said. "Everything else is a mystery."

He stood up, his breathing uneven, and began to pace the ground, his moccasins tamping the green grass. "What is a mystery to me is why the white men take our land. Why they are coming here to kill us. Why the woman who called me husband went away."

She could hear the bitterness mounting in his voice with each word he uttered. Rising, she went to stand before him, blocking his path so that his pacing ceased abruptly. She stood there, immobile, like a rock, until he was forced to look at her. And then she spoke in a soft voice, her eyes clear and bright, starkly contrasting the anger in the black gaze that was fixed on her.

"When I was a child, my father told me stories of a place far away on the other side of the great water, a place called Ireland where he lived with his family when he was a boy." She plucked a green leaf from a low-hanging branch as she reminisced and absently ran its rippled edge across her cheek. "I used to gaze at the mountains in the distance and try to imagine what was beyond them. I know," she said, "you do not dream of such things. You are content with who you are. But I was not." She paused, admitting, "At least I thought I was not."

Her gaze dropped to her feet, as if to find understanding of her actions somewhere among the blades of grass. "One day, when you were away on the hunt, soldiers came into the village. One of them told me about a woman who lived far away where the sun rises. This woman said she was my relative. My mother's sister. Until then I did not know I had any family left. I thought my family died on Blue Water. Do you know what it meant to me to hear that I had a family, a connection with one of my own kind?"

Green eyes peered up at him imploringly, searching for sympathy, but finding none in the hostile gaze focused on her. Fleetingly, she wondered how many of his enemies had seen that same heated stare. Was that it, then? she thought bleakly. Was she back to being his enemy? If not at this moment, then soon enough, when she told him the rest.

"And so, I went with the soldiers to find that connection. But also to save the village from attack, because the soldier told me if I did not go with him, that is what would happen." Here her gaze hardened like green glass. "Do you question me on what I had to do, when your whole life is devoted to acting on your true nature?" she challenged. "I did not plan to be away for so long, but my aunt was old and ill and she begged me to stay. I know now I should never have gone there, but there I was, and my aunt made me promise to remain there for one year." The leaf dropped from her hand and fluttered gently to the ground. "Would you have had me turn my back on her? Break my promise to an old, dying woman? Would you have done so?"

Her question was met with a flaring of his dark eyes before they lowered and turned away, giving her his answer.

"She died," Katie said, "and I came back. It was a mystery to me, all that lay beyond the mountains. But now I know that the answer to that mystery lies right here." She pressed her hand to her chest over her heart. "I have no need for big towns and pretty dresses, no desire to breathe any air but this." She drew a deep, lingering breath into her being. Softly exhaling, she said, "Like you, I am content now just to be. There is no mystery in that."

Black Moon remained for several minutes without speaking. She knew from the look on his face that he wanted desperately to believe her, to trust that she had always meant to return to him. She also knew that he was torn by the questions he wanted to ask. It would have been within his right to ask what she would have done if the old woman hadn't died, if she would be standing before him now speaking these words. Yet that would have been what any ordinary man would have asked, not a man who viewed the world according to what he saw, and what he saw right now was that she was here.

"I believe your words," he said. "But while we stand here with this river of misunderstanding between us, the soldiers march toward this place. You said it was Yellow Hand who told the bluecoats where to find us. How did you know that?"

She should have known his keen intelligence would tolerate no subversions and that he would go right to the heart of the matter.

"The soldier who came into the village told me."

There was no expression of puzzlement on his handsome face, no question in the eyes glaring back at her, only an unspoken command to tell all.

"His name is Josh McIntyre. He is a chief among the bluecoats. He is the one who told me about Yellow Hand. He also helped me save your life."

Tersely, Black Moon responded, "Why would he do that?"

"Because he and I are friends. He was in charge of the regiment that escorted me east to meet my aunt. He was also in the place called St. Louis where I lived with her. He returned to Fort Laramie soon after I arrived back there. I begged him to help me save you. He did so at great peril to himself."

"What white man risks his life for a Lakota?" Black Moon scoffed. "If he did so, it was for you, not for me. Why would he do that for you?"

Katie swallowed hard. There was no way to temper the truth. "Because he is in love with me."

He flinched. "And you? Are you...?" He could not utter the words.

"No," she said. "I am not in love with him."

"Then why did he do it?" he questioned. "The white man does nothing without getting something in return. This one cannot be so different."

"No, he is not so different. You are right. He wanted something in return. Something I promised."

Black Moon's voice dropped to a low growl. "Woman, you make too many promises."

"Be that as it may, I do not go back on my promises."

His eyes raked over her as if he were looking at her for the first...or last...time. He aimed a scornful look at the Arapaho dress she was wearing, and said, "We will get you a proper Lakota dress to wear."

"I promised him I would—"

"I do not want to hear it!" His voice thundered over hers, silencing her with a sharp gasp. "We will strike the lodges and move from this spot. Then, when you are safely out of the way, I will assemble the warriors and ride out to meet the bluecoats."

As he spoke, Katie shook her head with each word. "I will not be going with you."

"This is where you belong," he argued. "You said it yourself. I will take care of this thing and then we will go north for the winter moons."

"I am going back."

It was as if he didn't hear her. "They say there are still big buffalo herds up that way."

With each denial Katie's emotional turmoil swelled until at last it came bursting forth in a breathless rush. "I promised him I would be his wife."

Black Moon's eyes flared like a dark wind before a storm, and for one terrible moment it looked as if he would strike her as his fingers clenched at his sides. But he did not. His breathing quickened and he took a step back. The impact was swift, the pain as hot and acute as if he had been struck in the chest by an enemy arrow.

"I did it for you," she exclaimed. "I could not let them take you away or kill you."

"I am a warrior!" he bellowed. "I am not afraid to die. If that was what they planned for me, I would have met my death like a warrior. You did this thing not for me, but for yourself. Because *you* could not let them kill me. It was what *you* wanted."

"Yes!" Katie cried. "Because I love you and to lose you would be like losing my own life."

"But you will lose me if you go back," he cruelly reminded her.

"But you will be alive."

"Alive?" He snorted with contempt. "What kind of alive will I be without the one thing that gives me reason to draw breath?"

She rushed forward, but stopped short when he fired a look at her that warned her not to come any closer. Standing her ground before him, she said, "*This* is your reason to draw breath." She spread her arms wide and gestured to all that surrounded them. "With me or without me you are still who and what you are...a Lakota warrior. The land is your reason to draw breath."

Black Moon turned away from Katie's anguished look and the terrible truth she carried. "I knew there was the possibility you would leave, but never did I think it would be because you had promised to be another man's wife."

"Please," she begged, "try to understand."

"I understand very well what you are telling me. There is no mystery in it."

Her words flung back at her hit her with the force of a slap across the face. Into the taut, angry space that divided them she said, "I am doing this because I love you. Because I would die if anything were to happen to you." She ached to touch him, to place a hand on his brown arm, to feel his strong muscles tensing beneath her fingers. But the old shield of hostility was between them once again, and she knew he was unapproachable.

Black Moon glanced skyward to the clouds that stretched across the blue expanse. "The sun has reached half way past middle-sky," he said without emotion. "I must get back to camp and help get the women and children and old ones to safety." Yet he made no move to leave.

From the rapid rise and fall of his bare chest as he stood gazing at the sky Katie knew he was suffering. A terrible sadness washed over her, for she also knew that when she left this place, she would never look upon his proud, handsome face again, nor would she ever love another as strongly as she loved this man. She longed to tell him how much he had changed her life, how he had given her a reason to live when all reason seemed to have seeped from her spirit. Pain and sorrow welled up from the depths of her soul and lodged in her throat, making words impossible to utter.

Suddenly, a terrible abandon seized her. Mindless of the consequences, heeding only the commands of her heart, she rushed forward and flung herself against him. Her arms went around his neck. His black hair fell forward when she pulled his head towards hers and kissed his mouth with a fierce and violent energy.

Black Moon's breath came hard and fast, filling her mouth as he kissed her back, crushing her to him even as he tried to pull back at the same time. Her fingers splayed in his long, dark hair, her slender hips pressed against him, her lips were hot against his, her tongue moist and demanding. He made a little sound, half of despair, half of resignation, and yielded to the kiss.

When she felt his surrender, she softened her touch, hands moving from his neck to cup his face while she brushed his lips now with feather-light kisses. Pulling back at last, she opened her eyes and gazed at him. His black eyes, so close to hers, spiked with thick lashes, were half-closed with desire and pain.

Summoning the strength her kiss had robbed him of, Black Moon moistened his lips and turned his face away from hers.

Katie closed her eyes in anguish as her heart sank. Then, just as the tears were forming she felt his hand reach for hers, and looking down, saw his strong, brown fingers envelope her hand and draw it close to his side. They walked back to the camp together, hand in hand, neither speaking when there were no words left to say.

CHAPTER 32

*T*he morning mist drifted past the mammoth grizzly-shaped butte. Overhead, a narrow ribbon of indigo sky twined around the Black Hills as the cavalry advanced from the south, the swallowtail guidon flapping in the breeze.

As First Lieutenant of the Eleventh Ohio Cavalry, Josh McIntyre rode at the head of the column, leading his men into battle. Though in his heart he believed that the land belonged to the Indians, he believed just as strongly in the invincibility of the human spirit. In an age when men were only just beginning to discover the meaning of personal achievement, how could he tell the immigrants who flooded into the western lands from other parts of the world that they could not come here in search of opportunities denied them in their homelands? In this new land a man's potential was limitless, like the expanse of sky stretching over the endless plains, like his own future had once been.

As Josh led his men toward the battle, and some toward their doom, he could not help but view his future now as something without the bright promise he had hoped for. The plains had become a battlefield, and the last thing he wanted was to become another hard-bitten, steel-fisted old warhorse whose entire life revolved around regimental blue.

He had actually imagined a life for himself in St. Louis as a businessman with a family and a wife he adored. But he learned the hard way that dreams don't always come true.

The morning after his bitter reunion with Katie all hell broke loose with the news of the escape of the renegade, Black Moon. General Worth's bellow could be heard all the way from his quarters in Old Bedlam. Immigrant women ran screaming in fear for their lives even though Black Moon was long gone and no threat to their safety. Josh was grateful that in the pandemonium no one noticed his taut silence and the way he avoided everyone's eyes as he hurried over to the church to make hasty arrangements for the marriage. His own part in the escape, and the death of the sentry at the guardhouse, would remain forever imprinted on his conscience, but the thought that Katie would soon be his wife had pushed all else to the rear of his mind that morning.

He was scarcely aware of the trooper that had rushed up to him, crying, "Did ya hear? Old Yellow Hand's body was found outside the gates with his throat slit." He wasn't surprised. He'd heard the rumors that Yellow Hand murdered Black Moon's brother a few years ago. Apparently, Black Moon's vengeance ran thick in his blood. Josh would have preferred to have Black Moon shipped east to the Dry Tortugas rather than having him out there somewhere, his presence casting a dark shadow over Katie's heart. But once he got her back to St. Louis where she belonged, she would come to see that it was all for the best. And maybe, just maybe, she would learn to love him. After everything he had risked to help her, the least she could do was try. Despite his culpability in Black Moon's escape, the future had seemed bright with promise. Until he went to her room, and found her gone.

He had stood in the doorway, frozen like a wolf in the forest as the realization sank slowly and irrevocably into his brain that she had run off with that renegade. The pain and disbelief gushed up from his stomach and threatened to spill from his mouth. He felt like he'd been shot, not with bullets or cannon fire, but with deception. With a feeble shudder he had staggered outside onto the parade ground. A white hot rage seized him, and in that moment, he knew what he would do.

He had stormed into the general's quarters and asked to lead the Eleventh against the Sioux on Box Elder Creek, not in a week's time as had been planned, but the very next morning. General Worth had been only too happy to comply.

Now, as he rode at the head of the column of mounted soldiers in the direction of the Sioux encampment, Josh was oblivious to the beauty of the land around him, the sun high in the sky, the dew that tumbled from the leaves, the wild daisies blinking in the sunlight, the still summer air. He sat tall and erect in his McClellan saddle, his saber and Colt Navy revolver at his belt, his Sharps Carbine in its scabbard ready for action. His hands were tense in their kid gauntlets, his jaw was set in a hard line, his mouth a tight scowl, his heart frozen over like a river crusted with ice.

***

"Soldiers! Soldiers!"

At the terrified cry, Black Moon rushed from the lodge. A woman came running toward him, panting and pointing in the direction of the creek. Jumping astride his pony, he galloped to the top of a rise, where his coal-dark eyes fixed upon the flash of sabers from the approaching bluecoats. The dust rose from the hooves of their ponies, looking like a whirlwind. There was no time now to send the women and children to safety. He shouted for the people to take cover away from the lodges.

As he sat astride his pony's bare back watching the bluecoats approach, he did not understand the need of the white man to prevail over his environment to the exclusion of all other living things. The white way was an assault on his senses, an affront to his dignity. But most of all, it was an upheaval of all the balancing forces of the world as he knew them.

He turned his face toward the sun that was at the top of the sky, closed his eyes and called softly, "*Wakan Tanka*, have pity on the Lakota. Free us from this trap of the *washichus*."

Suddenly, a bugle blared. The infantrymen loosed their first volley as the bluecoats charged, a moving mass of blue against the summer panorama. Raising his thunder iron high over his head, Black Moon cried, "It is a good day to fight! A good day to die! Strong hearts, brave hearts to the front! Weak hearts and cowards to the rear!" Fueled by fury, he led his warriors down out of the hills to meet the enemy.

The sounds of gunfire echoed throughout the surrounding hills and the valley filled with smoke and dust. At every moment Black Moon was where the fighting was thickest. Spotting one of his braves in trouble, he lashed his pony forward to help. As he did, the blood from the mouth of a wounded horse splattered him in the face, blinding him momentarily. Just then he felt something hard strike his own horse and heard a grunt of pain. Wiping the blood from his eyes, Black Moon saw his old friend, Little Wound, on the ground. Little Wound had helped in the fight with the miners that had ultimately cost Black Moon the bighorn shirt. Black Moon knew in a flash that the thud he felt was Little Wound's body coming up against hundreds of pounds of horseflesh. Sliding off his pony, he raced to help him. Holding onto the jaw rope of his rearing pony with one hand, he reached for the fallen warrior, but it was too late. Little Wound was already dead. His head was twisted in a grotesque manner, and it was plain to see that his neck was broken.

Black Moon remounted, feeling sick. He did not blame himself for Little Wound's death. It was just the senselessness of it that sickened him. His blood ran hot in his veins and he felt consumed by a need more powerful than any he had ever known. Neither passion nor freedom had ever taken hold of him as strongly as this sudden need to kill. It did not matter who, only what.

He looked around for the nearest bluecoat. Through the blinding gun smoke and dust he spotted one and rode his pony straight at him. Uttering a murderous war cry, he hurled himself through the air, knocking the bluecoat off his horse.

The two men hit the ground and slid for several yards in the dust. They grappled with each other, rolling over and over. The white man fought desperately to evade the knife in the Black Moon's hand. Black Moon was equally intent upon plunging the blade into his enemy's heart. So violent were his emotions that he did not even realize he was fighting a soldier chief. He did not see the markings of rank on the blue uniform, only the pale skin beneath it.

The two men were evenly matched in size and strength. It was only Black Moon's blind fury that gave him the upper hand. He managed to get the bluecoat onto his back and straddled his chest. The knife was poised, aimed directly at the white throat.

But as the knife began its deadly descent, something froze Black Moon's hand in mid-motion, preventing him from driving the blade home. His eyes went wide with recognition. Around the white man's neck was the strand of love beads he had given to Katie.

The gray eyes that looked back up at him showed no fear, but rather blazed with a pride not unlike Black Moon's own. For one terrible moment he was paralyzed with indecision. This was the bluecoat Katie told him about, the one who had helped him escape. Every instinct he had told him he must kill this man, not just because he was his enemy, but because he was a rival for Katie's love.

For several tense moments their gazes locked before Black Moon released his death hold and pulled the white man to his feet by the front of his jacket. Grasping the string of beads, he ripped them sharply from around his enemy's neck and sent them scattering over the earth.

There was no mistaking the vicious look in Black Moon's eyes that said the next time they met on the battlefield, the white man's life would not be spared.

As Black Moon watched the white man disappear into the stinging dust, he was unaware of the rifle aimed at his back. A shot rang out and a bullet whizzed by dangerously close to his head. Whirling around, he saw a mounted bluecoat slump forward on his horse and the rifle in his hand fall to the ground. Through the biting dust Black Moon saw Katie. Her face was pale and beautiful. In her hands she held a rifle, its muzzle smoking. Their eyes met briefly across the battle-scarred distance before she turned and ran away.

From behind the cover of a jagged boulder, Katie fired her rifle into the ranks of pony soldiers that broke through the defense line to charge the village at full gallop.

A woman ran by, a cooking kettle still in her hands, then stopped short as a bullet ripped through her body. The kettle fell to the ground, its soupy contents spilling out. Steam rose from the pot to mingle with the smoke and dust. Katie saw this and felt sick inside. One part of her told her to run, while another part demanded that she stay and fight. Figures clad in blue were everywhere. Men, women and children fell like cut grass before the soldiers' long knives.

It was Blue Water Creek all over again. Now, as then, the air exploded with the deafening booms of the soldiers' guns and the cries and screams of the people.

A movement off to one side caught her attention. Looking up, she saw a child wander crying into the midst of battle. It just barely missed being trampled by stampeding horses. A figure darted out after it. Katie screamed. It was Good Deeds. By some miracle, Good Deeds managed to scoop up her son in her arms and run for safety. As she did, she did not see the blue-coated rider galloping straight for her.

From where Katie crouched behind the boulder she saw what was about to happen. Instinctively, she sprang into action, raising her rifle. It happened fast. Good Deeds staggered from the impact of the soldier's bullet just as Katie's own rifle roared. The soldier jerked his head up and pulled his horse to a stop. The horse walked slowly towards Katie, the man sitting straight and calm on its back. Then he pitched forward slowly, slid from the saddle and lay motionless on the ground at her feet while she looked on with horrified eyes.

When Katie reached Good Deeds, there was only enough strength left in the Oglala woman for her to push her child into Katie's arms. With her final breath, Good Deeds begged, "Do not let him forget his father."

Katie clutched the screaming child to her breast, the tears rolling from her eyes making crooked little paths in the battle grime covering her cheeks. She stared at the lifeless form of Good Deeds whose last thought had been of Fire Cloud. There was a strange smile on her lips as she lay there in stillness. She seemed happy at last.

***

The Lakota fought valiantly on into the afternoon, but just when it seemed they had the bluecoats on the run, another column was sighted coming up over the ridge. The reinforcements had to be diverted long enough for Black Moon to regroup his warriors.

"I will ride out as a decoy," he shouted to Lone Horn as they assessed this newest menace.

"No," argued the Minniconjou. "You are needed here to direct the battle. I will provide the diversion."

"What will you do?"

"What I must."

Black Moon reined his dancing pony in close to Lone Horn's and reached out to clamp a hand over the other man's arm. "There is no need for that, my friend."

"Can you think of another way?"

As a member of the Kit Foxes, a strong warrior society, Lone Hone was expected to exhibit valor in warfare to the point of death. As lance-owner within the society it was his place to stand by his lance and fight, retreating only when and if another warrior removed the lance from its stationary stand in the ground. With a heavy heart Black Moon watched his friend whip his pony hard in the direction of the approaching bluecoats.

Lone Horn raced like the wind back and forth before the soldiers' startled eyes, piercing the air with the cry of the fox. From his galloping pony he raised his lance over his head and sent it flying into the air. It struck the earth hard, standing erect in the ground. Jerking on the jaw rope, he brought his panting pony around sharply and galloped to the lance. With his thunder iron in one hand, his bow in the other, a buffalo-hide shield strapped to his forearm, he swung one leg over his pony's neck and dropped to the ground beside the lance.

Bullets whined around him. The song that issued from Lone Horn's lips was the song of the Foxes.

"I am a Fox.
I am supposed to die.
If there is anything difficult,
if there is anything dangerous,
that is mine to do."

A tremor passed through his body, stifling his song when the first bullet pierced his shoulder. Another bullet ripped through his thigh, crumbling his leg beneath him. Dark, sticky blood flowed from his wounds. Falling onto one knee, he threw his bow aside and fired his thunder iron, shooting a bluecoat off his horse, just as another shot ripped through his body, propelling him backwards. He staggered to his feet. There was a hole in his belly that went clear through to the other side. The hands he clutched over it filled quickly with his own guts.

The air crackled with exploding guns from all directions, turning the afternoon into a nightmare of dying men and horses. Black Moon pulled his pony to a halt when he spied Lone Horn through the biting dust. Something inside of him snapped. From the depths of his being a cry arose, a tortured, strangled cry that pierced the embattled air. "Hold on! I am coming!"

Digging his heels into his pony's flanks, Black Moon tore out after his friend. Their eyes met briefly across the flaming battleground, the look that raced back and forth between them speaking more than a lifetime of words could ever express. In the next instant it was gone.

Black Moon was oblivious to the battle raging all around him, the sounds of gunfire and screaming people and horses blocked out by the roaring in his mind as he sat astride his pony staring fixedly down at the body of his beloved teacher and truest friend. In his clenched fist he gripped the lance that he had been too late in pulling from the ground to save Lone Horn. Near his body lay the shield Black Moon would recognize anywhere. The figure of a fox was painted on the smoked buffalo hide. The eagle feathers on it fluttered quietly in the wind.

CHAPTER 33

From atop his hillside perch, Black Moon's anthracite gaze moved across the land he had fought for. The green valley along the gently winding river where the Lakota had moved their lodges was dappled with sunlight and painted with the colors of the earth. Beyond the river were high bluffs, some bare and brown, others overgrown with pink-blooming vines. The tawny hills were flecked with sagebrush. Here and there a Spanish dagger plant thrust its spike of flowers upwards. Lavender puff-balls dotted the land.

Deep in his bones was the sense of rightness over what he had done on Box Elder Creek. But the victory, now two moons past, however triumphant, was not decisive. He had won the battle but not the war. The real war, he knew, was just beginning.

Black Moon's gaze swept the horizon in a slow arc until it came to rest upon the brave little warrior beside him. His heart tripped at the sight of her. Her slender legs were wrapped around the girth of her spotted pony. With the hem of her elk skin dress hiked up to accommodate the animal's bare back, he had a good view of the tanned leather of the legging that reached to just below her knee, and of the column of bare white thigh above it.

The hardest battle he had fought was against the white woman who should have been his enemy but who was instead his love, his life. The realization of what she had become to him had come long before the fight on Box Elder Creek, but it had been solidified when he caught a glimpse of her through the thick smoke and black powder. Seeing her fighting as ferociously as he was, he had known then that she had made her choice. She was back to stay. His heart drummed hard at the victory. It was easy now to admit how much he loved the trader's daughter.

Just as four was a sacred number, the Great Spirit had planted four seeds in his heart that would flower into a love unlike any he had ever known. There was the emotional need he had for her, that desperate ache that went beyond all words. There was the spiritual affinity of their two hearts beating as one. There was the confidence she instilled in him that he could do anything. And there was the physical desire he had for her that had burned inside of him like a wild fire out of control since the first time he set eyes on her. Who was he to deserve the love of such a beautiful and courageous woman? In his heart he said a little prayer of thanks to *Wakan Tanka* for bringing her into his life.

The wind was blowing a little song through the needles of the pines. Black Moon felt as though he were at the center of the world. His heart swelled when he turned his head from the woman he loved to the land he loved. It was time to go up into the hills. With the new sun he would climb grizzly butte, using the rocks that formed steps to reach the summit. There, he would seek a new vision, for if there was any place in the world where the Great Spirit would speak to him, it was there. He would send his song to *Wakan Tanka* to be merciful to the Lakota. And maybe, just maybe, he would receive an answer for his people. But that was for tomorrow.

Black Moon's thought returned to the present. The silence of the summer afternoon filled with his strong, resonant voice. "We will raise the boy as our own son," he said. "He will be brother to the sons and daughters we will make together. Some day I will tell our children about the land and about the good men who fought and died for it."

His tone grew taut with suppressed emotion when he thought of his *kola*, Lone Horn. Those who understood knew that Lone Horn had not died in vain. Not only had his brave act given the warriors much-needed time to regroup and win the battle, but it had provided the Minniconjou with his greatest war honor and had assured the generations yet to come of a new tale of bravery told around winter campfires.

Black Moon's voice hardened like ice. "And I will tell them about the only promise the white man ever made to our people when he promised to take the land, and took it."

The fiery pride of the Lakota burned in his dark eyes. "The *washichus* underestimate us if they think we will not fight," he said with scorn. "But it is no less than what they would do. If the people living beyond the great water came to tell the whites that they must stop farming and killed all their cattle, would they not fight them? We were born naked and hungry into this world and we hunt to feed and clothe ourselves. It is right that we fight to stay alive. I am a Lakota warrior. I am ready for it. So are the others. Each day our numbers swell, with the promise of strong new leaders, men like Sitting Bull, the Hunkpapa, and among our own Oglala a youth of seventeen winters called Crazy Horse. They will be the leaders in the hard battles that lay ahead. Those are the stories I will tell our grandchildren."

There was no mistaking the vehemence in Black Moon's voice, but when he looked again at the woman he loved, his expression softened and a smile spread playfully across his lips, accentuating his proud handsomeness.

"And I will tell them about the green-eyed woman who stole the heart of this Lakota warrior." With a lusty laugh, he urged his pony into a gallop.

Those green eyes that set Black Moon's heart to drumming wildly in his chest were fixed upon the verdant valley. The sunlight flickered across the Belle Fourche, the water the Lakota called the thickwoods and McCabe used to call a sweet little river.

The day after the battle they had gathered up their dead, struck the lodges and left behind the steaming pit of dead soldiers and animals to pitch their lodges in this shady little spot in the shadow of the *Paha Sapa*, the sacred Black Hills.

A gentle summer breeze kicked up the ends of Katie's hair and brought clarity to her thoughts. She knew now she had been wrong to think the battle on Box Elder Creek was anything like the one on Blue Water Creek four years ago. The killing was the same, but she was different. She was stronger and somehow more resilient. Too much had happened between then and now for it to be the same. On Blue Water she had fought for her life. On Box Elder Creek she had fought for so much more.

It was the land. Always the land. Out here in this wild country of her birth life itself was equated with the earth and all the things that lived upon it. How could she do anything less than fight to keep the land from being taken? To take the land would be to destroy the best and truest part of herself. The future of the Lakota seemed uncertain. This last battle was only the beginning, she knew. Months and maybe years of warfare lay ahead. The outcome was anybody's guess. But Katie's path was chosen. Providence had led her every step of the way to this very moment in time…to this spot…to this man. If nothing else was certain, her future with Black Moon was no longer in doubt.

It came in a blinding flash during the battle when she chanced to look up in time to see a bluecoat aim his rifle at Black Moon's back. She had known in that fraction of time that nothing Black Moon could ever do to her would hurt her as much as losing him. Without thinking, acting on some inborn reflex, she had raised her rifle and fired at the soldier who would take from her the only thing that mattered.

Their love had come full circle and looked now toward the future, uniting them in a common fight to save the country of their birth where freedom abounded and the wild wind blew. Black Moon spoke of the children they would have. What he did not know was that his seed had already sprouted within her. She did not know when it had happened, only that she felt different somehow deep down inside. When she had lost everything else that mattered to her, this unborn child was something she could call her own. The child and the man who had set her world on end.

From the tragedy of Blue Water the road she traveled had been paved with bloodshed and tears, heartache and betrayal, bitter disappointment and grief. It carried her from the desolation of the plains to the glitter of St. Louis and back again, into the arms of the man who aroused her passion and ignited her spirit for life like no other.

She patted her stomach, where the child they had made together and the future of the people lay sleeping safe and sound. She could just imagine Black Moon's reaction when she told him he was going to be a father, the way his dark eyes would flash with happiness, how his proud, handsome face would brighten with a smile. How he would pull her into his strong embrace and tell her how much he loved her, not in her language, but in his.

If there was ever any doubt as to where she belonged, it was put to rest when she placed a hand above her eyes to shield them from the glare of the sun and watched him ride far out onto the plains. With the wild wind whipping through his long ebony hair, the sun reflecting off those smooth and sinewy muscles, he was a symbol of everything that burned strongly in Katie's own rebellious heart. She was a trader's daughter. He was a Lakota warrior. But they were made of the same stuff, and they were both renegades now. Whatever the future held for them, they would face it together.

The sound of Katie's laughter, as light as a summer breeze, rang out across the valley.

"Aye! It's good to be home."

And wheeling her pony around, she galloped off into the warm sunshine after him.

***

http://www.nancymorse.com

Printed in Great Britain
by Amazon

27310833R10139